Praise for Michael Baron:

"Nicholas Sparks fans will rejoice to hear there's a new male author on the scene who writes beautifully about love and emotionally charged relationships."
– _RT Book Reviews_

"I never thought a guy could write women's fiction this well. If you want deeply emotional, totally romantic novels that take you into the heart of a man, you need to read Michael Baron."
– _New York Times_ bestselling author Susan Elizabeth Phillips

"Michael Baron writes with deep sensitivity of the power of love to transform and heal in the face of overwhelming tragedy."
– #1 _New York Times_ bestselling author Susan Wiggs

"Michael Baron knows how to pull every string of a reader's heart."
– _Crystal Book Reviews_

"I love Michael Baron's books. He is such a storyteller!"
– Book Reviews R Us

Leaves

Leaves

A novel by

Michael Baron

THE
STORY PLANT

The Story Plant
The Aronica-Miller Publishing Project, LLC
P.O. Box 4331
Stamford, CT 06907

Copyright © 2012 by The Fiction Studio
Cover design by Barbara Aronica-Buck
Print ISBN-13: 978-0-9841905-4-6
E-book ISBN-13: 978-1-61188-011-3

Visit our website at www.thestoryplant.com and the author's website at
www.michaelbaronbooks.com

For information, address The Story Plant.

First Story Plant Printing: September 2012

Printed in The United States of America

To my family.

Acknowledgments

The idea for this novel was launched at the Deacon Timothy Pratt Bed and Breakfast in Old Saybrook, Connecticut, so I'd like to thank them for both their hospitality and their inspiration.

Thanks to my wife and children for their never-ending support, and to the rest of my family for providing the emotional foundation for this novel.

Thanks to Barbara Aronica-Buck for the beautiful covers she always provides.

Thanks to Sue Rasmussen for doing an excellent job of catching my dumb mistakes.

Thanks to my agents Danny Baror and Heather Baror-Shapiro for always being on my side.

Thanks to the countless musical and culinary artists who inspired Maria's and Deborah's scenes.

And thanks to the leaves. If you've never been along the Connecticut River Valley in the early fall, you owe it to yourself.

There's quite a bit of music mentioned in this novel. You can follow along by going to this link that The Story Plant has set up: http://open.spotify.com/user/laronica/playlist/59dqTdi7BJlKaEU7J1iWTX

Prologue

The car pulled up to the inn at the corner of Oak and Sugar Maple. The passengers came from Parsippany, New Jersey, but they could as easily have come from Boston or New York or Dayton, Ohio. They could even have flown in from Heathrow the night before.

The leaves were the reason that people came, whether it was for an overnight diversion or to settle for decades, raising generations of others who would remain nearby. The hundreds of miles of coastline, the dramatic topography, the distinctive architecture, and the Revolutionary-era history were all attractions, all contributors to a sturdy economy and buoyant property values. But the signature of the Connecticut River Valley was its October leaves.

Few places in America, or in fact, anywhere in the world, were capable of presenting a fall palette as varied and vibrant as this one. The warm, wet springs, the moderate summers, and early autumn days drenched in sunlight and crisped by cool evenings conspired to urge the trees into broad displays of color. The yellows of

the hickory. The bronzes of the beech. The pur-
ples of the sumac. The oranges of the sassafras.
The scarlets of the maple and the oak. The leaves
were an industry here, the vehicle that filled every town in the area for the entire month with
"leaf peepers," traveling from places where nature didn't provide such a rich visual bounty.

The visitors stayed in places like the Sugar
Maple Inn in Oldham, Connecticut. The Sugar Maple had opened its doors thirty-two years
earlier, after Joseph and Bethany Gold drove up
from Long Island and decided to stay in Oldham
the rest of their lives. It was known regionally for
the magnificent dinners it served, the homemade
cookies and chocolates it left for every guest, and
the artisan quilts that adorned each bed in its
dozen visitor rooms. But Joseph had been gone
four years now and Bethany had joined him in
the summer. In the days after Bethany's death,
the Gold children, all of who still lived in Oldham, made the reluctant decision to sell the Sugar Maple to an organization that operated country inns all along the Eastern seaboard. It would
officially change hands November first.

So as this month began, the Golds prepared
for the last days they would hold this property
that had done so much to define them, this physical centerpiece of their family. October was always a meaningful month to them, on occasion
even a momentous one. However, none could
have possibly anticipated just what this October
would bring.

For this October, certain threads would fray and certain binds would loosen. Unspoken words would be uttered at last while things that needed to be said would be withheld. Tradition would be honored and the past would be rejected. One heart would beat for another's for the first time, while one heart would stop beating forever. And a message would be delivered that was essential to all who heard it.

All before the last of the leaves came to ground.

One
Wednesday, October 6
Twenty-five days before the party

"Yes, I know I'm late," Tyler Gold said, not making eye contact with his brother or his sisters as he entered the common room of the inn. "I'm sorry."

"We'll get over it," Corrina said in the sharp tone he'd grown accustomed to hearing from her. It was difficult to know these days if she was angry with him for a specific reason or simply angry with him because he existed.

Deborah called out from the dining room. "Dinner's getting worse by the minute. Is Tyler here yet?"

He was a little surprised they'd bothered to wait for him and simultaneously wished they hadn't, though Deborah's cooking would almost certainly be the most pleasant thing about this evening.

"I'm here."

He made his way into the dining room with the rest of them, Maxwell clapping him on the shoulder as he passed by. These days Tyler felt more like the baby of the family around these people than he had since before he'd graduated high school. He had no idea why that was, given how world-weary the past year had made him feel otherwise.

Deborah ladled soup from a tureen, something orange and redolent of cinnamon and nutmeg. She topped each bowl with a dab of sour cream and snipped fresh chives over that. Ever the maestro, even in this crowd.

"Deborah, stop waiting on us," Maria said. "We're perfectly capable of serving our own soup."

Deborah simply smiled at her older sister, finishing at last and sitting with the rest of them.

Then the lights went out.

Just like when Dad died, Tyler thought instantly. It had been the night of the funeral. A beautiful but unsatisfying service that followed three days of communal heartache and eulogizing. Mourners came back to the inn with them that day, but at night the family gathered alone for dinner. Mom had been crying for a week, but just before the meal began, she stood at the head of the table, raised her wineglass, and said, "Joseph, what you gave us will be with us forever." Tyler touched his glass with the others and sipped through his tears. He knew what she'd said was true, but it didn't help him miss his father any less.

As Mom sat down after that tribute, the room went dark. For a moment, no one said anything. Then Maria started singing, her voice somewhat otherworldly coming out of the black. She sang "Autumn Leaves," Dad's favorite song. Tyler joined her, the youngest sibling attempting to lend ragged harmony to the oldest. It was the only jazz standard to which he knew all the words, in fact the only jazz standard on his iPod. Soon, all of them were singing, Mom's voice, nearly as mellifluous as Maria's, coming in last and with a purity that refuted her sadness. When the song ended, they sat in silence, Tyler half-expecting Maria to continue with another song, an impromptu concert to mark the occasion.

At last, Maxwell went to the basement, flicked a circuit breaker, and the power came back on. However, the tenor of the day, of that terrible week, had changed. After all the comfort they'd tried to bring each other at the wake and the funeral, it seemed to Tyler that this group song had managed to give them a modicum of peace.

Tyler didn't know whether anyone else seated at the table tonight flashed back to that previous power failure the way he did. All he knew was that the lights went back on of their own accord a few minutes later.

And this time no one sang.

❀❀∧∧❀❀

"I'm just saying that I think we're getting off to a bad start with the party," Corrina said, her fork poised outward above her plate. "We have less than a month – a lot less than a month, really – to get everything together."

And what happens if we don't get everything together perfectly, Tyler thought. *Will a huge hole open up and swallow us, taking all of Oldham with it?* The party meant a lot to him, too, especially this year, but Corrina had a way of making it sound like the fate of the free world depended on having just the right balloons.

Maxwell leaned toward Corrina's still-suspended fork. "I really would dedicate all of my time to it, Cor, but I kinda have this job thing that gets in the way. I mean if it wasn't for the annoying obligation to feed my family, I'd take care of the entire party myself."

Corrina scowled. "Yes, I have a job too, Maxwell. Yet I still manage to think about this function a little. It's called multitasking. Try it sometime."

"Great salmon," Maria said to Deborah in a stage whisper.

Deborah rolled her eyes toward Maxwell and Corrina. "Thanks."

"I can do more," Tyler said, not really stopping to think. The fact was he *could* do more. Without Patrice and with business as slow as it was, he had much more free time than he needed or wanted.

Corrina shook her head. "You have enough on your plate."

"Really, I don't."

"It's fine, Tyler. We'll get it all done."

There was no way to win with her right now. If he said he was maxed out, she would have criticized him for that. At least Ryan wasn't here to sneer at him tonight.

This was the first Wednesday in two months that all of them had gotten together for dinner. It hadn't been a weekly thing since before Mom got sick. Corrina, for reasons known only to her, wanted this particular one to be a siblings-only event. No spouses or kids. Tyler wondered how Gardner, Annie, and Doug felt about being excluded. Were they offended or relieved? Almost certainly the latter. Maybe they were even laughing together at a nearby restaurant.

"Let's just go over everyone's responsibilities again, so we're clear," Maria said.

Corrina sighed. "You're taking care of the entertainment, Maria. And it really is getting tight if you want to book a DJ. Deborah is doing the food, obviously, and we need to finalize the menu soon. Maxwell is in charge of promotion and publicity, and Tyler needs to take care of the decorations."

"It's all very doable," Maxwell said.

"As long as we really want to do it."

Maxwell narrowed his eyes. "Why wouldn't we want to do it? We all agreed to throw one more Halloween party."

Corrina seemed a little flustered by this confrontation. Tyler thought she might even cry. "It just doesn't feel like we're giving this our all."

Tyler stood up. "We'll get it done. We'll even get it done well. Maybe not as well as Mom and Dad always did it, but it'll be good. Listen, I have to run."

Corrina offered him a confused expression. "You're leaving already?"

"I know I should have cleared the whole night, but I couldn't. I need to get some shots cleaned up before tomorrow, and I'm already gonna be at this until just before dawn. Deborah, thanks; dinner was great. I'll see you all soon."

No one rose as Tyler left the table, which was just as well. At this point, he felt as though he needed a little distance from all of them. He stepped out of the inn and headed home. Maybe he truly would spend some time touching up some photos on his computer, though it could certainly wait until tomorrow or even next week.

It was an okay option if there was nothing good on TV.

Two

Thursday, October 7
Twenty-four days before the party

Tyler was dreaming of dancing pumpkins when the clock radio came on. For a moment, the pumpkins swayed to the rhythm of the song before Tyler realized what was going on. *Why'd I set the alarm? I don't have to be anywhere this morning.*

The song was James Taylor's version of "Up on the Roof," one of Maria's favorites. He remembered when she bought the album and played the song in what seemed to be an endless loop. It was the first pop song Tyler knew by heart – he was six at the time – and one afternoon, he found himself humming it while passing Maria's bedroom.

"Do you know what you're humming?" she said.

"It's that roof song."

She laughed. "Yeah, that roof song. You like it?"

"You play it all the time."

"But do you like it?"

"Yeah, it's good."

She seemed very happy to learn this. "Do you want to hear some more stuff like that?"

"Sure."

Maria invited him into her room and showed him her considerable record collection. She pulled out albums and played him a variety of songs: new stuff like Jackson Browne, Boston, and Bruce Springsteen, and cherished records like Cat Stevens' *Tea for the Tillerman*, Bob Dylan's *Blood on the Tracks*, and the Beach Boys' *Pet Sounds*. Tyler had heard some of this stuff before – Maria always had music on in her room – but he listened to it differently now as his sister pointed out the way a drumbeat changed in a certain place or the way the singer sang the same words differently each time. He thought key changes were the coolest thing in the world and loved the fact that none of his friends had any idea what he was talking about when he pointed one out.

After that, he and Maria became close music buddies. Every time she bought a new album, she invited him in to listen, and when she went off to college, she came back to tell him about all the new bands she'd heard. He loved that they had this between them, and he especially loved it when he got the opportunity to reciprocate by introducing her to new stuff as he got older.

When was the last time they'd gotten together to talk about new music? Did Maria even listen to new music now?

He finally got up the energy to shut off the radio, still trying to remember why he set it in the first place. He reached across the bed to flick the toggle. But the alarm wasn't set. The clock read four eighteen. Was he dreaming? His dreams were never that vivid.

James Taylor ad-libbed his way toward the end of the song, which faded out gently. Convinced now that he was truly awake – more awake than he would expect to be at four nineteen in the morning – Tyler wondered which song would come up next. What was the song that came after this one on the album? But the radio remained silent.

He lay back in bed, thinking, *this isn't a convenient time for me to lose my mind.*

❊❊∧∧❊❊

It's a funny thing. They're always at their most beautiful just before they die. The new photos had just come out of the printer, and Tyler found the richness and depth of color in them moving. The leaves in Oldham had just begun to change, but it was already obvious the foliage was going to be stunning this fall. He'd read in the local paper that conditions were near-optimal this year, though the media around here tended to say the same before relatively muted seasons. The local equivalent of propaganda. Still, if these first days were any indication, it would be a gorgeous month.

This was the first opportunity he'd had this year to photograph leaves as they came off the trees. There were three or four great shots here. A burnt umber sassafras set alone against a vivid blue sky, curling upward as though attempting to take flight. An almost coppery beech juxtaposed against a stand of trees across the park just beginning to be dotted with yellow. A lemony hickory as it pirouetted just inches from the ground. Those were the best of this lot, and they were very good. People would buy these.

If they were going to buy anything.

Tyler simply couldn't understand why this had been the toughest year of his career. The economy in Oldham and the entire surrounding area had rebounded extremely well, far ahead of the nation by all indications. Even the previous winter had been okay as far as tourism was concerned. But the demand for his work was decidedly down, coming off of his best year ever. Had he saturated the market? Were his photographs in too many galleries in the area? Were people tired of looking at his images? He'd pressed hard over the past few years to develop a distinctive style. Was this working against him now? Had that style become yesterday's news? If so, what was the next step? At thirty, retirement wasn't an option.

He could hardly consider it a surprise that his work life had gone badly for him this year. It was difficult to think of anything that had gone well in any aspect of his life. This was without question the most brutal stretch for him in memory, and the decline in interest in his work had only made a secondary contribution to this. His mother had wasted away so quickly and yet she also seemed to linger in a diminished state for an excruciatingly long time. Once Tyler understood that she was going to die, that no medical or spiritual miracles were coming, he had tried to come to terms with it. He even tried to convince himself that her dying was a preferable alternative to her suffering, and while at least that much was true, he was still completely unprepared when the inevitable happened. Knowing she was gone left an un-fillable chasm. That in itself was maybe the biggest sucker punch of the entire experience.

He'd started sparring with Corrina and her stepson Ryan during his mother's final weeks, and neither relationship had improved since, something he still found baffling. Ryan was fixing for a fight the day the kid went postal on him; of that much Tyler was certain. What he couldn't figure out was why. Of all people in the family, why him? And how was it possible that Corrina didn't see it for what it was?

It was not long after that when he realized he'd become an appendage in Patrice's life. It was one of those four-in-the-morning things where several images tumbled into his head at the same time – the way she no longer looked up when he entered the room, the way her eyes crinkled when he came to her with his troubles, the way her heart seemed to sag when she came home at night. When he got up the nerve to discuss it with her a week or so later, hoping she would convince him that he was imagining things, she thanked him for having the courage to say what she had wanted to say for some time. He had no option but to move out before what remained of their romance turned poisonous.

Yes, it had been a world-class awful year. However, fall had always been his favorite season. Maybe his fortunes would change color along with the leaves. Certainly if this latest set of photographs was any indication, things were about to improve. Though it was only nine thirty in the morning, Tyler had been at his computer for three hours already, waking up feeling much more motivated than he felt when he went to bed – even after that weird thing with the clock radio. Now, though, it was definitely time to get outside. He decided to take a walk to Henry's, taking his three best shots along with him.

Renting a place in town had some definite advantages. The cottage he'd shared with Patrice was beautiful, but it required jumping in a car to get anywhere, which meant sitting there freezing while the vehicle heated in the winter, and hassling with parking any other time of year. As a result, Tyler tended to go out less often than he liked, deciding it wasn't worth the bother. Now that he was living close to he middle of town, though, he walked all the time. He passed the house that Uriah Hayden built in 1687 – a fact noted on one of the white plaques so many of the houses in town displayed – which was followed by the one that Ezekiel Hamilton built two years later. There were plaques noting other Haydens and Hamiltons, as well as Simpsons and Partridges and others all over the town of Oldham, their homes having been converted into restaurants and coffee shops and boutiques. Some were even still homes. His own house was built by Nathaniel Essex, the first mayor of Oldham, in 1682.

Bob Ritchie was the owner of Henry's (so named for Josiah Henry, who built the place in 1701), the local art gallery on the far end of town. Bob had been selling Tyler's work since Tyler was twenty-one, claiming he was Tyler's "first patron." Certainly Henry's was the source of Tyler's biggest sales over the years and he always went there first when he had something exciting to show. There were already a handful of people browsing the shop at this time of morning, a sign that Bob's business was in good shape.

"Hey, how's it going?" Bob said, breaking away from a customer to pat Tyler on the shoulder. "Give me a couple of minutes and I'll be right with you. I just made coffee in the back if you want some."

"Thanks. I'll grab a cup and wait for you."

Tyler walked slowly toward the back of the store, finding a collection of some of his shots on a wall along the way. There were many new artists on display in the gallery since he was last here a month ago. Lots of misty watercolors.

Some faux Impressionist stuff. He noticed a new series of photographs of children playing. He'd never been able to photograph people well.

Tyler waved to Lanny, Bob's wife, as he walked into the office.

Lanny blew him a kiss. "You look good, Tyler. Lost a few pounds?"

"Yeah, maybe a few."

A few minutes later, Bob joined him.

"Did they buy anything?" Tyler said as Bob sat down across from him, picking up his own coffee cup.

"Lanny'll close the deal. They're trying to decide between a landscape and a still life. Both paintings are more than five hundred dollars, so whichever they take is fine with me. What's up?"

"I just finished processing a great session and I wanted to show you a few of the shots." Tyler opened his portfolio and pulled out the photographs, laying them on Bob's desk. "These are just test prints, obviously, but even before I start tweaking the output they look pretty good, don't they? Look at the movement on this one."

Bob leaned forward to look at the photos. "They're great, yeah. I love the angle you got here. Were you laying down?"

"Arched under. It was a lucky shot, to tell you the truth. I was focused on a different leaf when I saw this one float down. Closest I ever get to action photography."

Bob nodded. Tyler always knew he'd get a warm reception here. It was especially appreciated these days.

"Yeah, it's beautiful," Bob said.

"I'm glad you think so. I was pretty buzzed when they came out. I'll work on these a little and get you a set of prints to frame."

Bob pulled his coffee cup up to take a sip. "You might want to hold off on that for a little while. I have a fair amount of your inventory right now."

Bob had never said this to him before, and Tyler felt a little flustered, choosing to hide behind his own coffee cup for a moment. "Do you want me to take some of it back?"

"No, I would never ask you to do that. But I'm not sure I can handle anything else until some of this other stuff moves. We've got your display up and then there are the mounted pieces in the bin as well. I sold one last week, I think, so I'm sure I'll work through all of it in the near future. Then you can replenish the whole lot."

"What do you think is going on here?" Tyler said, failing to keep the concern from his voice.

"It's nothing. Don't worry about it. This stuff is cyclical. For a while people want nature photos, then they want watercolors, then they want abstracts, and then they want nature photos again. It always comes around."

Tyler knew Bob was trying to ease his mind, but business had never been cyclical for him. Every year, he'd sold more images than the year before. Until this one. He packed the shots back in his portfolio, feeling a sense of disorientation he'd never felt in Henry's before. "I guess so. I might have to give these to someone else."

"Yeah, of course. The lucky bastards. It's probably just something that's going on in this shop, anyway. They're probably burning through your stuff in Old Saybrook and they'll sell these in a week. I'm sure Penny'll call me to gloat." Bob stood as Tyler did to shake his hand. "Everything else okay?"

"Yeah, everything's fine."

"You settled in the new place."

"Pretty much, yeah. I don't have a lot of furniture, but my workspace is all set up."

"I'd like to see it sometime." Bob clapped him on the shoulder again. "I'll call you soon, right after we move a few more pieces."

Tyler hefted the portfolio. "That'd be great."

"Tyler, it's really just a cyclical thing."

Tyler offered a half-smile as he began to exit the gallery.

❀❀∧∧❀❀

This was as close as this town ever came to being hectic. It was barely past ten in the morning, and already a dozen or so people had stopped by the Oldham Visitors Bureau for information, brochures, recommendations or – in the case of one woman – simply to talk about the passing of her husband in the spring. Corrina Gold Warren laid out some local maps and a stack of cards announcing an upcoming tasting at the new gourmet shop and readied herself for a steady flow of traffic. She'd be alone until noon and then Perry and Jean would join her until Corrina left at four.

Corrina had been running the Bureau for the past six years and she knew October was always the busiest month. Most years, the increased activity excited her, gave her an approximation of the rush she assumed her husband Gardner got every time he started a new case. This year, though, it was just distracting. There was too much else to do before the end of the month. Too much that no one other than she could take care of, no matter what any of them thought.

Corrina turned as the door opened. A guy in his late twenties entered, looking around before settling his eyes on her.

"Hi, I'm wondering if you could help me."

"I'll do my best."

"I remember reading in *Connecticut* magazine a few years ago that there was a fife-and-drum museum in this town. I spent all day yesterday looking for it and I couldn't find it. Is it gone?"

"It's actually a couple of towns over in Ivoryton."

"Are you sure?"

"It's kind of my job to be sure."

The guy smiled. "Right, I guess it would be."

Corrina slid a map across the counter and took out a pen. "Here, I'll show you how to get there."

A few minutes later, he was on his way, armed with three brochures for places of interest related to the American Revolution as well as the title of Corrina's favorite history of the war. As he left, a woman in two-hundred-dollar jeans and a Versace sweatshirt entered with her Brooks-Brothers-casual husband trailing behind her.

"Can you tell me where I can get a facial around here?" the woman said.

A facial? Your valet couldn't make the trip? "There's a world-class spa in Old Saybrook that I'm sure has everything you're looking for."

The woman nodded. "And someplace quaint and New England-y for lunch."

Corrina knew exactly whom she was dealing with here. This couple had made the two-and-a-half hour drive from the Upper East Side to "get away" for a few days, dusting themselves with preconceived notions of these environs, but not willing to stray too far from their creature comforts. The restaurant recommendation was easy. There were any number of places in town that could provide precisely the experience they looked for. The local equivalent of a chain restaurant.

As they left, the husband pulled out his cell phone and glared at it. "Is there anyplace around here where the reception doesn't suck?" he said angrily.

"Sorry, sir. The Town Council has repeatedly fought the construction of a microwave tower in Oldham."

He shook his head and turned toward his wife. "Someone should tell these people what century we're in." The woman shrugged as they exited.

"You're welcome," Corrina said once the door was closed. It wasn't that she'd never heard the complaint before – dozens of times from Gardner, in fact – but she was just so much less willing to hear it from someone who didn't have the faintest notion why the Town Council might take that position.

The next fifteen minutes were surprisingly quiet, and Corrina pulled out her notebook and started compiling lists. Since Tyler left the dinner last night before they got all the details down, she was going to have to call him. She wasn't particularly fond of talking to him these days, and he also seemed so easily distracted that he could very well screw things up. She could of course get the decorations herself if she had to, but she didn't want him to drop it on her at the last minute.

When the door opened again, Corrina quickly closed the notebook, realizing it wasn't necessary when she looked up to see Etta Hawkins. Etta had been living in Oldham since she was a toddler and was one of her mother's closest friends.

"Hey, Etta."

"Hello, dear. How's the day treating you so far?"

"Just fine, I think. We've had a bunch of people here already this morning."

Etta took her hand and patted it softly. "It's good that they're keeping you on your toes."

Corrina smiled. Corrina had called this woman "Aunt Etta" until she was a teenager, and she was still tempted to do so at times. "It's nice to see you."

"And you too, dear, always. The reason I stopped by is that some of us were speculating yesterday and I figured I'd go straight to the source for the answer. Are you planning to hold the Halloween party again this year?"

For the past thirty years, the Sugar Maple Inn took no reservations for lodging on Halloween, instead opening its doors to the entire town for a huge celebration of the day, a holiday both Bethany and Joseph Gold had taken special pleasure in. The party had become one of the town's highlights of the season and was discussed with anticipation by the locals as early as August every year. With her mother's death and the pending sale of the inn, the common assumption around town had been that the tradition had ended. But Corrina wasn't ready for that, and in an increasingly rare showing of equanimity among her siblings, they'd all agreed to throw one more bash.

"Yes, we are. In fact, I was just drawing up a list of things to do for it when you came in."

"You *are*," Etta said with almost childlike pleasure. "I'm so glad. We all wanted it to happen just one more time. To say goodbye properly, you know? I'm sure the new owners mean well, but a corporation? It just won't be the same no matter what they do."

Corrina cast her eyes downward. "The party is important to all of us."

Etta reached for her hand, squeezing it tightly this time. "It's still hard for me to believe that Bethie is gone. Such a cruel disease. She would have wanted you to do this."

"I think so, too."

Etta held her hand for several moments longer, neither saying a word. Then Etta brightened, gave Corrina's hand one more tap, and turned toward the door.

"I have to go call Joanne and Martha. They're going to be so pleased." Etta stopped and looked at Corrina, beaming. "I need to start thinking about my costume!"

Corrina chuckled to herself as Etta left. Then she got back to her list. If she needed any further inspiration to make this party as special as her parents had always made it, her mother's old friend had managed to provide precisely that.

❀❀∧∧❀❀

We're not really going to have the parking conversation again, are we? Maxwell Gold thought as the meeting stretched into its second hour. In the eighteen months since he'd been elected president of the Oldham Chamber of Commerce

– not to mention the six years he'd been an active member of the board before that – the subject had arisen at every single meeting. Surely others in the room understood the futility of it and even the irony. But that didn't prevent the conversation from happening.

"You saw the results of the study," Charles Holley, the owner of The Grill Room, said. "The shop owners on Hickory Avenue are losing hundreds of thousands of dollars a year because visitors can't find adequate parking during the peak season."

"There were some serious problems with that study," said Susannah Melvoin, owner of Oldham Printing.

"It's easy to minimize the problem if you offer your customers pickup and delivery, Susannah," Will Champion, owner of Paperworks, the local stationery store, said. "It's a little harder for Carl or Darlene or most of the rest of us around the room to do that."

"My shop is entirely dependent on foot traffic," Maria Muldaur, owner of Fruits of the Kiln said. "If people can't park, they can't walk around. And if they can't walk around, they can't come into my shop."

Maxwell could have predicted the next several exchanges. He noticed Mike Mills, Publisher of the *Oldham Post*, shaking his head and doodling on the pad in front of him. Clearly, he too understood how ridiculous this debate was.

"We can't just make more space on Hickory."

"Yes we can. The town buys Imaginary Friend, razes it, and turns it into a municipal lot."

"Imaginary Friend sits inside a historical building that is more than three hundred years old."

"And three hundred years ago, the town didn't have a parking problem!"

"A municipal lot right on Hickory Avenue would be an eyesore. Should we commission a study to determine what would happen to our businesses if the town got ugly?"

It was obviously time for Maxwell to step in. He kept hoping debates such as these would occasionally lead to productive conversation, but they almost never did, and this one was going nowhere. He raised a hand to draw everyone's attention. "Listen, I know this is an important issue and I also know – as do the rest of you – that if there was an easy solution we would have come with it years ago. We're running late here. If the board will authorize it, I'll hire the Bittan Group to prepare a white paper offering alternatives."

The motion was raised and approved. Maxwell would call Roy Bittan this afternoon and the paper would be delivered within three months – which wouldn't prevent the same debate from happening next month, but might at least shorten it a little. Maxwell stood up and went for another cup of coffee while the others filed out of the conference room.

Mike Mills came up, taking half a cranberry muffin. "No matter how many times I hear that song, it still gets my toes tapping," he said.

Maxwell smiled. He'd met Mike when the man was a copyeditor for the paper and Maxwell interned there for a semester while a junior in high school. Even when Maxwell lived in Manhattan and worked on Wall Street, they'd stayed in touch.

"There were nine times today – I counted them – when I knew what someone was going to say before they said it," Maxwell said wearily.

"And still the meeting ran over by fifteen minutes."

"I need to make some changes to the way we do things here."

"Yeah, good luck with that. Listen, I have a great tidbit for you." Mike looked toward the door, which caused Maxwell to look in the same direction. If Mike was checking to make sure the coast was clear, he had something intriguing to say. "It looks like our paper is about to sweep the mayor into a little scandal."

Maxwell looked into Mike's eyes skeptically. Mike was clearly having fun with this. He'd been critical of the mayor since the politician had been nothing more than a local attorney. "Scandal?"

"The Water Line zoning might have taken a few shortcuts through Mayor Bruce's office."

Maxwell laughed. "You've got to be kidding me."

Mike held up a hand. "Now these are just allegations, mind you." His eyes twinkled when he said it. "But the *Post* feels confident enough in its sources to go to press with it tomorrow morning."

"Do you have a statement from Bruce?"

"He has until midnight tonight to return our calls. I'm guessing he won't."

Maxwell shook his head. "This is incredible."

"You're not really surprised, are you?"

"That Bruce might be involved in something shady? No. I'm just surprised he was careless enough to get caught. I mean, no offense, Mike, but you don't exactly have Woodward and Bernstein on your staff."

"I won't convey that comment to our reporters. They'd be devastated."

"Do you think anything is going to come of this?"

"You mean criminal charges? Unlikely. Bruce knows the law too well. He'll figure out a way around it. The allegations will still be there, though. Not the best thing for a reelection campaign."

"Jeez, you're right. He's up for reelection next year. I didn't even think about that."

Mike patted Maxwell on the shoulder. "Gotta think about these things." He walked toward the door, grabbing another half of a muffin on the way. "I need to get to the paper. You'll keep this under your hat until tomorrow, right?"

"Yeah, of course."

Maxwell speared a piece of cantaloupe before leaving the room. Stuff like this didn't happen in town very often. Mike would get front page news out of it for weeks.

❖❖∧∧❖❖

When she finally opened her eyes and looked at the clock on Doug's nightstand, Maria saw it was five minutes after ten. Fifteen minutes later than yesterday. *If I keep this up, I'll be skipping lunch in a couple of weeks.* She stretched, rolled over, and slowly raised herself out of bed. She thought she remembered Doug kissing her goodbye before the sun came up. That might have been yesterday, though.

What do we think, she wondered as she sat on the edge of the bed, *shower, brush teeth, breakfast? Breakfast, shower, brush teeth? Skip it all until a half hour before Doug comes home?* Maria made what could easily turn out to be the biggest decision of her day and headed toward the bathroom for the shower, brushing her teeth while the water heated up.

In the five weeks since Olivia had gone off to Brown University, Maria found herself utterly unmotivated for the first time she could remember. The initial few days, she was just sad at the thought that her daughter was grown and gone from the house. Then there was the day right after that when the realization she had nothing on the agenda seemed kind of liberating. Then a day of "taking time for herself" evolved into another day of the same, followed by yet another.

That this came on the heels of the most intense nine months of her life almost certainly added to her sense of displacement. All winter and spring she'd spent at least part of every day with her mother at the hospital and then at the hospice, talking to her even when Mom could no longer reply. Then the summer was spent letting Olivia go ever so slowly – drives into Manhattan or up into the mountains, excessive amounts of shopping, clam shacks and homemade pasta, movie marathons of Disney princesses, hunks-through-the-ages, and everything Susan Sarandon ever did – leading up to that last frantic week preparing for the trip to Providence. She and Doug cried most of the way back to Oldham and drank two bottles of wine that night over bad Italian takeout. In the morning, though, Doug had a stimulating, distracting job in Hartford to return to and she had decisions to make about whether to eat before showering. She had only recently turned forty, was years away from being able to expect grandchildren – "Mom, I'm not sure I'll ever want kids" was something Olivia had said far too often – and didn't have anything approaching a plan for what to do with the next phase of her life.

She toweled off, got dressed and booted up the computer while she waited for the coffee to brew. She looked out the window and noticed it was a gorgeous day.

I'll get outside. I'll walk into town; maybe spend some time at the bookstore.

Before eating, she decided to check her e-mail to see if Olivia had written back yet. There was nothing there but spam. She sat down at the desk to write another message.

Hi, Baby,

I hope things are going great for you up there. You never did tell me how your oral presentation went. Does your roommate still insist on studying to hard-core hip-hop? Anything more happening with THAT GUY??????

We're fine over here. Your dad is working his buns off, but that won't come as any surprise to you. Even though he's gotten two promotions in the first two years, he still thinks he needs to prove he's not some "country boy." Like anyone would ever think that about your father. He loves it, though. He's motivated in a way that I haven't seen since college.

I, myself, have a major day planned. I'm gonna go for a walk and I'm going to make dinner. Not sure how I'll cram it all in. I was thinking I might roast a couple of Cornish Hens with wild rice stuffing. Your father always likes that. Gee, maybe I should open a restaurant – just what this town needs (ha, ha!). Aunt Deborah and I could go into business together. I'm sure she'd love that.

I'm gonna go. I know you're really busy getting accustomed to all the new things at school, but write me back sometime. I realize we just talked on Sunday, but I miss you like crazy.

Love ya tons,
Mom

Maria sent the message and then wrote Corrina a quick note about the party. She threw an English muffin in the toaster and poured herself a cup of coffee.

It was time to start thinking about a job again. After botching things at the jewelry store and being bored to tears at the boutique, she was pretty sure retail was out. Maybe real estate? The market had been awful for a while, but it was starting to get better. Doug would hate it if she worked weekends, though. Maybe she could volunteer at Olivia's old elementary school. They always liked having her help out in the past and certainly she and Doug didn't need any extra money. Something to think about. She wondered if Dee Murray was still there. Olivia loved her.

The English muffin popped up in the toaster and Maria put it onto a plate. She opened the refrigerator and peered inside. Raspberry jam or apple butter?

So many decisions to make.

❀❀∧∧❀❀

Deborah had followed the traditional French preparation for Coq au Vin scrupulously, Marinating the chicken for two days in wine and aromatics, then browning it in butter and bacon fat, building the sauce by adding the marinade and vegetables to the pan, stirring in just enough flour, adding the mushrooms and onions, and then bringing it all together at the barest simmer for the past hour. Now it was time to play.

She looked around the kitchen, her two sous chefs absenting the room, knowing they would at best be in the way for the next fifteen minutes. Tarragon and mustard? No, much too French. She could dice some tomatoes and add a bit of cream. No, you'd barely be able to tell the difference. Cardamom would clash. Cinnamon could work – she'd keep it in mind. Dill? Not really. Horseradish? Please.

Cilantro? A definite possibility. It would brighten the dish without undermining all of her previous work. And now that she was going down this road, she thought a touch of cumin would add depth and thematic consistency. Yes, that could be very nice.

She crushed some cumin seeds in a mortar and pestle, and then, returning to the pan, she sprinkled it in and allowed it to blend with the dish while she chopped the cilantro. Ten minutes later, she added the herb and stirred just enough to incorporate it before taking the pan off the flame. She removed a thigh with a pair of tongs, cut a piece for herself and tasted. She'd pulled it off. The body of the original dish was still firmly in place, but the palate was surprised by the presence of the Mexican spices. She called her staff in for the daily "family meal" and they prepared the plates while she brought Paul a taste.

"Coq au Vin a la Mexicaine," she said dramatically as she handed the inn's manager a small dish. "Tonight's main course."

Paul glanced up from whatever he was doing at the computer to accept the plate. He sniffed at the dish before putting a forkful in his mouth.

"Mmm, thanks, it's good," he said before putting the plate down and returning to his work. Deborah knew that eventually Paul would eat the rest of it – and barely notice what he ate while he worked away.

It was a stupid habit, one that it was probably pointless to try to break at this stage. Whenever she finished inventing the night's meal, she took a sample of it out front. Of course, "out front" had always meant her father, or Doug, or until recently, her mother. All of them cared about food as much as she did and she knew they not only appreciated her work, but also enjoyed the game of guessing Deborah's secret ingredients or deconstructing the sauces she took special pride in innovating. Knowing they would be intrigued and delighted by this little moment was at least as much of an inspiration for her as satisfying the evening's guests. Paul had been working at the inn for the past two years, but until her mother died, he was always in a back room somewhere in the late afternoon.

Deborah headed back to the kitchen to eat with the three members of her staff.

"Great idea, Deb," Gina said, toasting her with a glass of sparkling water. "I wouldn't think to go this way." Gina was a recent graduate of the Culinary Institute of America and was taking a job at a restaurant in Vermont at the beginning of next month.

"You would have gone bigger, right?" The two of them laughed. Gina tended to want to make every dish more elaborate and it was the source of much spirited debate over the year she apprenticed at the inn.

Tim, her other sous chef, dabbed at his lips with a napkin. "Is the dining room full tonight?"

"Twenty-six," Deborah said. Only one table for four would be unoccupied this evening, which was unusual considering it was a Thursday and the inn itself was only half full. Word had gotten out. The kitchen staff at the Sugar Maple Inn was going to be changing along with ownership. Since Deborah had yet to decide where she would work next, people were unsure

where and when they would go to sample her regionally renowned cooking in the future. There
was a demand for a second seating on weekends
and Deborah agreed to comply. Except on the
thirtieth. She would allow only one seating for
the last meal she created at the inn.

The chicken was good. Her mother would
have loved it. Bethany Gold was especially fond
of the flavors of Mexico and China. She would
have brought her little tasting plate back for
more of this, perhaps guilting one of the staff
members into sharing some of his or her dinner.
Deborah would have laughed and reminded her
mother that she had other jobs to do and that she
could eat after the diners were served. Her mother would have then pretended to be chastened
and slink away – after which Deborah would almost certainly bring her some more a few minutes later.

In spite of the highly favorable reviews,
awards, and considerable regional attention she'd
received over the years, Deborah always considered her parents to be her most appreciative audience. It had been that way from the point she
discovered, at age fourteen, that cooking excited
her like nothing else. At first, she knew they were
simply being supportive of her finally having a
passion for something. Soon after that, though,
she could see they genuinely enjoyed what she
made. It was all very basic stuff back then – boeuf
Bourguignon, pasta Bolognese, sweet-and-sour
shrimp – but she prepared the dishes carefully,

sourcing dozens of cookbooks for the best techniques. As it became clear to her that her parents weren't just encouraging her because she was their child but because they thought she had a genuine talent, she found herself driven to learn everything she could, to understand the basics well enough to begin to develop her own style. The fact that she could talk to her parents about this, that they could challenge her with questions about her approach, was deeply satisfying.

When she graduated from the Culinary Institute, they paid her the ultimate compliment, asking her to take over the kitchen at the inn. Of course she took the job seriously. She would take any job seriously. But because her parents were behind her, because they gave this absolute indication of their faith in her, she dove into the job with utter devotion. She wanted not only to be good at what she did, but unique as well and they supported that completely – even on the occasions when the results were less than successful.

Now they were gone, though, as would soon be her days at the inn. Deborah finished her meal and got up from the table.

"Let's get moving," she said to her staff before heading outside. "I'll be back in a few minutes."

She walked onto the wraparound porch and leaned against the railing, looking out across the parking lot to their neighbor's expansive lawn. How many times over the past thirty-two years had she stood on this spot? How many times had she leaned precisely here? Her parents had opened the Inn when Deborah was four, and with the exception of her years at the Culinary Institute, she had been here in some fashion just about every day since. She always, even as a child, liked walking through the kitchen to stand out here.

A red Saab pulled into the parking lot and a couple emerged, walking arm in arm back toward their room. As they did, Sandra Peterson, who had been in Room 12 since Monday, strolled past on her way toward the street.

"Smells good in there," she said.

"Thanks."

Deborah knew she should get back inside. It was going to be a busy night. They'd all be busy from here on in. Until the first of November, when she would suddenly find herself somewhere else. Or even nowhere else if she couldn't make a decision. This kitchen, this porch, this railing, would belong to someone new then. Maybe eventually another person would love standing here as much as she did, would feel wrapped in its embrace, would develop comforting sense memories from the sound of tires on the gravel driveway, or the squealing little girl on the swing set across the way, or the slightly discordant church bells down the block.

Deborah had read that masters at meditation could slow their heart to the point where it was barely beating. She wondered if she could do the same with the passage of this last month. There were times when the thought of

starting everything anew suspended her, absolutely stopped her in her tracks.

She wasn't allowed to stop in her tracks right
now, though. She had diners to entertain.

Three

Friday, October 8
Twenty-three days before the party

Deborah startled as she got into the car. Staring at her from the passenger seat was a tiny field mouse, its nose twitching in the air. Deborah let out a little yip – she had always been squeamish around these things – and then wondered how a field mouse got there in the first place. She looked at the windows and confirmed that all of them were sealed shut.

Her mind flashed to a thunderstorm when she was maybe eight. The barrage of thunder had been relentless, making it impossible to sleep. The constant rumble had frightened Corrina and she'd run into Deborah's room for solace.

"How come it won't stop?" her sister said shakily.

Deborah listened to the sky crack again. "It's okay. It's a bad one, but it'll go away."

A huge clap rattled the windows. Corrina moved quickly to the edge of Deborah's bed. "Do you think I can stay here a while?"

Deborah pulled back her blankets. "Come on in. It'll end soon."

Corrina slipped in beside her. There was a long roll, followed by a split in the air that seemed to happen inside the room. Thunder never bothered Deborah, but it wasn't going to be easy to get to sleep with all this noise.

Corrina nestled a little closer. "I don't like this stuff."

"It's okay. It won't hurt you."

The storm raged for maybe another fifteen minutes. A couple more times, the walls shook. Then a long period of stillness ensued.

"Think it's done?" Corrina said.

"Sounds like it. Want to go back to your room?"

"I guess so."

"Come on, I'll take you."

Deborah pulled back the covers and reached a hand out to help her sister get up. As they exited the room, a beam of moonlight shone on a field mouse positioned in the doorway. Both girls screamed at once and grasped each other for protection. This must have startled the mouse, because it ran past them into the recesses of Deborah's room.

The two girls scurried out, dashing toward Corrina's bed and diving under her covers. With the blanket over their heads, they chuckled nervously.

"Did you see where it went?" Corrina said.

"It's in my room somewhere."

Corrina shivered. Deborah knew her younger sister was as wary of rodents as she was. "Wanna stay here tonight?"

"Yeah, maybe that's a good idea. That thing could be in my bed by now."

"Ooh, that's disgusting. Yeah, you stay here."

With the blanket still covering their heads, they'd nestled together on Corrina's pillow. Deborah had thought that the excitement would keep her awake, but she fell asleep in seconds, waking up the next morning with her little sister's head on her shoulder.

Now she walked around to the passenger side of the car to try to coax the mouse out. If she was lucky, she wouldn't have to touch the thing.

But when she opened the door, the mouse wasn't there. She was reluctant to search for it, but she was even more reluctant to have the thing appear again in her field of vision while she was driving. She looked under the seats and in every crevice of the car, even checking the glove compartment, though she knew that was stupid.

The mouse was nowhere to be found.

❀ ❀ ∧ ∧ ❀ ❀

On his way into town, Tyler stopped and picked up a fallen crimson leaf. It was still pliable and smooth, almost rubbery. In a few weeks, it would be heaped under thousands of others in a pile on the street, an ignominious fate for something so lovely – unless, of course some kids jumped in the pile the way he always had when he was younger. Then at least the leaf would serve its final role as the source of a child's fun. Not wanting to leave such a thing to chance, he decided to take the leaf with him on his walk.

He was headed toward his first meeting with the guy at Celebrations, the local party store. On the way, he stopped at BrewHaha, intending to get a cup of Sumatra, but deciding to get some warm apple cider instead. While he waited for his drink, he rotated the leaf between his thumb and forefinger, momentarily fixated by the red whirl. It took less to occupy his thoughts lately, which he supposed was a good thing.

He got to Celebrations a couple of minutes later, approaching the young woman behind the counter.

"Hi. Is Gene here? I have an appointment with him."

"Yeah, he's in his office. I think he's waiting for you."

"Thanks," Tyler said, handing her the leaf. She seemed confused, but she took it from him and even offered a polite smile.

Gene Buffett had come to Oldham a little more than a decade earlier to buy the thriving Celebrations from the widow of the previous owner. Rumor had it that he had been involved in some part of the music business before then, but he'd steadfastly refused to talk about his past. Tyler guessed it was because the truth was considerably less glamorous than the fiction. Still, his salt-and-pepper ponytail and his rheumy eyes suggested that "party" was a term that took on multiple meanings in Gene's life.

"Hey, Golden Boy," Gene said when Tyler knocked on the office door. "How's it going?"

"I'm doing all right. How are you?"

"Nobody's ever proven that it's worth complaining." He stood and shook Tyler's hand. "So the big fiesta is nearly upon us."

"The last one."

"Once more with feeling," Gene said loudly. "Your mother was great, I loved her. Coolest grandma in town. Sucks that she had to die."

"Yeah, that's just what the minister said when he eulogized her."

Gene smiled. "You know what I mean. She really was great." He looked down at his desk and picked up a couple of pieces of paper. "I pulled out the contracts for the last few years. We looking at the same kind of thing?"

"We can shake things up a little."

Gene nodded. "Wanna leave your mark on the event. I can respect that. So what are you thinking? Something darker? How Goth can we go here?"

"There are gonna be a lot of little kids there."

"How about a Goth room – adults only."

"Hmm, that might be a tough sell to the rest of my family."

"We're not talking chuckling pumpkins, are we?" Gene said wryly. He seemed genuinely disappointed that Tyler had rejected the notion of the Goth room. That was silly. He'd been to the inn's Halloween parties. He knew the vibe. Did he really think they were going to change it completely at the end?

"I was thinking about more motion."

"Radio-controlled bats!" Gene said, brightening and leaning forward in his chair. "I'll throw my nephew in free of charge to handle the swooping." He pantomimed the arc of a bat's flight.

Tyler smiled, following Gene's movements. "I like it. What else do you have?"

"Motion? I've got a hand that leaps out of the punch bowl, a ghostly mirror, creeping slime – hey, I can get you a skeleton that dances the Macarena if you want."

"Yeah, that's good. No Macarena, but the rest of it. I just want a little more action this year. Fun stuff, not gruesome stuff. But definitely more movement."

"Not a bang, but not a whimper," Gene said philosophically. "You got it. A bunch of the usual stuff to dress up the rooms?"

"Pretty much what my parents always did in that category."

"Same with paper goods?"

"Can the napkins not say, 'Happy Howl-a-ween' this year?"

"Your father loved that one."

"I think he'd understand."

Gene made a number of notations on a pad. While they talked, someone, presumably the person up front, put on the soundtrack from *The*

Rocky Horror Picture Show. "Time Warp" assaulted the room at surprising volume.

"Seasonal music?" Tyler said.

"It's in the rotation. We throw on some death metal in the afternoon when the teenagers come in for their costumes. And stuff like 'Monster Mash,' though it makes me want to vomit, around lunchtime when the old people show up. I'm just starting to work on my Christmas playlist. Someone told me that Blink-182 did a punk version of 'Jingle Bell Rock' at a concert last year. Any idea where I can get a bootleg?"

"Same place everyone else gets them, I'd guess."

Gene made a few more notations and then looked up at Tyler. "I think we're all set for now. I'll give you a call in about a week and we'll sit down again to go over prices and finalize the list. I'll look around a little and see if I can come up with some more fun stuff – stuff that moves – between now and then."

Tyler left the store feeling good about the meeting. Swooping bats would certainly be entertaining and he didn't think anyone else in the family would get bent out of shape over them. Corrina didn't explicitly tell him to follow Mom and Dad's template absolutely. If she had just wanted to go through the motions, she could have done it herself.

He walked back to his apartment and then decided to drive over to Corrina's to let her know what was going on. He didn't want Gene going out of his way to find stuff if she was only going to freak out about it. And if she liked where he was taking things, maybe she'd even lighten up with him a little. Walking on eggshells with her was getting a little old.

As he pulled up to the driveway, Corrina's sixteen-year-old stepson Ryan walked out the door. Tyler got out of his car and waved to him. "Hey, what's going on?"

Ryan simply lifted his hand slightly and said, "Hey."

"No school today?"

"Some staff development thing for the teachers." Ryan seemed to be going out of his way to avoid making eye contact. In fact, he seemed to be going out of his way to make sure Tyler knew he was going out of his way to avoid making eye contact.

"Where are you headed?"

Ryan looked at him then, but with an expression that screamed, *what the hell business is it of yours?* "I'm just going."

Tyler tilted his chin upward to let the kid know he didn't appreciate the dismissive attitude. He wished he could understand what was going on here. Was Corrina's house built over some kind of toxic substance that slowly turned everyone who lived there into jerks? Ryan never used to be like this. Gardner's son from his first marriage, he came to live in Oldham after his mother died three years ago. Tyler always liked the kid and once he lived here full time, they really connected. Ryan was pretty messed up about his mom and everyone else in the family treated him with kid gloves. Tyler thought it would be best to treat him like he had the rest of his life to live instead. He talked to him at length about his mother, but he also talked to him at length about everything else – school, music, friends, movies. He let him hang out with him while he worked on pictures (though the kid had no talent for photography whatsoever) and they often went for walks during family gatherings just to "get real."

Then during the summer at one of the increasingly rare Wednesday night dinners at the inn, things just snapped. Ryan was expounding on the exploits of a group of vandalizing pranksters in the school, with Maria's daughter Olivia egging him on. Something in Ryan's tone – the way he celebrated the thugs as though they were brazen anti-heroes – irritated Tyler enough to interrupt.

"Gee, do you think these guys want to be role models or are they just in it for the endorsement deals?" he said flippantly as Ryan laughed over another of the gang's exploits.

Ryan stopped laughing and turned to face Tyler, his eyes narrowed. "What's that supposed to mean?"

"I just wonder if these guys realize there are people out there who idolize them."

Ryan sneered. "I don't idolize them, if that's what you're saying."

Tyler took a quick glance around the table and noticed that all other conversation had stopped. "Sure sounds like it to me."

Ryan scoffed and then sat back in his seat. For a moment, it seemed the exchange was over. Tyler figured Ryan got the message and would dial it back, at least in front of this crowd. Conversation resumed, as others pretended they hadn't noticed the heated words.

Then Ryan stood up and confronted Tyler. "What the hell difference does it make if I do idolize them?"

Tyler was a little surprised by how contentious the kid was being. He held up a hand and said, "Ryan, chill."

"Don't tell me to chill. *You* can't tell me to chill."

"You're being a teensy bit over the top right now, don't you think, Rye?"

"Hey, I don't tell you what to think and you have no right to tell me what to think."

Olivia reached out a hand to calm Ryan and he pushed it away. For some reason, that action set Tyler off.

"Are you freaking kidding me? Because you're a big boy now? Because you have an absolute understanding of how the world works? Because you're old enough to draw your own conclusions?"

"Damn right I am."

"Then you're doing a pretty lousy job of it. You think it's funny that these kids are destroying school property, blowing up mailboxes, and breaking windows? Is that some kind of rebellious gesture to you? Some way of sticking it to The Man?"

"When did you become such a grown-up?"

"When did you become such an infant?"

Ryan responded as though Tyler had slapped him. He sat back down in his chair, and glared at him. Tyler glared right back, unwilling to simply let this go away. A moment later, Ryan, looking a little flustered, pulled back from the table and stalked out of the inn.

Corrina stood up and said to Tyler, "I guess we should all be glad you don't have kids of your own," before following after her stepson. Meanwhile, Gardner – the kid's actual father – just shook his head and the others looked away. Corrina came back a short time later, saying she was taking Ryan home. By that point, Tyler was all out of bluster and didn't even bother to look at his sister. He and Ryan hadn't had a civil conversation since, and Corrina was barely polite to him. He still had no idea how he became the villain of this piece.

Now, once again, Ryan was shoveling attitude at him. *I'm just going.*

"I meant that after I talk to Corrina, I would give you a ride if you wanted," Tyler said, attempting to take the high road.

Ryan shrugged and continued to walk down the drive, tossing, "Don't need ya" over his shoulder.

Tyler shook his head and started toward the house. He rang the doorbell and waited, then rang the doorbell again when there was no answer.

"She's not there," Ryan said.

Tyler turned to see the kid standing on the street. As he did, Ryan walked away.

"Thanks for letting me know," Tyler said to his back.

❀❀∧∧❀❀

The River Edge Café had been open for business since the late nineties, when a husband-and-wife team made a killing during the tech stock boom and decided to "chuck it all" and follow their passion for fine food. Located on the water between Oldham and Essex, it was popular for its ambitious menu, its beautiful setting, and its attentive staff. However, it had recently lost two executive chefs in quick succession, leading to rumors that the owners were impossible taskmasters and maybe even a little abusive. Deborah didn't necessarily believe these unsubstantiated stories, but they made her wary through the entire interview process, and even now in her third meeting with the couple, she wondered if there was something less than genuine behind Jenn Cristy's ubiquitous smile or Ray Graffia's persistence.

"We want you here, Deb," Ray said. People didn't really call her "Deb," but Ray seemed to insist on it. He had been doing so since they first met half a decade ago. "There are maybe two dishes on the menu we think we need to keep. The entire rest of the menu would be yours."

"It would be like having your own restaurant without the hassle of ownership," Jenn said. Deborah had been in precisely that situation her entire adult life, so she wasn't sure why Jenn thought this was a selling point.

"I'm completely willing to wait until the middle of November if you want to take a couple of weeks off between jobs," Ray said. "Trina's an excellent sous chef and she's doing a great job of holding down the fort for us. To be honest, if we weren't so intent on recruiting you, we'd give her the job right now."

"That's very flattering," Deborah said, wondering how resentful Trina would be of her if she decided to take the position.

This wasn't the first offer Deborah had received, though it was certainly the most aggressive. She'd gotten a couple of calls as soon as word got out about the sale of the inn. The people buying the Sugar Maple even made her an extremely attractive offer to stay precisely where she was. She never considered it seriously, though. It was hard enough cooking there now that both of her parents were gone. It would be impossible to take direction there from someone else, though, and even harder to watch the inevitable changes they made. Deborah imagined herself collapsing into tears the first time they replaced a table lamp. She was convinced that when she walked out of the inn at the end of the Halloween party she would never again set foot in the place just so she could remember it forever the way she wanted.

None of the offers she'd received so far had seemed very appealing. She knew she was running the risk of seeming like a prima donna and she also knew she should be eternally grateful for the attention, but she couldn't allow herself to take a position unless it sang out to her. She even considered trying to find a job in a diner or a coffee shop somewhere – something completely one-dimensional with little or no room for personal investment – just to recalibrate. But of course that was ridiculous. How long could she flip burgers before she started slipping exotic ingredients into the ground beef? She had enough money saved to get by for about six months, and if it took that long to find the right spot, that was fine with her.

"I'm not trying to flatter you," Ray said. "I'm trying to hire you. Your customers will flatter you every time the wait staff delivers one of your inventions."

Deborah smiled. The "Deb" thing aside, she'd always liked Ray and she wished the rumors weren't causing her to question his sincerity. That was the pernicious thing about rumors.

"The package you're offering is great," she said, nodding to both Ray and Jenn. "I've always been fond of this restaurant, and you have a great kitchen. I just need a couple of days."

"Of course," Jenn said. "Take as long as you must."

Ray patted her hand. "We're here for you, Deb. Call me anytime if you have questions. I gave you our home number, right?"

"You did, yes. I just want to take a little longer to think. I'll call you on Monday."

Deborah stood and shook their hands. In reality, though, she had already made her decision, but it didn't seem polite to turn them down flat. The River Edge Café was a fine restaurant and it did have a sensational kitchen. The more time she spent there, however, she realized there wasn't anything about this place that felt like home.

She drove through downtown Oldham on the way back to the inn. Waiting for a couple of pedestrians to cross Hickory, she noticed the sign for Sage, the gourmet shop that had opened a couple of weeks earlier. She couldn't believe she hadn't visited it yet. When a car pulled out of the parking space across from the store, she decided the time was right.

The store was in a moderately large space between a music store and a bookstore. Deborah had a hard time remembering what was in the space before (there had been several shops there over the past few years), but the new owner had done a great job of remodeling it. Lots of blond wood fixtures, warm lighting, and handwritten signage. There was a refrigerator case housing artisanal cheeses and sausages in understated, small-production packages.

Deborah liked being here immediately. Maybe it was the slack-key guitar music coming from the sound system or that one of the front tables was dedicated to the small Tuscan pasta manufacturer she had "discovered" a couple of years ago and had used exclusively at the inn ever since. Deborah knew this would be a place she'd visit often. She'd been to all the gourmet shops in the area, and was frustrated by the sameness of them. It was almost as though some food rep came along and set each one up based on some model. This place had a decidedly individual point of view, though. The shelf of spices was an asymmetrical jumble of bottles and tins of different sizes. Next to it was a card that read:

> This might not be the prettiest display of spices you've ever seen, but it's hopefully the best. I've compared everything on this shelf to the competition and only carry the ones I love the most.

Deborah agreed about the mustard seed, the za'atar, and the smoked paprika, but she would have chosen a different Telicherry peppercorn.

A man walked up to her while she was standing at the display. "Find anything you like?"

She turned to look at him. He was a little over six feet and lean. And he had very expressive eyes. "Krendahl has better peppercorns," she said.

"You're right, but they only sell from their catalog. I tried, believe me. They also import this fabulous five-spice powder, but again, I couldn't get it. Think I should change the card in the spirit of full disclosure?"

Deborah laughed. "Your secret is safe with me. You're the owner?"

He extended his hand and Deborah took it. "Sage Mixon."

"Deborah Gold. So the store is named after you and not after" – she reached for a bottle – "Brookfield's hand-rubbed Albanian."

He smiled. "You obviously know your spices. Are you in the food business?"

"I'm the chef at the Sugar Maple Inn – at least I am until the end of the month."

"Moving on to bigger and better things?"

Deborah rolled her eyes. "That part isn't at all certain at the moment." She turned toward another display. "I've never seen these preserves before."

"They're incredible. They're all made by a single dad out of a barn in New Hampshire. He sweetens them with a 'proprietary blend' of fruit juices and balances each with some kind of spice or infusion. The lemon marmalade is mind-boggling." He picked up a jar and handed it to her. "He adds a touch of Thai basil. It's amazing what happens."

Deborah examined the jar in her hand. If nothing else, Sage was an excellent salesperson. Of course she would buy this. Before she did, though, she spent another half hour in the store walking from display to display. Sage stayed with her when he wasn't helping other customers, and it became obvious that there was a story behind everything he carried. She hoped the visitors who flitted in and out appreciated the thought that went into every selection in this store. More important, she hoped that – appreciative or not – the visitors were plentiful. Oldham needed more places like this one.

By the time she'd finished shopping, Deborah had the marmalade, a salsa from Nogales, a bottle of raspberry thyme vinegar made a half-hour away, and a package of stroopwafels made in Montana, of all places. She didn't need any of it. She certainly had access to just about everything she wanted from the network of suppliers she'd developed over the years. But it was fun buying here and she definitely wanted to support the establishment.

"Come again soon," Sage said as he packaged her purchases.

"I will. Definitely. Hey, come by the inn for dinner sometime in the next month."

"I might just do that. I mean if you know this much about food, you might actually be able to cook."

Deborah laughed. "Yeah, it's a possibility."

He smiled and his eyes danced. Deborah would definitely be back soon.

❀❀∧∧❀❀

Maria couldn't remember the last time she was in McGarrigle's Music Center. She figured it was at least a whole McGarrigle ago. When she was seven, she came here every Wednesday and Saturday for guitar lessons. The elder McGarrigle seemed like an old man to her then, though at that point he was probably only a few years older than she was now. With his closely cropped grey hair, thick waistline, and fascination with old jazz tunes, she would have guessed him to be sixty, if not a hundred. He gave her the lessons himself for the first six months, talking to her like she was a baby and making her play inane songs. It was a real chore to get through the sessions and even more of a chore to practice this music that seemed so pointless to her at home. As much as she loved the sound of the guitar and enjoyed picking out her own rudimentary melodies, she probably would have quit if Roger hadn't become her teacher. He went to Yale, and he had gorgeous long golden hair, and he taught her how to play the Beatles, and Joni Mitchell, and James Taylor. From that point on, Maria practiced at least an hour a day, more than that on Tuesdays and Fridays because she wanted Roger to keep telling her how much better she was getting.

It always seemed funny to her that Loudon McGarrigle's youngest child Martha was the one to take over the family business. Martha was a year ahead of Maria in school and she constantly complained about how "dead" her father was. Yet when it was time for him to retire and everyone thought he was going to sell the store, Martha stepped in and did her old man proud.

The store had an utterly different vibe now than it had when Maria was a kid. Back then, everyone came here to get their school instruments, and Mr. McGarrigle drove the point home by featuring a large display of brass and woodwinds up front. Now Maria needed to peer all the way into the back of the store to find those things. Up front were keyboards, guitars, amplifiers, and quite a bit of the kinds of electronic equipment that Maria often saw on television but still barely understood.

In addition, of course, there was the DJ stuff. This was a business that hadn't even existed for McGarrigle's Music Center when Maria was growing up. Now, though, if you were having a party and you wanted dance music, this was where you came. Martha could even provide dancers to motivate your guests onto the floor if you wanted that sort of thing.

Maria tried to remember when they started having a DJ at the Halloween party. Somewhere along the line, it stopped being enough to simply play music from a portable stereo, even though there was no official dance floor. "It's more exciting, don't you think?" she remembered her mother saying. Of course she was right, and another frivolity became a necessity. Now it was Maria's job to make the arrangements – and as Corrina so succinctly reminded her, time was getting tight. So she came to see Martha, a woman she'd barely seen in the past few decades. As it turned out, she wasn't going to see her today, either. Business had taken her out of the store and Martha's manager was going to handle the meeting instead. The only issue was that the guy was with a supplier. He asked if Maria could wait a few minutes. It was a few minutes that stretched to nearly a half-hour.

To entertain herself, Maria walked over to the guitars and picked up a Martin acoustic. A sign said this was the "Eric Clapton Model." She positioned the guitar on her propped-up leg and wrapped her left fingers around the fret board. The act made her think of the music store scene in the movie *Wayne's World* and she halfway expected to turn to see a poster demanding "No Stairway Allowed," a joke about amateur guitarists' propensity for playing the opening chords from "Stairway to Heaven" when trying out an instrument.

Now that this was in her head, she couldn't think of anything to play, and she just plucked a D chord randomly for a moment. She hadn't picked up a guitar since Olivia was in fifth grade and lost interest in hearing a song at bedtime. Finally, Maria started playing Joni Mitchell's "The

Circle Game," botching the third chord change
a couple of times before remembering it. There
was no question she was out of practice, but she
felt comfortable with the instrument. Whether
Eric Clapton ever played one of these or not,
she could see why he'd lent his name to it. When
someone came up to her to tell her that the manager could see her now, Maria stopped the song,
but she did a couple of runs before putting the
guitar down. She flubbed them, of course, but
it felt good to use her fingers this way, to have
the sound and sensation come back to her. Her
fingers tingled from the friction of the strings. It
was like the excitement of running into a sorority
sister after a decade apart.

Later, when she was back at home, the DJ
arrangements made, the contracts signed, Maria
went to the closet in the guest room and pulled
out her old guitar and songbooks. The Paul Simon and the Dan Fogelberg. The Suzanne Vega
and the Sarah McLachlan. And of course the spi-
ral-bounds. The guitar's strings were creaky and
brittle and she was certain one would snap when
she tuned it. But they held, and she strummed a
few chords to get a feel for the instrument again.
The tingling in her fingers became more uncomfortable as she played. Her hands had gone soft
over the years, and she was going to pay the price
for that now. But sitting there on the guest bed,
the Paul Simon book open next to her, it didn't
matter.

She played the chords to "American Tune" and "Duncan" and then decided to sing along on "Something So Right." She always sang – around the house, to the iPod in the car, to Muzak in stores – but singing to her own accompaniment was still a journey back for her, like visiting her old high school or reentering the house she and Doug had rented just after Olivia was born. She moved on to "Leader of the Band" and "Same Auld Lang Syne" from Dan Fogelberg and then "Marlene on the Wall" and "Gypsy" and "Luka" from Suzanne Vega and "Ice Cream" and "I Will Not Forget You" from Sarah McLachlan. She laughed when she forgot how to play a chord, and laughed even louder in triumph when she remembered how to make an Fdim. This was so completely not like riding a bicycle, but she was amazed at how much she retained and at how the simple performance of these songs drew her back to another stage in her life. Olivia smiling at her sleepily. Doug sitting on the couch, head tilted, wineglass in hand, desire brimming from his eyes. Family gatherings where she provided the entertainment, at first embarrassed and then proud when someone requested an encore.

With some trepidation, she opened one of the spiral-bound notebooks. Her original songs were here, lyrics with chords written above the words. She knew from the memory of these songs that they weren't entirely awful, but she also knew that some of them were simply terrible. She turned to a protest song about baby seals and cringed at the clichés and the indignation. There was the fragment of a lyric that stopped dead because Maria couldn't think of a word to rhyme with "orange." Here too was a song that was a blatant rip-off of The Police and yet another that was a laughable attempt to infuse her work with "soul."

Some of the stuff *was* good, though. There was "Paradox," the song she wrote a week after Jimmy Jilson said he would call her and didn't. And there was "Mumbledy Man," which she wrote about her father's habit of muttering incomprehensibly when he didn't want to do something. She found the newest notebook, which started with the poem she'd written while still in the hospital after having Olivia. She ultimately worked it into a song, but the refrain was never as strong as she wanted it to be and it made for better reading than singing.

The last song in the book was "What Can I Say?" which she wrote about Olivia growing up a month after she'd stopped singing for her at night. It was the last song Maria had written and she remembered that, as she composed it, she pondered how two phases of her life were ending simultaneously. At the time, it was the most vulnerable moment in her life. She sang the first verse, but choked up on the chorus and decided maybe this wasn't the right time to play this particular tune.

She put down the guitar and got ready to get up from the bed. Enough of this little diversion.

But then she flipped through some of the song-books and picked up the guitar again. It wasn't until the darkening room made it difficult to read the pages that she realized how much time had passed. She looked at her watch, laughed, and flipped on a lamp. Then she bent toward the guitar again and improvised a bit.

I guess Doug is taking me out to dinner tonight.

Four

Sunday, October 10
Twenty-one days before the party

Because their two-year-old son Joey was a relentless early riser, Maxwell and Annie had a deal. Annie could sleep in on Saturdays and Maxwell got to do it on Sundays. Though the challenge of keeping the increasingly boisterous child quiet while one of them slept was considerable, the system seemed to work. They each got one morning every week to try to catch up on all the sleep they'd been denied the previous six days.

This was the first thing that surprised Maxwell about Annie walking into the bedroom at seven forty to throw on some workout clothes. The second surprising thing was the way she sat down on the bed, plopped Joey next to him and said, "I've just gotta get out of the house for a while."

"What time is it?"

"It's a quarter to eight. I'm sorry, but I've just gotta get out." She stood up and headed through the bedroom door. Within seconds, he heard the front door close.

Maxwell wasn't processing things very efficiently yet this morning, and he certainly couldn't process Annie's attitude. Did something happen this morning while he was sleeping? Was Joey being impossible? He'd find out later when his wife finally explained her cut-and-run to him.

He rolled over to find his son's face inches from his own and bearing a huge smile. "I don't suppose I could convince you to go back to sleep with Daddy for a while, huh?"

In response, Joey, who still didn't speak much, scrambled up and began jumping on the bed.

"Yeah, that's what I thought." Maxwell pulled down the covers and made his way into the bathroom. It wasn't all that early – he was up by six fifteen during the week – but his head was a little foggy. He probably shouldn't have stayed awake until one in the morning watching *Sleepless in Seattle* on Comedy Central. Annie had gone to bed early and he had planned to do so himself, but he made the mistake of flipping through the channels and then he was hooked.

"Hey Pinball, shower time." Maxwell came up with the nickname for his son not long after Joey started walking (and within days running) and showed a strong tendency to bounce off things, most notably walls and furniture. Maxwell stood in the doorway and motioned for his son, who was still jumping. Joey did an awkwardly executed seat drop and then hopped off the bed.

Maxwell and Joey showered together most mornings these days. It wasn't exactly the same experience as the showers he'd taken with Annie before the kid was born, but it was usually entertaining. This morning, Joey was occupying himself drawing on the shower walls with soap. The little bar slipped from the boy's hand in the process and he thought this was hilarious, so he repeated the act over and over again.

Eventually, Maxwell took his own soap (it was beyond pointless to share a bar with the kid) and cleaned him off.

"No hair," Joey said as Maxwell positioned him under the showerhead to rinse off.

"Yes, hair."

"No hair," his son said more emphatically.

"You haven't washed your hair in something like three days. We're washing it today." For someone who approached life with utter abandon, Joey was unusually skittish about getting shampoo in his eyes. "We'll do that thing where you tilt your head back like I taught you." Of course Joey was incapable of maintaining that posture through the entire process and grew frantic when any suds touched his face. Maxwell rinsed him off quickly, after which the boy, forgetting the torture of moments past, resumed drawing on the walls.

Once they were dressed – yet another adventure, as Joey chose to dance away from his father after putting on each article of clothing – they headed into the kitchen for breakfast. Maxwell spent some time staring into the refrigerator and trying to come up with something to eat, but what he really wanted was some of Carmen Twillie's coffee cake.

"Pinball, come on. We're going into town."

Downtown Oldham was a half-hour walk from their house, and keeping Joey in his stroller that long would make alligator wrestling seem relaxing. Still, it was such a gorgeous morning that it seemed silly to drive. For the first half of the walk, Joey sat contentedly, pointing to leaves and squirrels and some things Maxwell couldn't pick out. He got antsy after that, though, and when he turned completely around in the stroller, tangling himself up in the straps, Maxwell carried him on his shoulders the rest of the way.

Carmen Twillie's bakery, The Open Hearth, had been turning out world-class breads and pastries since 1970. Ever since he was a boy, Maxwell maintained an absolute passion for her coffee cake. Moist and spongy underneath and topped with dense, cinnamon-laced crumbs, it was an unparalleled morning starter. When he lived in Manhattan, he woke up some mornings longing for it. Even after Maxwell entered his thirties and realized he needed to be more careful about what he put into his body, he still stopped here at least once a week.

"Cake," Joey said from atop his perch as they entered the bakery.

Maxwell ordered two squares, a large coffee, and a cup of milk, and they settled down at one of the three tables inside the bakery. Joey immediately took to deconstructing his piece, squeezing crumbs between his fingers and occasionally getting some into his mouth.

"No, look Joe, it's best if you eat the cake and the crumbs together." Maxwell took a small piece and fed it to his son. The boy ate it, smiled, and then continued to tear his piece apart. Maxwell shrugged. Everything in time.

"Boys having a little morning outing today?" elderly Bill Black said as he walked by.

"Hey, Bill," Maxwell said. "How are you doing today?"

"I'm awake and walking around, so I guess I'm okay. So what do you make of that little incident with the mayor?"

"I think we might want to get a little more information before we cast any aspersions."

Bill laughed. "You sound like a real politician."

Maxwell jokingly covered Joey's ears and said, "Please, Bill, my son can hear you." Joey pulled away from him and took a huge gulp of milk, of course spilling half of it onto his shirt. Maxwell quickly blotted it up with a napkin.

"Great kid you got there, Maxwell," Bill said.

Maxwell swept the littered table with his eyes. "I just wish he wasn't such a neat freak."

Bill patted him on the shoulder. "Well, you two have a great day."

A few minutes later, Maxwell had Joey back in the stroller as they walked through town. Maxwell waved hello to Mrs. Crest and Steve Wilkins and his son when he passed them on the street, and stopped into Carl Edwards' hardware store to make sure that Carl wasn't still upset about the confrontation they'd had at the last board meeting. It was always good to bring a two-year-old along when you did that kind of thing.

Afterward, they took a right turn off of Hickory and toward Arbor Elementary School. It was the best playground in town by far, thanks in no small part to the efforts of the Chamber of Commerce. Because the weather was so warm for the season, the playground was packed even though it wasn't even ten o'clock yet. Maxwell waved to a few more people and spent a minute chatting with Elise Fetters while he pushed Joey on a swing. But what he really wanted to do was play. That was, after all, what you did at a playground, wasn't it? He took his son on multiple trips down each of the three slides (the spiral one was his favorite), rocked with him on the teeter-totter, and tried to teach him how to climb the rope ladder. Joey most seemed to enjoy sliding down the pole with his father holding his butt. After a while, the kid decided it was time to run. Without warning, he took off into the park with Maxwell trailing behind. When Maxwell caught up to him, Joey stopped short, looked up at his father, and then yelled, "Go!" running off again. They did this for several minutes until Joey suddenly sat down to examine an orange leaf. This held the boy's complete attention for perhaps a minute and then he was off and running again.

Maxwell remembered reading somewhere that an experiment was once done in which an Olympic athlete mimicked the movements of a toddler for as long as he could hold out. After an hour and a half, the athlete was exhausted but the child was still going strong. As Maxwell slowed to allow his son to run ahead, he sympathized.

The walk back through town involved a half-hour at the toy store and then a tense couple of minutes when Joey ran into Fruits of the Kiln and endangered every piece of pottery in the shop before Maxwell corralled him. Joey finally agreed to go back in his stroller and they headed home at a moderately leisurely pace. By the time they got back to the house, Joey was asleep and Maxwell settled him into his crib. Amazing kid. One minute he's the Tasmanian Devil and the next you couldn't wake him with a marching band.

Maxwell walked into the den and flipped on the television. The football pre-game show would be on ESPN by now.

Annie still wasn't home. "I've just gotta get out of the house for a while," she'd said.

For the first time, it dawned on Maxwell that she hadn't said where she was going. Or for that matter, when she would get back.

❀❀∧∧❀❀

Tyler had tossed and turned most of the night, finally at some point falling into a deep sleep which kept him under until late morning. As a result, when he got out of bed a little after eleven, he felt more rested than he'd felt in a long time. He lounged around the apartment for a while and thought about doing some work on Lightroom. It was too gorgeous a day for that, though. Who knew how many of these were left in the year?

His walk through town ultimately left him outside the door of The Sweetest Thing, Patrice's candy shop. He'd passed it so many times, his pace quickening as he did so, over the last few months. But whether it was the Indian summer weather, the panoply of colors dressing Oldham, or the simple fact that he wasn't as tired today as he'd been lately, Tyler felt compelled to stop into the store this time.

For most of the five years they had been together, Tyler was more natural around Patrice than he had ever been with anyone. She was amazingly easy to talk to, and because of that it was so easy to express his emotions, his affections, and his desires. Even with his own family, Tyler felt there were certain barriers he couldn't cross. There were no such obstacles with Patrice – and because of this, he was wide open with her.

Then at some point in the last year, it all changed. Never having been in a serious relationship before, Tyler had no idea whether this kind of thing happened all the time, but he realized one day that they'd exchanged the sense of intimacy they always had between them for the assumption of intimacy. He thought everything was fine because it always had been. It was then that he realized Patrice was telling him less about what was going on in her life. That they hadn't had a meaningful conversation for longer than he could remember. Some of this he chalked up to his mother's illness and his grief over losing her (and certainly, after spending so much time with Mom over the years, Patrice grieved too). But when they began sniping at one another – something they'd never done before – it became impossible for Tyler to ignore the fact that something had been eating away at their relationship from the inside. It meant a lot to him that they still loved each other enough to end it before it got ugly. Still, what remained was a feeling that Patrice had left him behind. That she'd been in the process of distancing herself for a while. That in her mind he was gone before he was gone.

A customer came out of the store and held the door for him. Tyler considered that an invitation and fought the last bit of trepidation he'd been feeling. He walked in.

A half-dozen people were in the store. Patrice was attending to a couple of them while the others browsed displays of chocolates, sugar confections, glazed fruits, and boxed assortments. The Halloween display took up the entire front table with marzipan jack-o-lanterns, gummy spiders (and this year's new addition, *sour* gummy spiders), white chocolate ghosts, and dark chocolate vampires. Tyler glanced at the displays for a minute before walking over to the counter. Patrice didn't seem to notice him until she completed the sale she was working on. When she did, she seemed pleasantly surprised.

"Do I still get free candy when I come in?" Tyler said with a little more tightness in his throat than he'd anticipated.

"Dark chocolate butter toffee?" she said, smiling.

The smile warmed him. "With almonds?"

Patrice walked down the counter to get him two pieces. She handed them to him, reaching over to kiss him on the cheek as she did so. "How have you been?"

"I've been good. Just took some new shots that I really like, doing a bunch of other stuff. How about you?"

"I'm good. Frantic, a little. You know what this place gets like in the fall."

As if to punctuate the point, a customer walked up with two boxes and ordered a pound of truffles. Tyler took a bite of his candy while he waited, watching Patrice the entire time. At one point, she looked up to let him know she'd be right back. She never used to do that. Even in the early days when things were insanely passionate between them, Tyler became invisible when a customer showed up.

"You look good," she said when she returned. "Lost a couple of pounds?"

"I think I might have. I'm doing a lot more walking now that I'm closer to town." The fact that he was also doing a lot less eating and a lot more worrying since he moved out was something he didn't feel the need to mention.

"You look good," she said again.

"Thanks. You look spectacular, as usual." Patrice always looked beautiful to him. Even as he packed to move out, he saw her face and thought about how beautiful she was.

"Thanks," she said with a demure smile that only made her look more appealing. "You like your new place?"

"It's really nice. Older than our place, but really well maintained. You'd hate the kitchen, but it's fine for me."

"In other words, it has a microwave."

"You got it."

Two customers came up at the same time with two more right behind them. Tyler stepped to the side and watched Patrice's brow crease as the first customer sent her in multiple directions to choose a single piece of this chocolate and then maybe just one of that chocolate and then quizzed her on several others without choosing any of them. When the customer again took her in his direction, Tyler said, "Do you want me to give you a hand?"

Patrice faked a swoon and said, "I'd love that."

Tyler moved behind the counter and helped the next several people in line. He'd been around the store enough that answering questions was easy. By the time Patrice finished with her first customer, he'd taken care of everyone else.

"Thanks," she said when the little rush was over.

"You're welcome. Where's Lindsay?"

"Ithaca. She's in college now."

"Jeez, I forgot she graduated. So who's doing weekends with you?"

"A girl named Marisa. She's usually here by now, but she needed to come in at one thirty today."

"Good thing I stopped by then, huh?"

"Yeah, good thing." She smiled again and Tyler realized he desperately wanted to kiss her.

"I don't work free, you know," he said. "This is going to cost you a bag of sour gummy spiders."

"Take two."

"Yeah, maybe I'll do that." He watched her watching him. He couldn't remember the last time Patrice's eyes had lingered on him this long. He felt a little buzzed by the experience.

He wished they could be alone together. There was no one else in the store at the moment, but he had a much longer respite in mind. Tyler knew it would get busy again soon and a lot busier later in the afternoon, especially given the weather.

"Want me to stick around until Marisa gets here?"

Patrice broke eye contact to look at her watch. "She'll be around pretty soon. I'm sure I'll be okay. Not that I'm kicking you out."

Tyler wasn't sure if that meant he should stay or go. In the past, he never worried about outstaying his welcome in the store. Certainly Patrice seemed comfortable enough with his being here now. And he definitely didn't want to leave. It felt good to be here with her.

Then he thought about the new girl coming in and wondered what kind of introduction Patrice would make. She'd probably just say, "This is Tyler," like he was someone she hung out with occasionally. That wouldn't work for him.

"I've got a bunch of things to take care of, actually," he said. "I was just passing by the store and thought I'd see how you were doing."

"I'm glad you stopped in."

He reached over and hugged her, kissing her cheek as they separated. He walked around to the front of the counter as another customer came into the store. He turned back to Patrice.

"You want to maybe have dinner sometime?"

"I think I'd like that."

"What are you doing Tuesday night?"

"I might be available," she said with an expression that indicated that she knew she was.

"I'll give you a call."

"Sounds good." Again she held his eyes. He loved the way she looked at him when she was paying attention to him. "Hey, I'm really glad you dropped in. And thanks again for the hand. Don't forget your gummies on the way out."

Tyler walked over and picked up a bag. "Got 'em. Maybe you can bring me the other bag on Tuesday."

"I'll do that."

The customer walked to the counter and pulled Patrice away from him. Tyler waved and walked outside.

It really was a gorgeous day.

❈❈∧∧❈❈

It was just after noon and Deborah had been at the inn for a little more than a half-hour. She didn't need to be here this early today. The stock was already prepared for the Chicken Miso Soup that was tonight's appetizer. She wouldn't pat the spice rub for the seared tuna onto the fish until an hour before she cooked it. And the pears poached in caramel and Marsala would be cooked while diners ate the rest of the meal. Still, she didn't have anything going on at home, so she was just as happy to be here.

She wanted to give some thought to the October thirtieth menu. It would be the final formal meal she served at the inn and she wanted it to be a memorable one. As silly as it sounded, she thought better about food when she was in this kitchen than anywhere else. Maybe it was the ready access to the hundreds of cookbooks she'd collected and stored here (she was going to have to figure out where she was going to put these in her apartment). Maybe it was that she could smell an ingredient or heft a piece of equipment for inspiration. Or maybe it was just sheer force of habit. This was where she'd always thought about her menus.

It was never difficult for Deborah to put a menu together. When a dozen German dignitaries talked her mother into an impromptu opening of the dining room for lunch once, Deborah improvised effortlessly. When a shipment of Dungeness Crabs failed to arrive one night, she shifted direction without missing a beat. However, this upcoming menu was giving her fits. All she'd decided so far was that she would serve six courses rather than four and that she would give the diners a little something to have with their breakfast the next morning. It was her way of saying, "To be continued." Beyond that, she had no idea what to present. Maybe she should throw darts at a list of ingredients and just put a meal together out of that.

While Gina toasted walnuts in vanilla sugar for tonight's salad, Deborah sat at the table in the kitchen with a pad and created columns for the six courses: salad or soup, appetizer, fish course, first meat course, second meat course, dessert. Maybe just looking at the columns on a piece of paper would get her started in the right direction. She wrote various ingredients into the columns with the same thing in mind.

While she was writing, Paul popped his head through the kitchen door to tell her she had a phone call. It was unusual for anyone to call her here on a Sunday. Most of the calls she got were from suppliers, and none of them would be around today.

"Deborah, hi, it's Sage Mixon from the gourmet shop."

"Oh, hi," she said brightly. "The marmalade was great, by the way."

"I had a feeling you'd like it. Listen, if you aren't too busy over there, I'm having a tasting this afternoon for a new line of dessert toppings. I thought you might be interested in stopping by. There'll be ice cream and my homemade pound cake. It's from two to three thirty."

"Sounds great. You hit me on a good day. I'm usually knee-deep by three o'clock, but the menu is easy tonight."

"I'm a lucky guy. I now know at least one person will show up."

"Are you kidding? You're giving away food at the height of tourist season. I just hope you have enough."

Deborah was certainly right about how much of a crowd one could draw by giving away free tastes. By the time she arrived at two twenty, there were a couple dozen people in the store, all crowded around Sage and one of his assistants as they doled out little servings. Deborah laughed to herself as she heard Sage tell various customers about where the company that made the toppings got their chocolate and how they made their butterscotch. He was such a foodie. Deborah knew many people who loved to eat as much as she did, but she rarely met anyone who shared her passion for the process of cooking.

Sage made eye contact with her and she waved, but she stayed on the periphery of the crowd until it began to loosen. Clearly this tasting was good for business. Customers walked up to the cash register not only with a dessert topping or two, but also with several other items from the store. When she got to Sage, he handed her a small scoop of ice cream and two squares of pound cake, each with a different topping.

"To get the most out of it, you should try the caramel first, then the butterscotch, then the fudge," he said.

Deborah nodded as she took the plate.

"You knew that already, didn't you?" he said sheepishly.

She just smiled and took a bite of the pound cake with caramel sauce. The sauce was rich and unusually creamy, almost like a dulce de leche. The butterscotch had the same consistency and the butter flitted over the sugar pleasantly rather than overwhelming it the way so many did. The fudge was robust and dense, edging just close enough to bitter to make the taste memorable.

"These are very good," Deborah said. She read the descriptive handwritten sign Sage had posted next to the display. "They're from Michigan? How'd you find them?"

"My sister went to college with the woman who started the company. We're the first store on the East Coast to carry them."

Deborah spooned a final bit of fudge sauce. The after notes were really pleasant.

"Want more?"

"Nope," she said, smiling. "I want a piece of your pound cake with nothing on it."

"That almost sounded obscene," he said, handing her a square. Deborah was a tiny bit embarrassed by that comment, but hid it by popping the cake into her mouth.

"Pretty decent," she said. "A touch of nutmeg, some orange peel. What kind of vanilla?"

"Madagascar. Beans, not extract, of course."

"Goes without saying." Sage really knew his stuff. She hadn't met many people like him since she left the Culinary Institute. She'd "talked food" with numerous restaurateurs over the years and her staff, of course, and she'd discussed technique with numerous appreciative patrons of the inn, but Sage was a breed apart from all of these. It didn't hurt that he had such expressive eyes, either. "I guess a few people showed up after all."

"They did, yes," he said, looking around the crowded store. "I'm still getting the rhythm of this place."

"Where did you say you came from?"

"I don't think I did, actually. I'm from Delaware."

"Did you have a shop there as well?"

He chuckled. "I was Chief Technology Officer for an insurance company."

Deborah laughed out loud. She would have been better prepared if he'd told her he was once the bearded lady at the circus. "You're kidding!"

"Sort of what I ultimately realized. I decided to follow my bliss."

"Good choice."

"Not everyone agrees, but that's a story for another day."

His station got busier again, and at one point he needed to go to the back room to get more ice cream, but Deborah stuck around. She told herself she should probably be back at the Inn by four o'clock, but she knew she could stretch that a little if necessary. She liked watching Sage interact with customers.

When the pound cake ran out, Sage closed down the tasting. Over the next fifteen minutes, the store slowly emptied.

"The treats are gone and so is my clientele," he said as he cleaned up.

"Well, nothing attracts like free food."

"I can't complain. I think this has been our busiest day yet." He wiped down a counter with a damp cloth and then returned a display of gift baskets there. "I'm really glad you could come."

"Me too. Hey, I feel the same way about free food as everyone else. Definitely invite me to these things whenever you have them."

"You'll be the first call on my list." He looked directly into her eyes, looked down for a second, then looked back up at her. "What if I invited you somewhere else?"

Deborah felt a little charge. "What did you have in mind?"

"A drink sometime this week?"

"I think I'd like that."

He smiled. "When are you available?"

"It would have to be pretty late. Unless you want to go on Wednesday. The dining room is closed that night."

"Wednesday would be great."

Deborah nodded. She didn't want to make too much out of this, but she was thrilled at the opportunity to get to know Sage better. She noticed the clock on the wall and that it was a quarter to five. "I definitely need to go. My staff is probably wondering what happened to me. I'll see you Wednesday?"

"Absolutely. I'll give you a call."

Deborah waved and then exited the store. She'd meant to buy a couple of the toppings before she left, but thought it would seem foolish if she went back in now. *Maybe I'll ask him to bring me some when I see him on Wednesday*, she thought.

Five

Maxwell got up in the middle of the night because he had to go to the bathroom again. Decaffeinated coffee didn't keep him awake because of the caffeine; instead it kept him awake because he had to pee. Most people learned these things earlier in life.

He flicked on the bathroom light, closing the door as quickly as he could. He didn't want to stir Annie, but at the same time, he'd learned from messy experience that he wasn't very good at doing this kind of thing in the dark. He stood for a second in the room to allow his eyes to adjust. As he looked down, the random pattern of the floor tiles seemed to readjust into a checkerboard. He blinked his eyes and shook his head, but the image held.

His first thought was *what the hell?* Then another memory followed it almost immediately. It was of playing checkers with Tyler when Maxwell was twelve and the kid was just four.

Some aunt who didn't know much about what boys played with at that age got Tyler a checkers set for Christmas. Tyler seemed befuddled by the thing, and one afternoon Maxwell saw him with the board out, stacking the checkers on top of one another with no sense of purpose. Maxwell decided to show him how to play the game, which took some doing. The concepts of moving only in diagonals and only in one direction were a little hard for someone Tyler's age to retain. Tyler seemed to like doing this with him, though, and he regularly brought the board out when Maxwell got home from school, hoping for a game.

Maxwell let Tyler win most of the time, foregoing obvious opportunities for multiple jumps and being kinged. Then one day, maybe seven or eight months after they'd started playing, Maxwell realized Tyler was winning the game they were playing on his own. In fact, while Maxwell had barely been paying attention, his little brother had pulled off a triple jump. The game was already lost at that point, but Maxwell played the rest of it aggressively, laughing out loud when Tyler's three kings backed down and captured his final piece.

"Nice game," Maxwell said proudly.

"Thanks," Tyler said, beaming. He wondered at that moment if the kid knew that Maxwell had been going easy on him. He also wondered if the kid knew that those days were through.

Over the next few months, they played checkers nearly every afternoon. Maxwell won more often than he lost, but he never won easily. That Christmas, Maxwell found a handmade wooden checkerboard with brass pieces at one of the local craft shops and bought it for Tyler. It was a ridiculously elaborate gift – much more expensive than anything he got for his sisters – but he got it with the money he'd earned doing small tasks around the inn and the expression on Tyler's face when he opened it was priceless.

They continued playing until Maxwell went off to Penn and even picked up the game the first few times Maxwell came back during breaks. Eventually, they both had other things going on when Maxwell was around, and the checkerboard became an accent piece in Tyler's room, covered over with CD cases and photography books.

Maxwell hadn't thought about those games with Tyler in years. He wondered if Tyler even remembered they used to do that together and what it had meant to both of them.

Finally Maxwell moved from the spot in the bathroom where he'd stood fixed. He noticed that the floor was back to normal, the checkerboard some three-in-the-morning illusion.

He really needed to stop drinking coffee of any kind at night.

❀ ❀ ∧ ∧ ❀ ❀

A year after Janice died, Corrina was in a store with Ryan, who was fourteen at the time.

Within Ryan's earshot, the elderly sales clerk helping them said, "Your son is so handsome." Corrina smiled and said, "He is, isn't he?" When she glanced over to toss Ryan a teasing look, though, the expression of reproach on his face was unmistakable. It said, "I am not your son." It chilled Corrina to see it. She'd never presumed to be his mother and certainly never as much as suggested she could replace Janice. She simply agreed with the sales clerk because it was such a non-moment and it didn't seem necessary to explain that Ryan was her stepson. Watching Ryan appear so appalled at the notion made an indelible impression on her. She would never make a mistake like that again.

Her relationship with Gardner's son had been mostly cordial, but it rarely extended beyond that point. Ryan was three when his parents split up, four when she and Gardner started dating, and five when they got married. Janice moved him to Concord, Massachusetts, and Corrina and Gardner saw Ryan only once a month and three weeks in the summer after that. He was cute, bright, and likable, but Corrina felt that in many ways she'd never gotten to know him. The visits were too brief, and when he was here he was too removed from his normal life to be the kid he really was.

Then Janice died suddenly. All at once this teenaged boy only seventeen years her junior was dropped into her household. He was filled with grief, adolescent confusion, ambivalence about his father, and reticence about his stepmother. His mother had never remarried. They were a team. In an instant, the team had been broken up forever, and Ryan was cut loose into the world.

Ryan came into their home all attitude and defenses. He and Gardner had never gotten further than being "buddies," and given the fact that Gardner had been busy building his law practice for the three years of Ryan's life in which he was married to Janice, they had no practical experience living together. Gardner's response to his son's delicate situation was to heap material things upon him. It was more of a well-meaning gesture than anyone other than Corrina understood, but it left more than a few unfilled spaces. Corrina took it upon herself to try to provide the rest: structure, boundaries, a sense of family, and most importantly a safe harbor. She was still aching from the string of miscarriages that all but guaranteed her childlessness, and while she knew that caring for Ryan couldn't be a substitute, it soothed her soul a little. And as much as he struggled to project the opposite, Ryan needed people to make him feel at home. In an odd way, that defining incident with the sales clerk had made it easier for Corrina to understand her role with him – he wasn't looking for a new mother and she didn't need to pretend to be one. It was enough for her to be the nearest adult female in his life and let him know she was around.

The past year had been both the easiest and hardest between them so far. Ryan was sixteen and testing his limits. He spent much more time alone in his room. He was out with friends every weekend. His disposition had taken a dramatic change in the past six months. At the same time, though, he was more willing to help around the house, especially in the kitchen. And he was surprisingly sensitive after Corrina's mother died, asking questions about her, pulling humorous stories from Corrina that made her mother feel just a little bit more alive. Corrina was deeply grateful for these gestures, and for the first time she felt a kind of tenderness toward Ryan that extended beyond responsibility. She doubted this was what maternal love felt like, but it was different from anything else she knew.

"Need someone to chop?" he said as he came into the kitchen while she prepared the evening's stir-fry.

"Yeah, I'd love it. You take the carrots, the peppers, and the squash. I'll do the garlic, the lemongrass and the onions." Corrina knew Ryan wouldn't want to chop the onions because it wasn't acceptable to have her see him with tears in his eyes, even if they were artificially induced.

He pulled out a chef's knife and cutting board and began slicing the yellow squash into half moons. "What's tonight's theme ingredient?" They often watched "Iron Chef America" together on The Food Network on Sunday nights.

"Something especially challenging. It's chicken."

"Ah, the rare delicacy found only in the American specialty shop known as the supermarket."

"I thought I'd throw in some of that Thai Basil sauce I found at Sage the other day."

"Nice. Way to push the envelope, Cor."

Corrina finished slicing the onion and moved the bowl to the other counter, wiping at her eyes while she did so.

"Tough onion?"

"Nah. I was just moved by your compliment," she said sarcastically.

He grinned. He really was a handsome boy. Lean and angular like his father, but softer around the eyes and mouth. Many girls would fall for those eyes. Many might have already, for all she knew. She wasn't allowed to ask such questions.

"So a friend of mine got tickets to the River concert at Madison Square Garden and asked me if I wanted to go."

"Madison Square Garden? That's a hell of a long ride from here."

"It's not that far away."

"Doesn't River play shows that go on for something like four hours?"

"Yeah, something like that."

"School night?"

"It's a Friday."

Corrina nodded. If he went to the show, he wouldn't be home until three in the morning at the earliest. Gardner and she had never let him stay out anywhere near that late before. What she knew of the audiences at River concerts was that they tended to be relatively relaxed – but this was largely because of a liberal use of marijuana. She'd talked to Ryan a couple of times about drug use as casually as she could. So far, she'd gotten no indication that Ryan was taking drugs or even thinking about experimenting with them. Still, she knew the temptation was everywhere.

"What do you think?" Ryan said.

"I hear they put on a great show."

"Yeah, that's what I've heard too."

"It would be tough to miss out on a show like that."

Ryan smiled.

"You'd have to bring me back a T-shirt, you know," Corrina said.

"Maybe. If you're good."

Corrina thought this was one advantage to their relatively small age difference. While Gardner was hardly ancient at forty-five, his pop culture touchstones were vastly different from his son's. It was Led Zeppelin and George Carlin and Harrison Ford for him rather than the White Stripes, "South Park" and Channing Tatum. Corrina actually listened to River. She even found "South Park" funny, though Gardner thought it was offensive. It gave her another way in which she and her stepson could relate, a topic of conversation they could fall back on.

"What do you think Dad'll say?"

"Depends on how the day went at the firm."

Ryan's expression darkened. "Is that what it depends on?" Corrina arched an eyebrow at him. "I mean, really, is that what it depends on? I always got the impression the code was a lot harder than that to break."

Did he really want to get into this? And if he did, what should Corrina say? She had her opinions about the way Gardner and Ryan dealt with each other, but she rarely expressed them to Gardner and never to his son. She looked into Ryan's eyes to gauge how serious he was about this discussion, but he broke contact with an angry chortle and returned to the cutting board. When he was through chopping, he went up to his room.

"Thanks," she said, calling after him.

"You got it."

Corrina finished getting dinner ready. Gardner had a rare early night. The firm's caseload was building to the point where they were considering taking on another associate – one of these days – and the three of them hardly ever ate together anymore. He came into the house a few minutes later. The first time Corrina met him, Gardner was wearing a fine suit, and she never stopped admiring how good he looked when dressed professionally. He was cute enough in jeans, and he kept himself in the kind of condition where he looked great wearing nothing as well, but a well-tailored suit embellished him. He walked into the kitchen and kissed her tenderly.

"I'm glad you were able to get out of there tonight," Corrina said.

"Me too," Gardner said, kissing her again. "We're starting depositions on the Mansfield case tomorrow, so we might want to enjoy this while it lasts." He reached over and pulled a spear of pepper from a bowl on the counter. "I'm starving."

"We'll have a nice early dinner," Corrina said. "Followed by a nice early bedtime?"

"Are you propositioning me?"

"Depends. Will you take me up on it if I do?"

He smiled unabashedly. "I think I just might."

"Then I definitely am."

Gardner pulled her toward him, at which point Ryan came down the stairs.

"Hey, Dad."

"Hey, Rye. Good day in school?"

"The usual."

"A lot of homework?"

"Done. So did Corrina tell you about the River concert?"

"I just walked in the door. What about a River concert?"

"Andy Summers got tickets to see them at Madison Square Garden and asked me to come along." Ryan glanced over at Corrina and Gardner did the same.

"He's buying me a T-shirt," she said, hoping to deflect them away.

"Madison Square Garden?" Gardner said.

"Yeah. It's gonna be a great show."

"That's a long way from here, Rye."

Corrina could see Ryan's face tighten. Certainly, she hadn't given him permission to go to the concert – that was his dad's call – and she knew Ryan hadn't interpreted their conversation that way regardless of how he made it seem now.

"Andy's older brother is driving," Ryan said. "He's twenty-two and a total grownup."

"That's not really the issue. The issue is that you're sixteen and going all the way to Manhattan for a rock concert isn't really appropriate."

"A lot of my friends have done stuff like this already and they're sixteen."

"I'm currently trying a case against two sixteen-year-olds who robbed my client's house and killed her dog. There are many things sixteen-year-olds do that I wouldn't condone."

Ryan looked in Corrina's direction again, but she didn't make eye contact. She knew Gardner had ruled unilaterally here and there was no chance he was going to change his mind. As much as she knew Ryan wanted to go to this show, arguing was a waste of time.

"So you're telling me flat-out I can't go."

"It's just not a good idea, Rye."

"Well, I appreciate your looking out for me, counselor," Ryan said snidely, turning to leave the room. Before he did so, though, he leaned toward Corrina and said, "Thanks for your support."

Corrina opened her mouth to say something – though she wasn't at all sure what that would be – but didn't get the chance. Ryan had already pivoted and pounded out of the room.

❊ ❊ ∧ ∧ ❊ ❊

While Maria waited for Doug to arrive at the restaurant, she thought back on the first few times they went out after Olivia was born. For some reason the baby, who would sit contentedly in her high chair at home for seemingly any period, abhorred public places. So Maria would eat her salad while Doug walked Olivia around outside to keep her from wailing. Then they would switch places. This happened a handful of times over the first nine months of the little girl's life before they decided that if eating out together was impractical, they wouldn't do it at all. For a while after that, "date nights" involved getting Olivia to bed at a reasonable hour and then ordering Chinese takeout.

Since they'd taken Olivia to Brown, Doug wanted to go to restaurants all the time. Part of the reason was that they were free to do so in a way they hadn't been even when their daughter was a teenager and could take care of herself. Part of it was because for the first time in their lives together they had a decent disposable income. Things had been so tight in the early days. The unexpected pregnancy and the marriage that came at least eighteen months before they'd planned it set both of them off of their career courses. Maria's parents had been there with a good job for Doug at the inn, but even when he was promoted to Business and Marketing Manager, his salary had allowed for few extravagances. Then two years ago, with her mother's blessings, Doug took a marketing position with a company in Hartford. The two promotions and the bonuses he received since then not only made paying for college considerably easier than they'd expected, but gave them a cushion for the first time.

That was how she found herself sitting in the Hampshire Inn in Essex sipping a glass of Chianti. Doug had called as she got out of her car to tell her there was an accident on Rte. 9 that was slowing him up and that he'd be about fifteen minutes late. Maria spent the first couple of minutes looking over the menu – she'd decide between the citrus roasted duck and the Moroccan-spiced halibut when it was time to order – and then the next several glancing around the room. Most of the tables were full, most likely with out-of-towners enjoying a long weekend. Several were taken by business associates, their body language juxtaposing the discomfort of unfamiliarity with the desire to appear approachable. There was an older couple holding hands across the table, and another couple around her age that barely acknowledged each other's presence.

A Michael Feinstein CD played softly in the background. The tune in Maria's own head was Tracy Chapman's "Baby Can I Hold You?"

a song she'd nearly forgotten until she played it for the first time in years that morning. She hadn't picked up the guitar the entire weekend, but after Doug went to work this morning, she sat down with it again. As was true on Friday, hours melted while she played. It was like having your long-lost best friend show up on your doorstep. She had absolutely no idea how much she'd missed playing until she started doing it again. She mentioned it casually to Doug on Friday, not wanting to admit to him how completely she'd let time get away from her that day.

"Sounds like fun," he'd said. "I wish I could play an instrument." The conversation ended at that point.

Twenty minutes after she'd gotten there, Doug entered the room. He had a huge smile on his face when he saw her and he kissed her deeply before he sat down. "I'm so sorry I'm late. The whole thing was caused by rubbernecking, if you can believe it. The accident was on the other side of the highway. People should get tickets for doing that kind of thing."

"It's okay, I was just daydreaming. Have some wine and relax."

Doug poured himself a glass from the bottle Maria had ordered and took a quick sip. Maria knew he felt guilty about making her wait, but he would settle down before their appetizers came.

"Did you have a good day?" he said.

"Yeah, you know, I did some stuff around the house, talked to Corrina about the party, finally heard back from Olivia."

"I assume she's been able to find the bathroom without you," he said with a glint in his eye.

Maria smirked at him. "Yes, she has. She's also managed to find *Brad* without me."

Doug's brow furrowed. "Who's Brad?"

Maria smiled to herself. Doug never liked hearing that his baby was interested in boys. He was too evolved to pepper her dates with questions and thinly veiled threats, but not so evolved that he didn't mention the idea to Maria after Olivia left the house.

"Nothing more than a flirtation from what I can tell."

"This is the part about her going to college I'm not going to do well with."

Maria laughed. "She has a great head on her shoulders. She knows how to keep the bad ones at bay. Tell me about your day."

Doug seemed lost in thought for one more moment, took another sip of wine, and then leaned forward in his chair. "It was really good. We pitched the new promotion campaign to Rob Krieger – you know the one where we partner with the candy companies? – and he reacted really well. He gave us a bunch of little suggestions just to put his stamp on it, but we have the green light."

"That's great news. You've been working on that project for months."

"And as recently as last week, I was convinced he wanted to go in an entirely different direction."

"Wow, really? You never mentioned that to me."

"I was too nervous about it to mention it."

"But now you're on, right?"

"I'm on." Doug beamed. The pleasure and pride he took in his work was unmistakable. He had never been this way when he worked at the inn. He loved Maria's parents and he took his job with them very seriously, but in all the years he worked there, Maria had never seen the expression he was wearing now.

"I'm proud of you," she said.

"I'm kind of proud of myself." He reached out and squeezed Maria's hand. He looked around the room. "I love this place. Remember when we came here for our fifteenth anniversary? It was such a huge deal, and now we're just here on a Monday night. I know you miss Liv sometimes, Babe. I do too. But I'd be lying if I said I wasn't loving what we have now. We have our whole lives in front of us. My work is stimulating, we can do whatever we want with our nights, we can walk around the house naked whenever we want – something I strongly recommend we do more of, by the way – and we can be so spontaneous."

Maria raised Doug's hand to her lips and kissed it. He smiled at her fondly and then looked down at his menu.

"Do you know what you're having?" he said.

"I've narrowed it down."

"Let me just take a look."

Maria watched him amusedly as he glanced through the menu and commented enthusiastically on several of the selections. It tickled her that Doug was embracing life with such brio these days. He'd made the transition to "empty nester" so easily. It wasn't that he didn't love Olivia or that he wanted her out the door. In fact, Maria knew that when Olivia came home for the party he would hang on to every moment they had together. But he was ready to face the rest of his life. For him, this was the reward for struggling through his early twenties with a baby and a mortgage – just turned forty, rippling with energy, and wise enough and worldly enough to enjoy it.

Still, there was a tiny bit of Maria that was jealous of how smoothly Doug had moved on to the next stage. He wasn't struggling over what to do with the rest of his life. He didn't need to redefine himself. As wonderful as it was to see him having this much fun, it was also a reminder of how much work she had to do to get where he was.

He closed his menu. "Baked oysters and then the filet," he said. He leaned forward conspiratorially. "Then maybe a little port at home, some Marvin Gaye, some slow dancing, and who knows?" He moved toward her and kissed her lightly, seductively, on the lips.

She really did love seeing him like this.

Six

Tuesday, October 12
Nineteen days before the party

Maxwell remembered the first party thirty years ago more vividly than any other event in his childhood. It was the first time he'd concluded that his family was remarkable.

He'd turned eight that summer and remembered the fall for his first organized football games and for the continuing quest to make it up the hill on Aspen Drive on his bicycle without stopping. Like presumably every other kid his age, he spent hours contemplating his Halloween costume and more hours than that anticipating the loot he would bring in when he went trick-or-treating. When his mother mentioned that the family was going to be throwing a huge party at the inn, he couldn't help feeling cheated. Instead of ringing doorbells all over the neighborhood and collecting pounds of candy, he would give out treats instead. He had no way of knowing at that point that he was in for the time of his life – and more important, that many of the guests would bring candy for the Gold kids so that he would wind up with more than he ever had before.

The family had always operated well together, a byproduct of two parents running a business out of their home. Chores were always executed efficiently, games organized and played smoothly, favors easily doled out and reciprocated. However, something kicked up a level as that Halloween approached. His mother and father seemingly designed the entire event not only to show guests a good time, but also to allow their own children to have as much fun as possible putting it together. Dad offered nightly updates on the progress of the plans while Mom solicited suggestions from each of the kids. Goodies to be served were "tested" weeks ahead of time and repeatedly offered to make sure they "got it right." Secrets regarding surprise activities were shared as long as each child swore silence. Best of all, the kids all got to stay home from school on October thirtieth to help with the final preparations.

It was during this time that Maxwell perceived in some sense the value of his siblings as a unit for the first time. Maria, ten, could be trusted to handle certain arrangements over the telephone and she served as unofficial entertainment director. Deborah, six, offered outspoken advice on candy and beverages, and even figured out how to make ghost treats out of marshmallows. Corrina, only three, insisted on drawing pictures and placing them strategically throughout the inn. Tyler had only begun to crawl that October and was at once the least prominent member of the family and the center of attention. Maxwell remembered a friend of his mother's suggesting that maybe it was unwise to hold a party of this magnitude with a baby in the house, but his mother simply dismissed such talk. She was so tickled with the idea of doing this.

Once he got past his initial trepidation, Maxwell found himself swept into the spirit of the event. One afternoon, he heard his parents worrying that no one would show up and he appointed himself the role of promotion director. He tapped classmates, older siblings of friends, teachers, and even local shop owners to help him publicize the event. He commissioned a handful of his cronies to play a role in certain activities without letting them know exactly what those activities would be – further increasing the sense of anticipation.

When the day arrived, it was clear that Halloween at the Sugar Maple Inn was an event for the ages as far as Oldham was concerned. The place was crowded within minutes after they opened the door at six o'clock and was still packed for the final "haunting" at ten. Two of the workers at the inn had come down sick that day, and it all could have been overwhelming to do this short-staffed, but again the kids came through. Maria operated the tape player and organized the children's events. Deborah transported trays of appetizers and kept the punch bowl filled. Maxwell served double duty at the coat check and as supervisor of the "spook chamber" (as one of the downstairs guest rooms had been renamed). Even little Corrina served a hugely important role by playing with Tyler, allowing the babysitter to fill in elsewhere.

That Maxwell's friends (and he would later learn, much of the town) continued to talk about the party weeks later was satisfying enough. That the event put the inn on the map regionally was something he didn't understand at the time. But what he remembered the most – and so many of the images were still so strong, but this was the strongest – was the way the family sat together in the common room after everyone else had gone. Tyler was asleep in Maria's arms and Deborah was sprawled out semiconscious on one of the couches, but all seven of them were together at nearly midnight, even though there was school the next day.

"Bethie, this was a crazy idea," his father said from an armchair.

"It was, wasn't it?" his mother said, gathering Corrina up next to her. "Do it again next year?"

"Hell, yes!"

Maxwell and Maria laughed. Deborah grunted something that sounded like assent.

"You kids were great tonight," his father said. "Real clutch performers. This whole thing might have been a disaster without you." Maxwell remembered his father looking him squarely in the eye at that point and nodding to him, sending a little electric charge of pride through his young soul.

"We'd better get you kids to bed so you can get some sleep," his mother said, at which point Deborah snored loudly to indicate that such formalities were hardly necessary.

Now sitting in the reception area of the offices of the *Oldham Post*, Maxwell couldn't help thinking about how much had changed in the thirty years since that first party. Foremost of course was the passing of both of his parents. But somewhere along the line, the shimmer of the party had dimmed for him. It still meant a lot, but more for its historic value than any resonance it could provide in his life these days. Maybe if they held onto the inn for a couple more years and he could see Joey there at a point when he understood what was going on, some of the unalloyed joy Maxwell once felt might return. But holding onto the inn for even one more day was impractical, and they had gotten a very good price in the sale.

Mike Mills walked out to greet him, extending his hand. "Sorry to hold you up. It's been crazy here the last few days."

"That stuff with Bruce?"

Mike smiled at him knowingly. "Yeah, that stuff with Bruce. Our readers are a little fascinated."

"Hey, no such thing as bad publicity, right?"

"I don't think that applies in this case. Come on back to the office." Mike gestured toward a door and then guided Maxwell through a series of cubicles. The newsroom was certainly buzzing, much more so than any time Maxwell could remember from his days here.

"So what's up?" Mike said when they were seated in his office.

"I'm hoping you'll do me a favor."

"What? A pillar of our community asking for special favors? This is the kind of thing that has Bruce in hot water."

Maxwell laughed. "Not that kind of favor. I guess you could say that I'm here to pitch you a story."

"Shoot."

"You know that we sold the inn and the new owners are taking over at the beginning of November, right?"

"Yeah, of course I know. I'm already negotiating an ad contract with the new guys."

"And I know you know about the Halloween parties we've had over the years, because I've seen you there scarfing down goodies."

"Your sister's a great chef."

"Well, we're doing it one more time and I was hoping you'd consider running a little feature piece about it maybe the week before."

"You got it. I'll have John McVie call you to discuss angles in a couple of days."

"Really? That's it? I figured I'd need to be more persuasive than that."

"Nah, don't be ridiculous. I loved your parents, the inn's a freaking institution in town, and as you yourself pointed out, I've enjoyed more than my share of your hospitality over the years. I'm kind of ashamed I didn't think of it myself."

"Thanks," Maxwell said, standing and shaking Mike's hand.

"Don't mention it. Besides, I figure it behooves me to stay on your good side."

Maxwell didn't have a clue what that meant, but he figured it was best not to ask.

❊ ❊ ∧ ∧ ❊ ❊

It didn't dawn on Deborah until she got there that she hadn't been to Corrina's house in months. That dinner for Ryan's birthday when he went postal on Tyler. Since then, they'd spoken dozens of times and gotten together for a few Wednesday night dinners at the inn, but Deborah hadn't been in this house since the early summer.

There was a time when Corrina had the entire family over for brunch nearly every Sunday. Mom and Dad would let Larry Mullen handle things for the afternoon so they could be there, and more often than not Maxwell and Annie would come up from Manhattan to join them. Mimosa in hand, Corrina would toast the family and then each person sitting at the table would talk about their highs and lows for the week. It was a great way to keep everyone in the loop and let people know what was on your mind. It was also a useful tool for soliciting advice if you needed it.

Then Dad died one Sunday morning and it was a month before anyone had the heart to do anything on a Sunday again. Not long after that, Ryan's mother died and he moved in with Corrina and Gardner, and that adjustment period began. By the time it was over – Deborah assumed it was over by now – the brunch was little more than a memory.

"Are these new?" Deborah asked as she examined the coffee mugs she and Corrina drank from.

"They're great, aren't they? I got them in Boston a couple of weeks ago."

"Is that when you went up for that lawyer's convention?"

"That was months ago. No, this was when we took Ryan to visit some of his old friends. Gardner got us a hotel room at the Fairmont and while Ryan hung out with his buddies we reintroduced ourselves."

"I guess it's tough for you two to have time alone with a teenager around, huh?"

"The teenager's nothing, really. These days he's often invisible. But Gardner has been working insane hours just about every night. I really feel it when I've been alone all day and then he doesn't come home until nine. At least the money is really good. So how's the menu coming for the party?"

"I think we're okay. The treats for the kids are easy and I'm playing with a bunch of appetizers."

"You're not doing anything too out there with the sweets, right?"

"No, I've learned my lesson. No marzipan or ribboned sugar this year. Chocolate, peanut butter, marshmallow – I'm sticking to the basics."

"You can be more adventurous with the adult stuff. Those sherried mushroom turnovers were great last year."

"You liked those? I could do them again, I guess."

"And those hoisin chicken tarts. People flipped over them."

"Yeah, I guess I could make those again as well." This was classic Corrina, telling you to take care of something and then directing every move you made. How did someone at the back end of the birth order become such a control freak?

"You should. We want everything about this party to blow people away."

"It'll be great, don't worry. To tell you the truth, I'm much more concerned about dinner the night before than I am about this."

"Why's that?"

"It's the last formal meal I'm serving at the inn. A cocktail party is a totally different thing. But this dinner – this is what I've been doing for the last fifteen years. How do I sum up my entire life in this place in six courses?"

"You can't, so don't worry about it."

Deborah was surprised by how dismissive Corrina sounded. "Is that really your advice?"

"You said it yourself. You can't sum up your entire life at the inn in six courses. So don't even try. You'll make yourself crazy."

This from the person micromanaging every element of the party.

"Thanks," Deborah said thinly. "I'll take that under advisement."

Corrina sipped her coffee and for a short while Deborah thought they might have run out of things to say to one another. Even the party wasn't enough of a conversation piece these days. Corrina had dispatched her instructions – had she really needed to see Deborah in person to say what she'd said? – with a few terse sentences and then their "business" was done.

"What would Dad have said?" Corrina said as Deborah examined a new handmade clock on the far wall. Corrina was certainly being acquisitive these days, wasn't she?

"Excuse me?"

"What would Dad have said about the last dinner at the inn?"

"There wouldn't be a last dinner at the inn if Dad was still around."

Corrina smirked at her. Deborah couldn't remember the exact point at which her younger sister started acting like the senior sibling, but by now she had become accustomed to such expressions. "Are you telling me you don't have conversations with him in your head?"

Deborah smiled, some of the tension abating. "You do that too?"

"Of course I do. Whenever I need a little advice. He's even better at it in the afterlife than he was before." Corrina let a small grin come to her lips. "Sounds more like me."

"You would like that."

"So what would he say if you asked him about it?"

Deborah furrowed her brow. "He'd tell me to follow my heart. To figure out what I was trying to accomplish and then head directly toward that goal." Deborah laughed. "Then he'd make me experiment with three dozen different dishes – all of which he'd 'volunteer' to taste – until I came up with exactly what I was looking for."

Corrina nodded. "I guess you should have asked him, then, huh?"

Deborah nodded her head. "It's not that easy. If anything, it's worse because I can feel him in my head, but I need him in person."

Corrina studied her mug. "I've been missing him a lot lately. Mom all the time still, but I really miss Dad again. I'm sure it has to do with selling the inn and with the party and everything. And maybe because I've been having so many conversations with him these days."

Corrina looked her straight in the eyes at that point, and Deborah expected her to elaborate. Why was she talking to Dad so often? What did she need his advice about? Instead of taking this further though, Corrina looked down at her coffee, then out the window, and then stood up.

"Did I show you the new centerpiece I got when we were in Boston?" she said, moving toward the dining room.

Had Corrina been expecting Deborah to ask what was troubling her? They'd never needed to prompt each other in the past. Deborah took one last sip of coffee and got up to follow her sister into the dining room. She'd leave directly from there. If Corrina wanted to reach out, Deborah would be there, but she wasn't going to chase after her.

❀❀∧∧❀❀

Tyler couldn't remember ever laboring over which restaurant to go to with Patrice. Early in their relationship, every place was new – places Tyler had previously thought about going with dates as he passed them or read about in the paper. Not long after that, they developed a collection of favorites, places they could go if they just felt like getting out, along with others for special occasions. Even toward the end of their relationship, they were comfortable with the old standbys and could even find a bit of an oasis in someplace new.

However, choosing a restaurant for their dinner this time was proving confounding. Did it suggest too much if he decided on someplace they used to frequent? Was he willing to risk a bad meal or bad service at someplace previously untried? Maybe he should have let Patrice pick the place; it was unlikely she would have turned this into the angst-fest he'd turned it into.

Finally, he decided on The Phoenix Grill. They had gone there many times before, but the restaurant had hired a new chef in September and the menu had changed dramatically from the last time they'd been there. It was like going somewhere new and old at the same time.

Picking Patrice up from the cottage was a bit surreal. It was so familiar – he'd lived here for nearly half a decade – that he felt entirely out of place waiting in the foyer while Patrice got her jacket. Shouldn't he be sitting on the couch watching the news while she finished getting ready? Or maybe making sure he didn't leave the light on in the bathroom or something like that? Tyler chose to focus on the print Patrice had put up in the hallway to replace one of the framed photographs he'd taken with him when he moved out. It was a watercolor of a daylily. A little generic for Tyler's tastes, but it certainly brightened the spot.

Now sitting at the Phoenix sipping a margarita, any uneasiness had sloughed away. Patrice looked fabulous and she seemed genuinely glad to be here with him. They talked about work and caught each other up on the lives of their friends. Precisely the kind of thing they would have done if they were in the middle of their relationship rather than at its coda.

"I miss this," Patrice said during a break in the conversation.

Tyler reached out for her hand and squeezed it. He wondered if he should keep it there or if that would make her uncomfortable. "I do too."

Patrice took his hand in both of hers. "We were pretty good buds, huh? I mean on top of all that other stuff."

Tyler smiled. "Yeah, we were good buds. You were kinda fun to hang out with."

"Especially on Monday mornings." Patrice's shop was closed on Mondays and she and Tyler often stayed in bed until after noon, making love, holding each other, listening to music, and just replenishing. On most winter Mondays they would never leave the house, while afternoons the rest of the year were devoted to errands and other necessities to get them through the week. As a rule, though, they spent every Monday together unless a conflict couldn't be avoided.

Tyler risked locking eyes with his former lover. "I think I really miss Mondays."

Patrice closed her hands over his and neither said anything for a long moment. "You're doing okay, though?"

"I'm okay. Like I said, I wish I was selling more pictures and, well, it's been a year, you know? But I'm holding up all right." He liked feeling his hand embraced by Patrice's and was thankful that she didn't have any qualms about touching him this way. "How about you?"

"Six-and-a-half on a scale of ten."

He nodded knowingly. "What would make it better?"

Patrice squeezed his hand and then tilted her head to the side. She was gorgeous from any angle. "More of this."

Was she saying what he thought she was saying? "More of...us?"

She wrinkled her nose. "I'm being ridiculous, aren't I?"

"No, why is that ridiculous?"

She shook her head. "Oh, I don't know."

"I think more of this would make me better, too."

She looked right into his soul this time. If it were possible to allow her deeper, he would have. "Do you really think so?"

"Patrice, you were the definition of 'better' for me."

"Until I wasn't."

"No. Always."

They actually managed to finish their meals, but Tyler had no idea what he'd eaten. All he could think about was being alone with Patrice, about recapturing the best of what they were together. He recognized the feeling building up in him, the hunger for all of her, for a seamlessness between the two of them. It wasn't that long ago that he felt it regularly.

They drove home quietly, Patrice playing with the hair on the back of Tyler's neck while Tyler wished he'd picked a restaurant closer to the cottage. When he stopped the car, there was no question about where the evening was going.

Patrice leaned over, kissed him deeply and said, "Let's go inside."

They embraced in the very foyer that had seemed so strange to Tyler earlier. They kissed and pawed at each other, barely remembering to close the front door first. Slowly, they sank to the floor. The bedroom was perhaps forty feet away, but it was miles further than Tyler was interested in traveling at that moment. So underneath the daylily, they explored each other, passionately and hungrily. The suppleness of Patrice's skin, the curve of her knees, and the softness of her breasts were wonders to him, something he knew so well but thrilled to as though he'd never experienced them before. Tyler hadn't as much as kissed a woman since he'd split with Patrice, and now he wondered if anyone else could possibly make him feel this way. In this moment, though, that wasn't an issue. Maybe it never would be again.

Eventually they made it to bed and began making love again. Tyler couldn't remember the last time he had been this voracious. Afterward, they lay facing each other, Tyler's fingers running along Patrice's back as he kissed her forehead, the bridge of her nose, her exposed shoulder.

"I am so glad I forgot what that felt like," he said dreamily.

"What do you mean?"

"If I remembered what making love to you felt like while we were apart, I think I might have jumped off a bridge."

Patrice kissed him passionately again and the thought came to mind that it might not yet be time to go to sleep. "I don't want you to forget it again," she said.

"No, I definitely think I'll remember it this time."

She nuzzled against him and he kissed her hair. Holding her was nearly as much of a pleasure as any other physical act between them. "You can stay, right?" she said.

"There's no place else I want to be."

Seven

Wednesday, October 13
Eighteen days before the party

Maria's affection for James Taylor bordered on the obsessional. Since she had been a teenager, JT had been the one singer-songwriter guaranteed to affect her mood precisely the way she'd hoped. If she needed to raise her spirits, she could always turn to "Whenever I See Your Smiling Face," or "Only One," or his great cover of "Up on the Roof." If she needed to feed her melancholy, there was always "Fire and Rain," or "Millworker," or the entire *Mud Slide Slim* album. If she needed a little romance, JT was there for her. If she needed a little thoughtful contemplation, JT was there for her. Her relationship with JT was one of her most reliable, really.

Still, she'd forgotten how edifying it was to play James Taylor. Clearly, she couldn't sing like him, and no one replicated the guitar sounds he created, but the songs filled her in an entirely different way when she was able to bring them to life herself.

She was into the third verse of "Gaia," one of JT's most profound sociological songs, when the phone rang. Maria thought about letting the call go to voicemail as she'd done a couple of times a few hours ago when she'd first started playing, but the interruption had taken her out of the song. She might as well answer it.

As soon as she did, she wished she hadn't. It was the credit card company calling to confirm some recent charges. Doug had gone online last night to buy them both tablet computers, which triggered the company's alert systems. As an electronic voice asked her to confirm everything from their dinner the other night, to the produce she'd bought yesterday, to the gas Doug had obviously gotten on his way to work this morning, Maria wished she were back singing JT. She was all for fraud protection, but couldn't they program their computers not to worry if a big electronics sale one night was followed by nothing more than a stop at the neighborhood Gulf station the next day?

Finally satisfying the machine she'd spent the last seven minutes with, Maria returned to the den and her guitar. Should she try "Gaia" again or move on? That song was all about the emotional build, and it wouldn't feel the same if she tried to recapture that feeling so soon after she'd last gone after it. As she sat down on her stool, though, she noticed that the song on the music stand was "Something in the Way She Moves." That was odd. The songbook was in alphabetical order, so this song was nowhere near "Gaia," and she'd used the book so often over the years that the spine was completely broken. There was no chance that the book would have flipped to those pages because of some movement in the room.

The thought of the new song stirred a memory of Deborah from something like fifteen years ago. Deborah was having her first serious crush – Cal, or Carl, or Kurt, or something like that – and she would ask Maria to play the song incessantly while she mooned over the boy. Maria pretended to play the song grudgingly, but she was secretly tickled at the idea of providing the soundtrack to her sister's love life. She also enjoyed the far-ranging conversations they'd have afterward, conversations that always started about the boy – Clark! That was his name – but would evolve into talks about family, friends, careers, food (of course), music (*of course*), or even recent movies. They could talk for an hour or more barely stopping for breath. When was the last time their conversation went for more than four minutes without trailing off?

For that matter, when was the last time Deborah mentioned a man? Had she even dated anyone since those regrettable few weeks with Tom from the hardware store? That had gone so badly that the entire family still had to drive to another town if they needed a screwdriver.

Looking down at her guitar, Maria played a few lines from "Something in the Way She Moves," remembering how Deborah's eyes sparkled when she used to talk about Clark. She hoped her sister got another chance to sparkle like that soon. Maybe that's why the book had magically flipped to this song; maybe Deborah was dating someone.

The phone rang again and Maria stopped playing. She got up and checked the caller ID. It was an 800 number. There was no chance she was going to deal with a credit card company and a telemarketer on the same day. She let the phone finish its programmed five rings while she went back to the stool.

When she got there, she found the songbook page turned to "Gaia." She took a deep breath and exhaled slowly. Maybe it was time to switch to a different songwriter today.

❀❀∧∧❀❀

The small talk rarely went this deep into the meal. Whenever Maxwell had lunch with a Chamber board member, there was always time for sharing pictures, bringing everyone up to date on the family, and chatting about sports. Usually, though, by the time entrees arrived, the conversation got more intense and even confrontational. Not today, though. When the waiter came over to take coffee orders, the topic was lawn maintenance. Just three buddies chewing the fat. What was the agenda here? Were Will Champion and Mike Mills planning to ask Maxwell to go steady with them?

"So was I the only one who thought Bruce looked pretty ragged at the Columbus Day parade?" Mike said as his cappuccino arrived. He pulled the cup up to his lips and peered over it at Will.

Will moved in his chair as though Mike had kicked him under the table. "Well, I think your paper's little exposé has him very nervous."

Mike spoke through his coffee cup. "He should be nervous." He put down his drink and leaned toward Maxwell. From the corner of his eye, Maxwell could see Will doing the same thing. "Don't you think so, Maxwell?"

They'd obviously moved on to today's key topic. Maxwell still wasn't sure what the agenda was, though. "You're not thinking he's going to get indicted, are you?"

Mike shrugged broadly. "It isn't inconceivable."

Maxwell tipped his head toward first Mike and then Will. "It's inconceivable to me. Bruce might be a small-town politician, but he has the savvy of a ten-term congressman. There's no way he doesn't slither out of this."

Mike nodded slowly. "It might not be as easy as you think for him to escape this time."

Maxwell chuckled. "Your judgment is a little suspect in this area – though you've never told me why you have such an obsession with Bruce." He looked over at Will. "You don't think he's going to hang over this, do you?"

Will looked down at his coffee, then over at Mike, and finally at Maxwell. "Hang as in be removed from office or go to jail? Nah, there's very little chance of that. Next November is another story, though."

Maxwell finally reached for his own coffee cup. "Really? That's more than a year from now. This isn't the first time Bruce has been implicated in dirty stuff, and he's been reelected twice. You don't think the town will be over this by then?"

Mike smiled slyly. "Not if the media does its job."

Maxwell laughed. "What *did* he do to you?"

Mike put up a hand. "That's not the point. The point is we have reason to believe the mayor might truly be vulnerable to opposition this time."

Maxwell remembered similar talk three years ago. Bruce took sixty-four percent of the vote. "If anyone is crazy enough to oppose him."

Will put a hand on Maxwell's forearm. "'Crazy' is a strong word, Maxwell."

Maxwell found the solemnity in Will's tone surprising. "Are you telling me that one of the two of you are thinking about running? Is that why the *Post* is going after this story so hard?"

Even Joey would have been able to read the conspiratorial glance that passed between Maxwell's two lunch companions then.

"Neither of us has the right constitution for politics," Will said slowly. "You, on the other hand, have both the mettle and the vision."

Maxwell was so unprepared for this conversation, that he thought he might have heard the stationery story owner wrong. "The mettle and the vision for what?"

Mike leaned forward. "Don't try to tell me you've never considered political office."

Had he ever considered political office? In many ways, being president of the Chamber was exactly that. Certainly, it was political enough. "Are you guys saying what I think you're saying?"

Mike smiled at him. "If you think we're saying you should seriously consider running for mayor next year, then yes."

Maxwell felt his gut tighten. Mayor? Him? It wasn't as though he'd never considered the idea of some day pursuing an elected position in Oldham. He'd been so focused on enterprise, though. The Chamber position was a nice bridge because the policymaking was all about business. Would he have an equal passion for education, civic affairs, security, and the like?

"There are a lot of people who would rally behind you, Maxwell," Will said.

Maxwell guessed that was true. The merchants in Oldham were extremely vocal, and monthly spats aside, he'd been a strong advocate for them.

While he was still wrapping his mind around the idea of running for mayor, he had to consider the possibility that running might lead to winning, even if Bruce had crushed his other opponents. If he won, his life would change dramatically. This meant that Annie and Joey's lives would change as well. Maxwell was sure the toddler could handle it. After this weekend, he wasn't positive he could say the same about his wife.

"Well, I can honestly tell you that this is the last thing I thought we'd be talking about today, guys. You're going to have to give me a little time to absorb this."

❅ ❅ ∧ ∧ ❅ ❅

Maria had no idea why she hadn't thought of this sooner. Providence was only an hour and a half from Oldham, which meant she only needed to get out of the house by ten or so any time she wanted to have lunch with her daughter. Olivia had seemed so far away since she went to college, but Brown was actually closer than either Manhattan or Boston, and they'd taken day trips to both cities numerous times over the years. And getting out of the house was much less of an issue for her the past week than it had been since late August. On most days, Maria would find herself stirring when Doug got up for his shower, and by the time he was off to work, she'd be gearing up for a session with her guitar and her songbooks.

Shawn Colvin's album of cover songs was on the iPod for the drive. Listening to a distinctive singer-songwriter like Colvin interpreting other songwriters was inspirational for Maria, making her realize she needed to infuse more of herself in the songs she chose. Many of the artists Maria admired covered the work of others on occasion – several of JT's most successful songs were covers – but for some reason it never struck her until now that she should be doing what singers did with the best covers, performing the song as though she'd written it herself.

Between Colvin's silky voice and Maria's rumination on interpretation, the drive seemed to last no more than a few minutes. In fact, it seemed to take as long to navigate through the traffic around the campus, as it had taken to make the entire trip up I-95.

Maria wanted to surprise Olivia with her visit, so she hadn't let her know she was coming. Now that she was out of the car, though, she had to call Olivia's cell phone, since she wasn't sure where her daughter might be. Wednesdays were good days to visit Olivia, because she had a ten o'clock class and then a long break until her class at four. Wednesdays would in all likelihood be the days Maria came up when she wanted to take her daughter to lunch.

Olivia picked up on the third ring. "Hey, what's up?"

"Nothing," Maria said, trying to keep the playfulness out of her voice. "I was just thinking about getting some lunch."

"Gee, Mom, thanks for sharing that. Did you post it on your Facebook page?"

"I appreciate the reminder. What are you up to?"

"I hung back to talk to my professor for a few minutes after class and I'm walking back to my dorm now. I'll probably grab some lunch myself pretty soon."

"Sounds good," Maria said, hearing the smile in her voice. "So where should we go?"

"Huh?"

"Well, I was in the neighborhood, so I thought I'd hit a greasy spoon with my daughter."

There was a pause on the other end, and Maria imagined Olivia's wide-eyed expression at the thought that her mother had made this trip just to see her.

"You're here?" Olivia said after ten seconds or so.

"Isn't that cool?"

"Yeah, cool. And you want to have lunch?"

"Well, it's about noon and we're both hungry, so it seems like an option we should consider."

"Uh, yeah, great. There are a few places just off campus I've been wanting to try. I just need to drop my stuff off in my room."

They set up a place to meet and Maria strolled around the campus for fifteen minutes while Olivia did whatever she needed to do. It was windier up here than it had been in Oldham this morning, and Maria wished she'd brought a heavier coat. None of that mattered, though, when she enfolded her daughter in her arms.

"I can't believe you just got in the car and drove up here," Olivia said when they started walking toward the restaurant.

Maria smiled broadly. "It was really easy. This could be a thing we do, you know? I know I don't usually like to drive too far by myself, but this was a piece of cake, really."

Olivia just nodded, cinched up the collar of her coat, and they walked to the restaurant without saying much else.

They wound up at an Indian buffet that Olivia hadn't been to before. "I hear it's good," she said, "and we won't have to wait for our food." They got a table, went up to fill their plates, and by the time they returned, their waiter had come by with naan and pieces of tandoori chicken.

"I'm not going to want to have anything for dinner tonight," Maria said, examining the bounty she'd put on her plate. "Your father's going to have to get by with leftovers."

"So Dad's good?"

"Your dad's great. He misses you, of course, but work has been fantastic lately."

"Yeah, he mentioned that the last time we talked. How's everybody else?"

Maria did a quick rundown of the family, including the latest on the party planning. "Also, I have a feeling that your Aunt Deborah might be seeing someone?"

Olivia brightened. "Really? Have you met him?"

"I'm not even sure if there *is* a him, but I just have a feeling."

"Are you having *visions*, Mom? That's not exactly like you."

Maria frowned. "I'm not having visions. Just intuition. And what do you mean it's not exactly like me? Creative people trust their imaginations."

"I'm sure creative people do," Olivia said slyly.

"What's *that* supposed to mean?"

Olivia waved her hands dismissively. "Nothing, never mind."

Olivia concentrated on her food for several minutes after that. Her last comment had thrown Maria off balance. Did her daughter think she was an automaton? Didn't she remember the guitar playing and songwriting? Had Maria spent so much time away from her instrument that her daughter didn't associate her with the guitar at all? Maria wanted to tell Olivia about starting to play again and about the new songs that were starting to simmer in her brain, but something held her back.

The conversation picked up again a few minutes later, but stayed very much at the surface level: the differences in the weather between Providence and Oldham, what the Halloween decorations looked like on Hickory Avenue, how limited the salad bar selections were in the dining hall, that sort of thing. Maria had been hoping for conversation closer to the great heart-to-hearts she and Olivia had regularly the month before Olivia left, but there was time for that. Olivia didn't have another class until four, so maybe they'd find a coffee bar to kick back in for a while before Maria headed home.

That plan evaporated as soon as Maria signed the credit card receipt. Olivia stood up quickly and shrugged on her jacket.

"I gotta get back," she said.

"Really? I was hoping we could go for a little walk, maybe grab some coffee."

Olivia scrunched up her face. "I'm in the middle of my day, Mom."

Maria looked down at the table and then back up at her daughter. "But you don't have another class for a while."

"And I have to prepare for that class. One of the things I've learned very quickly is that I can't just show up here the way I did in high school. Besides, I'm supposed to meet a friend at three."

Maria's heart grew heavier. "You can't reschedule because your mother drove an hour and a half to see you?"

"If you'd have let me know you were coming, I could have set things up differently. You kinda surprised me here."

"That was sort of the point."

Olivia's shoulder's slumped. "I know, Mom, and it was really nice of you, but I'm kinda in the middle of things."

There wasn't much else to say about this, so Maria got up from the table and asked Olivia if she would walk with her to her car.

As she opened the car door, Maria remembered the tear-soaked goodbye she and her daughter shared in late August. Now, Olivia was practically shutting the car door on Maria's legs.

"You're still planning to come down for the party, right?" Maria said as she started the engine.

Olivia bobbed her head quickly. "Yeah, of course. I've been planning to come down all along."

"Just making sure."

Olivia reached through the rolled-down window at that point and hugged her. "I love you, Mom."

"Love you, too, Liv."

Maria pulled out of the space and waved to her daughter as she drove off, realizing as she did that she would probably never make a visit like this again.

❀❀∧∧❀❀

Deborah figured Sage and she weren't likely to run out of conversation, something that often concerned her when she saw someone socially for the first time. In Sage's case, though, they had a nearly endless number of prompts if things bogged down. All she'd have to do is mention a food item – mustards maybe, or perhaps Ventresca tuna – and they'd be good for another fifteen minutes. That made her that much more comfortable about the idea of their getting drinks together.

It was therefore surprising to find herself off the topic of food entirely, only minutes after her glass of wine arrived.

"Yes, I get it," Sage said with the same intensity with which he'd sold her on preserves when they'd met, "and I'll grant you it's nice to see a museum where an abandoned warehouse used to be, but don't you think it's a little *artificial*?"

"Well," Deborah said with a coy smile, "it's a building. They're rarely organic."

"You know what I mean."

"I don't, actually."

Sage tipped his head toward her, acknowledging that he knew that she knew that he knew she was playing with him. "The museum has nothing to do with the rest of the neighborhood."

Deborah glanced at him over her wineglass. "You know where that kind of thinking leads, don't you?"

"Logical growth?"

"I was thinking entropy."

Deborah wondered where that retort came from. She wasn't sure she'd ever said the word "entropy" aloud before.

Sage shrugged. "Yeah, you're probably right."

"Wow, I never win arguments that easily."

"You must be arguing with the wrong people."

Deborah considered that, and then tried to remember the last argument she'd had at all — not that this exchange about the recently erected modern art museum in the former industrial town of Creston Mills counted as an actual argument. She'd yelled at one of her produce purveyors a few days ago about giving her paltry parsnips. Was that an argument? She'd won that one as well. Maybe she *did* usually win arguments this easily, at least when they were entirely innocuous.

Sage caught her eye and smiled at her, acknowledging that he'd noticed she'd drifted off for a moment.

"I was doing some reading about the Sugar Maple Inn," he said. "Did you know that it was the headquarters for a prohibition opposition group in the early twenties."

"I might have heard something about that, you know, since I've spent nearly my entire life there."

"Yes, I guess you would have. There was quite a bit about your parents at the historical society."

Deborah's eyes widened. "You went to the historical society to research my family? Do you do this with everyone you meet."

"Not everyone. To be honest, I was there to look up some information about *my* building. I'm trying to come up with a way to incorporate some history into the store's merchandising. While I was there, I decided to look up the legendary Golds."

"Does that mean you were a little bit awed about having drinks with me tonight?"

Sage grinned. "Yes, but not for that reason." He took a sip of his Laphroaig. "Your parents were honest-to-goodness icons in this community. That's very impressive."

"And you can bet I use it shamelessly to my advantage. Just the other day, I threw my name around to get the best treadmill at the gym. I'm thinking about using it to get an invitation to lunch at the White House next."

Sage nodded slowly. "I get it; you don't like to talk about your family's place in the community."

Deborah put up a hand. "No, that's not really it at all. It's just that Oldham has a lot of icons. It seems that two-thirds of the people here have been around for decades."

"Ah, so I'm dragging down the average."

Deborah smiled. "Yeah, between you and the new owners of the Sugar Maple, the whole town is going to hell."

The conversation detoured away from Oldham at that point. First toward a speech about nanotechnology that Sage saw on YouTube, then toward national politics, and eventually even toward condiments, though not specifically mustard. Three glasses of wine later, they strolled out onto the street, where both of them had remarkably found parking spaces. They stopped by Deborah's car and she pulled out her keys.

"I had a great time tonight, thanks," Sage said.

Deborah reached out to touch him on the arm. "Me too."

"Your officially my best friend in Oldham now. You snuck past the mailman in the last half-hour."

"I'm honored."

They locked eyes at that point and neither said anything for a very long moment.

Sage leaned toward her. "Can we do it again soon?"

"I think I'd like that."

"Would it bother you if we called our next evening a 'date?'"

Deborah felt her face warming. "I'd be good with calling it that."

He leaned over and kissed her softly on the cheek. Deborah strongly wanted to pull him toward her, but she knew it was smarter to leave things at this.

"I'll call you tomorrow," he said, taking her hand for a brief instant before turning toward his car.

Eight

Thursday, October 14
Seventeen days before the party

Maxwell felt a little embarrassed to realize that he hadn't been inside the kitchen of the Sugar Maple Inn in years. He couldn't count the number of meals he'd had at the inn during that time, but he'd always been satisfied with waiting for the food to come out. He hadn't gotten the gourmand gene that it seemed most of the rest of the family had, and he rarely had any interest in either seeing how food was prepared or helping with the process. In that regard, Annie and he were a perfect match. Their kitchen was largely decorative, somewhat like the house's fourth bedroom that they used for storage.

When he entered, Deborah was working over a huge slab of fish with tweezers, pulling out bones. The fish looked like salmon to Maxwell, but knowing Deborah, he assumed it was some rare cousin of salmon, sustainably caught in a small inlet in Newfoundland. Around her, three of Deborah's assistants worked intently, one chopping onions, another stirring something in a pot, the third throwing all of his strength at a large ball of dough.

Deborah didn't appear to notice him, so he said, "Hey." When that didn't elicit a reaction, he moved closer to her and said it again.

Deborah glanced up. It appeared that the sight of her brother momentarily disoriented her. Maxwell could practically see her thoughts. Maybe she was trying to remember the last time he'd been in this room.

"Hey," she said. "What are you doing here?"

"There's something I wanted to let you know about."

Deborah's face creased. "Please tell me it's not a job idea."

"What?"

Deborah shook her head quickly. "Nothing. It just seems that every time someone wants to tell me about something these days, it's about where I should go for my next job."

"I'm staying out of that one, sis. If you're comfortable going out on the high wire without a net, I'm with you."

"Thanks. That was a metaphor I hadn't considered. It makes me feel so much better about my future. So what's up?"

At that point, something clattered to the floor, causing Maxwell to startle. He wouldn't last an hour in this environment. Of course, Deborah probably wouldn't last long at one of the Chamber meetings. *One man's torment is another's pleasure, I suppose.*

"Do you think we can talk someplace less... under siege?" he said.

Deborah offered a tiny shrug, put the fish back in the refrigerator, washed her hands, and gestured him out toward the dining room.

"So what's going on?" Deborah said, sitting.

"I was following my orders from Corrina and I sat down with Mike Mills at the *Post* to pitch him on doing a feature piece in the paper about the party. He's going to run it on the Friday before Halloween."

"That's great. I'm sure Corrina is thrilled."

"Not that she'd ever admit it. There's more, though. Mike loves your cooking, you know."

Deborah brightened. "It's great when Mike comes here. He'll eat anything I send out. He has excellent taste." She paused for a moment, her brows lowering. "Or maybe he doesn't have any taste buds at all."

"Let's go with the former. Anyway, he decided he wants to do a completely separate piece about the last meal you're serving at the inn to run the week after the new guys take over."

"Wow, really?"

"I figured you'd be happy about that. The ink can't hurt, right?"

Deborah offered him a forced smile. "Yeah, it's great."

Maxwell had no idea what was going on. "You know, I realize it isn't *The New York Times*, but I'm guessing most people would be a little more excited about something like this."

Deborah glanced past him out the window. "No, it's good."

"Sis, what am I missing?"

Deborah's gaze at the distance deepened. Maxwell was beginning to wonder if "feature piece in the *Oldham Post*" was somehow code for "we're going to have to amputate your left leg."

In a week of improbabilities, what happened next was the most improbable thing of all. A tear started running down the face of Maxwell's ultra-composed, eminently competent sister. Was this some kind of delayed reaction to all the onions her assistant had been chopping?

"I can't figure it out," Deborah said, wiping at her cheekbone.

"Can't figure what out?"

"That dinner. I can't figure out what I'm going to make for the last meal at the inn. And now we're going to have a reporter here chronicling my crash-and-burn."

"Deborah, how many times have you crashed and burned here?"

Deborah turned to face him, her eyes wide. "Enough times, believe me. But I'm saving my worst for last. I can't think of a single thing to serve. I'm going to be sending Fruit Loops out to the dining room."

Maxwell took a deep breath and exhaled slowly, as he always did when someone was having a crisis in front of him. It had been his experience that exuding calm actually helped to calm down others.

"You'll figure it out," he said. "You always do."

Deborah threw her hands up. "How do I know? I've never had to make a meal like this before."

There was no chance he was going to make any progress with this conversation. Maybe not having a job to turn to was affecting Deborah more than she had let on. Maybe there was another issue at play entirely. Regardless, Maxwell knew that talking about it more wasn't going to improve Deborah's outlook. Instead, he just sat with her.

A few minutes later, she told him she had to get the rest of the pin bones from her fish, and she escaped back into the kitchen.

❈❈∧∧❈❈

A few days ago, when Maria had made the appointment to take a music lesson, she had an entirely different purpose in mind. Back then, she thought brushing up on her playing would be a fun way to pass a little time. Today, though, as she sat in the waiting area at McGarrigle's, she realized the lesson was going to serve as a critical diversion. She was still hurting over the way her "surprise" with Olivia had turned out. Her daughter e-mailed her that night saying it was "great" to see her, but not suggesting that she was looking for an encore any time soon. Meanwhile, Doug tried to be sympathetic, but he couldn't hide the fact that he thought dropping in on one's eighteen-year-old daughter was rarely a good idea. The entire experience left her feeling squeamish, as though she'd shown up at a formal party in cutoffs.

What she needed right now was something to take her mind completely off of this. Playing at her music stand helped a bit, but it was too easy to let her thoughts overwhelm her at home. That wouldn't happen with a teacher in the room with her.

"Maria?"

Maria turned toward the voice to find Martha McGarrigle standing five feet away with a bemused expression.

"Martha, hi. How have you been?"

In a town like Oldham, it wasn't easy to be a local and to go a long stretch without seeing another local, but it had to have been years since Maria had spoken with Martha. The woman looked great, slimmer and more casually put together than Maria remembered.

"I'm doing really well. This place is a blessing and curse, as always, but things are good. How about you?"

"Everything is fine. I'm dealing with a bit of an empty-nest thing right now, but my husband and daughter are great."

"Wow, I can't believe you have a kid out of the house already. My oldest just turned seven."

Martha gestured toward Maria's guitar case. "Is that yours?"

Maria patted the case. "Yeah, I'm here for my first lesson since I was a teenager."

"Wow, I completely forgot that you played."

Maria nodded. "I haven't played seriously in a while. I decided I wanted to pick it up again, and it seemed like a good idea to get some pointers."

"Yeah, makes sense. Can you play something for me now?"

Maria looked around the waiting area. The only other person there was a woman who seemed to be in her late fifties who had a piano book on her lap. Maria knew the store would get much busier later after school let out.

"Really?"

"Yeah. I was on my way back to my office to pay bills. This sounds like much more fun."

Feeling a bit apprehensive – she was here, after all, because she knew her guitar playing needed work – Maria opened the case and pulled out her guitar. Checking the tuning, she suddenly couldn't think of a single song she knew. How foolish would she seem to Martha if she couldn't play more than a line or two?

Finally, Dar Williams's "The Babysitter's Here" popped into her head. It was a song from the perspective of a child whose beloved babysitter was going off to college. As was true of so many songs Maria loved, this one had evolved in meaning for her over the years, and as she began to sing the first verse, she realized it had shifted yet again.

Thinking about this caused her to botch a chord change in the refrain, but she finished without stumbling again. The lyrics made her a little teary, as they always did, leading her to wonder if it were the best choice to play for Martha, but Martha smiled at her when Maria was finished.

"That was really good," Martha said. "You have a nice touch. And you sing well, too."

Maria looked down at her guitar. "Thanks. My voice isn't quite as rusty as my playing, but both could use a lot of work."

"Not as much as you think." Martha leaned toward her and spoke conspiratorially. "You wouldn't believe what some of the 'advanced' students play like."

They chuckled together, and then Martha tapped the neck of Maria's guitar. "I've gotta go. This is great that you're doing this. Who's your lesson with?"

"Colin."

"Oh, good. He'll push you once he realizes how good you are. This is great. I'll see you again soon."

With that, Martha left to pay her bills. Maria fingerpicked a few more chords on the guitar before putting it away, just in time for Colin to come out to greet her.

❉ ❉ ∧ ∧ ❉ ❉

The peepers were out in full force. This was the weekend every year when the masses decided to descend on the Connecticut River Valley. It had been busy the first two weekends in October and it would stay busy through Halloween, but the media always hyped this weekend as the peak viewing time and that always pulled in the crowds.

Corrina had been working at the Visitors Bureau long enough that she knew to gird herself for the onslaught. It always started around lunchtime on Thursday and stayed intense through Sunday brunch. She'd been answering questions nonstop for the past three hours. If there weren't three people waiting in line in the office, there was someone on the phone. She'd answered questions about museums, craft shops, scenic views, and historical points of interest so often that she felt as though she were activating some digital recording device rather than actually speaking. The predictability broke only occasionally when someone came in asking for a toy store or for a specific type of restaurant. This year, there were decidedly more people asking how to get a table for dinner at the Sugar Maple Inn, something not even the chef's sister could provide at this point, unless the prospective diner wanted to stick around until Monday night.

At two thirty, Corrina got a modicum of relief from Lita Ford, a "cool grandma" who worked at the bureau about fifteen hours a week. Lita entered while a peeper from New Jersey was dominating Corrina with questions about seemingly every brochure in the office, and she quickly took care of the other patrons. It was ten minutes before Corrina could even say hello to her.

"What was that all about?" Lita said when the Jersey guy finally left.

"I think it was about the entire history of the Valley. That guy definitely wanted to make sure he got the peak experience."

"Man, I'm glad I didn't get here five minutes earlier."

"Try fifteen."

Lita's eyes widened. "You were talking to him for fifteen minutes already?"

Corrina sighed. "Maybe more. It felt like an hour and a half."

Lita shook her head slowly. "You definitely need a break. Why don't you go get some coffee? I'll hold down the fort."

Lita didn't need to twist her arm. Corrina grabbed her sweater and headed out, holding the door for yet another patron as she did.

The traffic on Hickory Avenue was predictably thick. Corrina noticed license plates from four states while she stood at the crosswalk. Under normal circumstances, she could be certain oncoming drivers would stop for a pedestrian in the crosswalk, but with so many out-of-towners here, she wasn't sure, so she waited for an opening, glancing longingly at the coffee bar across the street as she did.

At that moment, a couple of teenagers came out of the deli next to the coffee bar. Corrina instantly recognized Ryan. What she couldn't place as easily was the carefree smile on his face. It had been years since she'd seen him with that expression, and seeing it now reminded her how handsome the boy could be when he lightened up.

The cause for the expression was easy to identify, though the subject was not. It was the bright-eyed girl with shoulder-length brown hair who'd just laid a kiss on Ryan's cheek. Ryan responded by kissing the girl on the lips and then wrapping his arm around her shoulder as they walked down the street away from Corrina.

Ryan had a girlfriend? He'd never once mentioned a girl – any girl – to Corrina, and she was fairly certain he hadn't said anything to Gardner, either.

The traffic let up enough for Corrina to cross, which she did briskly. When she got to the other side of the street, she searched for Ryan and the mystery girl again, catching them just before the girl yanked on Ryan's chuckling form and pulled him into another store.

Ryan. Chuckling. Wow.

❀❀∧∧❀❀

Tyler enjoyed stopping by Maria's house for coffee – everything except the *coffee* part. For the most part, his sister had very good taste, but she made her coffee comically weak. For a long time, Tyler assumed this was a nod to frugality, but even when the money started flowing for Maria and Doug, the brew remained absurdly light. It finally registered on Tyler that Maria simply didn't like coffee. Why serve it at all, then? Did she think he'd be insulted if she gave him a cup of tea or even a glass of water instead? It was one of those things he might have actually questioned her about at some other point. Instead, he just used his imagination.

"Is business picking up at all?" Maria said as she brought their mugs and sat across from him.

"Nah, nothing. One of the galleries in Essex took a couple more pieces on consignment, but who knows if they'll sell them."

Maria pursed her lips. "I don't get it."

"Imagine how I feel."

"Are you gonna be okay financially?"

Tyler shrugged. "For a little while. It's not like I have an elaborate lifestyle. I'm really glad I invested in all of that equipment a couple of years ago when things were flying. I don't know what I'd do if I needed a big upgrade now."

Maria took a sip of her coffee, probably wondering if it would be better with a tablespoon less of grounds. "Things will start turning around for you soon."

Tyler offered a tiny grin. "I think they may have already started, at least in my romantic life."

Maria leaned toward him. "Oh really? New girlfriend?"

"It only feels new. Patrice and I got together the other night. We didn't stop 'getting together' until the next morning."

Maria practically did a spit-take. "What? How did that happen?"

"I stopped by the store, we decided to have dinner one night, and things just took their course."

For easily the fiftieth time, Tyler smiled at the thought of Tuesday night. He'd spoken with Patrice on the phone twice since, and he'd stopped by the candy store earlier. Tomorrow, they were going away for the night.

"So are you guys thinking about getting back together?"

Tyler had momentarily forgotten he was in the middle of a conversation with his sister. "I think we're already back together."

Maria arched her brows. "Huh."

"What does that mean?"

"Nothing. I like Patrice very much."

"And yet your reaction to our getting back together is, 'Huh.'"

"I'm just taking this in."

"What's there to take in? We won't be the first couple to realize we're better off together than apart."

Maria frowned into her coffee and then took another long sip, putting the mug down in slow motion afterward.

"It's just that the two of you seemed pretty done by the time you split."

"We did? I didn't feel like we were done at all. In case you didn't notice, I was pretty bummed about the whole thing."

"I know you were. You still seemed bummed about it a few days ago. People have different reasons for feeling that way, though. It sure didn't seem to me that yours was because things had ended too soon."

"Gee, thanks for the buzzkill, Maria."

"Look, I hope I'm wrong. Just watch your heart, okay?"

What was he supposed to say to this? Was this how everyone in the family was going to react? Was he going to feel even weirder being around them now that Patrice and he were together again?

"My heart's fine. In fact, it's freaking great."

"Don't get pissed at me, Tyler. I'm just looking out for you."

Tyler got up from his chair. "I've got this one covered, okay? You know, I was feeling really good about this until now." He pushed his chair back under the table and turned toward the door. "Thanks for the dirty water."

Nine

Friday, October 15
Sixteen days before the party

For the second time this week, Deborah had decided to make a significant change to the night's menu in the hour before she entered the kitchen. A salad of thinly sliced candy-striped beets would be a much better starter than the truffled chickpea soufflé she had originally been planning, especially since tonight's entree was duck breast. Fortunately, the staff wouldn't have started on the prep for the soufflé yet.

As she pulled out the beets and readied them for roasting, she decided that a walnut oil vinaigrette would dress them well. The only issue was that she wasn't certain she had enough on hand. None of her purveyors would be able to get her any tonight – though she could always call on Sage in an emergency.

Once the beets were in the oven, she went to the pantry to check. There, among her many fragrant oils, she found a bottle of pomegranate molasses and she wondered how the bottle wound up stocked in the wrong place. She didn't even recall having any of the stuff, as she couldn't remember the last time she'd used it. She used to do a pork tagine with it, but that had been years ago.

The thought of the molasses reminded her of the time Maxwell had brought her a bottle on his return from a trip to Manhattan. Bringing her presents wasn't a common thing for him and she found it touching until she realized it was Maxwell's attempt to soften what came next.

"Sit down for a couple of minutes," he'd said. "We need to talk about something."

Deborah grew apprehensive instantly. First there was the surprise of the gift and now the grave timbre of her brother's tone.

"What's going on?" she said as she moved to one of only two chairs in the kitchen.

"The news on Dad is worse than we originally thought."

Deborah felt the air go heavy around her. "What do you mean? I thought it was just anemia."

Maxwell closed his eyes and shook his head very slowly. "It's cancer, sis. Fourth stage."

"How is that possible? Dad never misses a checkup."

"The doctor didn't catch it. His numbers didn't indicate a problem until his latest blood work."

Deborah felt increasingly disoriented. As she struggled to make sense of this, though, the thought came to mind that her parents had been home all afternoon. She'd spoken with them when she first arrived at the inn. Why hadn't they said anything? Did they think this would go better if the news came from Maxwell?

"It's inoperable?"

"Stage four usually is."

"How much time are they giving him?"

Maxwell took a deep breath before answering. "Somewhere between six months and a year."

Deborah put her head in her hands at that point, soon feeling her brother's arms around her.

Minutes later, she rose up, noticing the molasses on the table next to her.

"That was supposed to make me feel better?" she said, pointing to the bottle.

He offered her a soft smile. "I guess I was trying to sugarcoat things – literally."

Deborah wiped at her eyes. "That might have been the worst timing for a pun ever."

"Sorry."

She leaned her head into Maxwell's chest and they stayed that way silently for several minutes. Eventually, the two of them went out to see Dad together.

Was the bottle of pomegranate molasses she found today in the pantry the same bottle? Deborah had been moving bottles around while she was lost in thought, finally finding an unopened bottle of walnut oil.

When she went to put the molasses in its correct place, though, she couldn't find it anywhere.

❀❀∧∧❀❀

Sage actually showed up at the kitchen an hour later carrying a bag with his store's logo.

"If there's pomegranate molasses in there," Deborah said, gesturing toward the bag, "I'm going to have to lay down for a while."

Sage reached into the bag and pulled out a jar. "Black bean paste, which I guess is good news. Does pomegranate molasses always make you swoon?"

"It's been known to happen, but this was about something else entirely. Since I'd prefer that you not think I'm crazy, I'm not going to explain."

"I can live with that. A certain amount of mystery is exciting."

He put the jar back in the bag and handed it to her.

"Thanks," Deborah said. "You don't need to bring me presents when you come to visit, you know."

"This just came in and I thought of you instantly. It's artisanally produced by a woman in San Jose. About seven layers of depth. Not salty at all."

Deborah removed the jar from the bag again and examined it. "Hmm. Sounds like a great ingredient to use to finish a sauce."

"Exactly. A little of it would add roundness without imparting too much of its own flavor."

Deborah gazed at Sage admiringly. Just minutes ago, she'd been feeling melancholy over the memory of her father. Melancholy definitely wasn't what she was feeling now.

"You're very sexy when you talk sauces, you know," she said.

"You bet I know. I used to have this great pickup line about bordelaise."

Deborah faked a shiver. "You'd better stop now or I might do something irresponsible."

Sage moved toward her at that point and kissed her with remarkable tenderness. For a second, Deborah thought about the fact that her sous chefs were in the kitchen with her. Only for a second, though. It was probably close to a minute before Sage stepped back.

"Was that the kind of irresponsible thing you had in mind?" he said.

Deborah smiled drunkenly. "Sorry, what were we talking about?"

Sage laughed and pulled her close to him. In the past, she would have felt uncomfortable with these displays of affection in front of colleagues. They'd probably have fun teasing her later – and she'd have fun along with them.

"Thanks for thinking of me when the black bean paste came in," she said.

"I don't need black bean paste to make me think of you."

"Thanks for that, too."

"Are you going to be too tired after service tonight for me to see you?"

"I really don't think I'm going to be tired at all."

※ ※∧∧※ ※

Corrina tried to keep her voice steady. "I don't understand what there is to contemplate. They've given the restaurant rave reviews and even back then they talked about how we were a fixture of the community."

The evenness in Maxwell's tone was considerably more aggravating than if he'd been screeching at her. "They get pitched a lot of stories."

"But this is our moment. Our *last* moment. They can't decide to do this story next year."

This debate had been running for five minutes now. Maxwell had called to report on his lack of progress at getting the *New York Times* to do a feature story about the last party at the inn for their weekend Metropolitan section. Corrina was beginning to regret having assigned this task to her brother.

"I've told them exactly that in about five different ways," he said. "They keep telling me they have to think about it. I think we have to accept the possibility that this isn't going to happen."

"I don't want to accept that possibility. Call in bigger guns. Use your resources. Isn't that what guys like you do? There's gotta be someone in town who has a friend high up at the *Times*."

The line was silent for several seconds. "Sorry, you lost me after 'guys like you.' What were you saying?"

"You know what I mean."

"I'm not sure I do."

"*Political* people."

There was another pause. Maxwell didn't usually let any silence creep into conversations. "What makes you think I'm political?"

Corrina tapped her forehead once with the receiver. "Maxwell, you run the Chamber of Commerce. That's the most political operation in Oldham other than the mayor's office, and the mayor's office isn't as much political as it is evil."

"Don't condemn the office because of its current resident," Maxwell said sharply. Where was that coming from?

Corrina paused this time to allow the air to cool. "Do you think we can get back to the topic at hand?"

"Hey, I'm a politician, Cor. Skirting the issue is what I'm all about."

Corrina shut her eyes. "Maxwell, it would be great if the *Times* did a story, okay?"

"Message received, captain. I'll do everything in my power."

Corrina got off the phone less than a minute later. Why did she feel as though she'd been mugged after every conversation with her family lately? She went to the kitchen to get a glass of water, though what she really wanted was a margarita. Then she headed toward Gardner's office.

Ryan was out with friends – she wondered if one of the friends was the girl she'd seen him with yesterday – so they were alone in the house.

Gardner looked up from his work when she came in. "Hey," he said. "You look flustered. Everything okay?"

Corrina dropped her head and walked over to her husband for a hug. "Party stuff."

Gardner pulled back and offered his version of an understanding expression. "Maybe it's not such a bad thing that this is the last of these."

"Don't say that. I'm not ready to think that way." Corrina looked down at Gardner's desk. "Do you have a ton to do tonight?"

"The usual, which is about five times as much as I would like."

Corrina moved closer to Gardner again. "It's Friday night, you know. And Ryan definitely won't be back for hours."

Gardner chuckled. "I know where you're going with this, but –"

"– Maybe just a little snuggle afterward. You could be back at your desk in an hour...or so."

Gardner put his head against her chest. "You know I can't do that, babe. I always get so mellow afterward. I'll never get my edge back."

Corrina looked skyward. "I'm going to try to take that as a compliment."

"Let me just get through a little more of this. An hour and a half, two hours at most. I'm all yours after that."

Corrina was sure that two hours would become three or more. Gardner had no sense of

time when he was working. She kissed her husband on the top of the head and left him to his
papers.

✿✿∧∧✿✿

In the cottony moments after lovemaking,
Tyler had two revelations about the word "away."
One was that going away had very little to do
with distance. The inn where he and Patrice now
lay took less time to get to than it took to drive
to the beach nearest to downtown Oldham on
a busy summer weekend. Yet he still felt transported, as though they'd gone off to the northern
reaches of Maine or down to the Virginia coastline. Simply being out of their normal environs
constituted all the "away" he needed.

Of course, this was only true because of the
other thing he realized about the concept: whom
you were away with was fundamental. This
overnight at a nearby B&B felt like a vacation
because he was here with Patrice. In any other
situation, it would have felt pointless.

They'd had dinner at a Thai place Tyler had
read about in *Connecticut* magazine. The review-
er had gushed about the drunken noodles, and
both Patrice and Tyler concurred. Of course, after six bottles of Singha between them, the noodles weren't the only things that were drunken.
Fortunately, the restaurant was within walking
distance of the inn. Equally fortunate was that
the alcohol had no effect on Tyler's focus once
they got back to their room. When they'd made

love earlier in the week, Tyler had felt an overwhelming sense of reunion. Being with Patrice that night was all about acknowledging and recapturing what he'd missed. Tonight, though, reminded him of what it had been like during their best times together – an irreducible sense of *nowness*. Tyler was feeling everything, experiencing everything. There was no need to rush, no need to finish at all. Being in this was everything.

Ultimately, they did finish, though there was always the promise they'd begin again. Whether they did or not wasn't critical to Tyler. In many ways, with Patrice in his arms aimlessly playing with his chest hair, they were still making love. He'd always loved these moments with her.

"That was delicious," Patrice said, the first words either had spoken in more than a half-hour. That was another thing that distinguished his connection with her. In the first stages of lovemaking, they spoke endearments, even a few humorous comments. As it went further, however, they stopped speaking, as though they'd moved beyond the need for words.

Tyler kissed her hair. "Almost as delicious as the Pad Krapow."

Patrice lifted her head from the pillow. "Only 'almost?'"

Tyler smiled. "The Pad Krapow was very, very good."

"So that was the highlight of the evening, huh?"

Tyler turned toward her, their faces now centimeters apart. "This moment is the highlight of the evening." He paused for a second. "No, sorry, *this* moment." He paused again. "No, wait...."

Patrice kissed him surprisingly passionately then. It was the kind of kiss that stirred him in unexpected ways, only one of which was sexual.

"Okay," he said, "that might have been the highlight."

"Well, at least we've moved the Thai food down from the top."

They kissed again, languorously this time, the kind where their lips seemed to run together like two streams joining at a river.

Tyler drew Patrice as close to him as he could physically manage. "I can't tell you how happy I am to be here with you."

Patrice hummed softly. "This was a very good idea."

Tyler kissed the top of her head. "All of this was a good idea. You have no idea how much I want you."

Patrice chuckled. "I have *some* idea."

"I don't mean in that way – although in that way as well. I just *want* you. Your presence, your nurturance, your joy. I thought I was just missing you when we weren't together, but that's only a piece of it. I'm physically healthier when I'm with you."

Patrice squeezed him. "We're good together."

"We are. So good."

What happened next was both spontaneous and, in a manner, carefully considered. As Tyler turned to look at the woman he loved, he realized his subconscious had been considering this for a very long time.

"Marry me," he said as he locked eyes with Patrice.

Patrice's expression electrified. "What?"

Tyler laughed. "I had no idea I was about to say that – but I totally mean it. Marry me, Patrice. Let's do this forever."

Patrice looked at him as though he'd suddenly turned into a cartoon character; she seemed both bemused and startled.

"That might have been the last thing I was expecting to hear from you," she said.

"Well, I can promise you it wasn't premeditated."

She kissed him deeply again. This time, Tyler wasn't at all surprised he was getting aroused.

"Is that your way of saying yes?"

Patrice had started kissing his chest and was now moving lower. "I'm too busy planning to bring you to the heights of ecstasy right now to bother with such trivialities."

Seconds later, Tyler's mind was on other things. They could deal with the "trivialities" in the morning.

❀❀∧∧❀❀

Saturday, October 16
Fifteen days before the party

As he shrugged on a light crew neck sweater, Maxwell realized his dress casual wardrobe could use a bit of updating. He'd gotten several new suits in the last year, and he had plenty of jeans and sweats, but he couldn't remember the last time he'd shopped for something nice to wear on a Saturday night. Probably because he had so little need for something nice to wear on a Saturday night these days.

Maxwell didn't want to look unfashionable, but then he put this in the context of where they were going. There would be any number of people at their twentieth high school reunion that looked far more unfashionable than he did.

Annie, however, would not be one of them. As he reached for his sports jacket, she walked in from the bathroom wearing a cobalt cocktail dress that stopped about two inches above her knees. She wore her long blond hair in a French braid that accentuated her slim neck. Her neck and her knees were two of Maxwell's favorite places to kiss, and he felt a strong urge to do so to both immediately.

Maxwell hadn't seen Annie this done up in a while, and he found himself crossing the room and reaching for her without even realizing he was moving.

"You look mind-bogglingly beautiful," he said, drawing her close to him.

"As good as I looked in high school?"

In his mind, Maxwell flashed on the teenaged girl he'd first fallen in love with, even though they didn't start dating until after college. "Annie, you were gorgeous in high school, but even when I was seventeen, I think I would have chosen this version of you over that one."

Annie kissed him softly and intently. Kissing her had always been one of his purest pleasures.

She pulled back slightly. "You do know that was exactly the right thing to say, don't you?"

They kissed again, Maxwell's head flitting between wanting to continue to see his wife dressed this way and wanting to remove everything she was wearing as quickly as he could.

The sound of Joey playing downstairs with the babysitter jostled Maxwell a bit. "I think maybe we should blow off the reunion and go get a hotel room instead. A bottle of Champagne, some soft music…" He let his voice drift off as he embraced the vision.

"Sounds great," Annie said, pulling back a bit, "but I have some old acquaintances I want to make jealous."

"You sure?"

"We can't skip out on this, hon."

"Next Saturday, then. Duffy seems great. I think we should book her every Saturday night until Joey goes to college."

Annie kissed him on the cheek and then pushed him away gently. "I like it when you're horny."

A half-hour later, they were inside a massive tent on the grounds of the botanical gardens. The band was playing U2, Nirvana, and Red Hot Chili Peppers, though Maxwell knew that fluffier songs from the nineties would be arriving soon, especially when the band was trying to coax people out onto the dance floor.

Dancing was going to have to wait for Maxwell and Annie, though. Nearly as soon as they entered the tent, they peeled off in separate directions, Maxwell to catch up with Beck, a lacrosse buddy he hadn't seen in at least a decade, and Annie to show off in front of a couple of former cheerleaders.

❀❀∧∧❀❀

Annie knew she was going to have a good time tonight. It all started with the dress. She'd been apprehensive about putting it on ever since she brought it home. Yes, it looked good in the store, but she'd been fooled by that sort of thing before. This time, though, the dress looked better than she remembered, and she just knew the evening was going to go right.

It didn't hurt that Cynthia Robinson and Georgeanna Tillman fawned over her for ten minutes after she showed up. They made her feel so good that Annie could put Georgeanna's pending judgeship in perspective.

She'd just left them to get another drink when she felt a light touch on her bare forearm. She turned, expecting to find Maxwell. What she found instead was decidedly not her husband.

"Oh, God, your hair still does that amazing floaty thing when you turn around."

It took her a second to register Marty. Not that she'd ever forgotten what he looked like, but she'd never seen him in a suit – a very expensive suit, from what she could tell – and while he still had longish blond hair and a full beard, the hair was professionally styled now, and the beard was cropped very close to his face. Based on a quick glance, this wasn't the original Marty, but a very impressive upgrade.

Annie squealed – a sound she rarely made – and threw herself into her old boyfriend's arms.

"I had no idea you were coming tonight," she said as she stepped back.

"I didn't know myself until a couple of days ago. I didn't even know this was *happening* until a couple of days ago."

"You mean you didn't get any of the dozens of reminders the committee sent out?"

Marty smiled in the lopsided way Annie re-membered well. "I think they might have lost track of me. But now that I've seen you, I'm very glad I found out about this little party."

Marty made no effort to hide the way he was ogling her. A long-buried memory surfaced of the way he used to drink her in with his eyes when they were in bed together.

"Annie, you look remarkable."

Suddenly, the praise from Cynthia and Georgeanna seemed paltry. "Thank you. You've cleaned up pretty nicely yourself."

Marty swept his eyes quickly over his suit. "Yeah, I have a few of these now."

"I'm guessing you decided to do something other than classic car renovation."

He chuckled, causing his bangs to sweep in front of his face. "Yeah, you might say that. Let's put it this way: I had a very good idea about five years ago and things sorta took off from there."

Annie leaned toward him, feeling his heat even from a distance of a few feet. "Your good idea wouldn't be illegal, would it?"

"Not even a little bit. In fact, the government and I have become very good friends."

Annie couldn't imagine the Marty she knew ever saying something like that. This was the new and improved model for sure.

"So, have you moved back to the area?"

"I'm scouting locations. Right now I'm set up about an hour outside of Vegas."

"How long are you around?"

"Not sure yet. I might be convinced to 'scout' a little longer in the vicinity. I'm swinging back in this direction toward the end of the week. Any chance you're free Thursday afternoon?"

Annie nearly said she needed to make sure she could get a babysitter. This wasn't the time to mention Joey, though. She'd work it out.

"I can be free."

Marty grinned at her. "Then I will definitely be in Oldham on Thursday."

A few minutes later, someone Annie didn't recognize whisked Marty away. She didn't catch sight of him the rest of the night, but they'd already made arrangements for Thursday.

She just knew she was going to have a good time tonight.

Ten

Doug rolled over onto his back with a satisfied laugh. "Making love to you is a pleasure any time, babe, but making love to you first thing on a Sunday morning has always been a special treat."

When they'd first fallen in love, Maria and Doug would often make love when they woke on the weekends and then spend most of the rest of the morning in bed. After Olivia, that became impractical and for the most part impossible, and it became one of the many pleasures they exchanged for the different pleasures of parenthood. She wasn't sure what brought it back to Doug's mind this morning, but she remembered now that it was an awfully good way to bring on a new day.

Maria snuggled up next to Doug, resting her head on his chest. Back in the pre-Olivia days, she often dozed off at this point, but she didn't feel sleepy at all now. At the same time, she didn't have any interest in getting out of bed.

"We don't have anything going on today, right?" Doug said, kissing her hair.

"Not a single thing."

He drew her closer. "The day just keeps getting better."

Neither of them said anything for the next several minutes. Doug lightly stroked her arm with his fingernails while she played with the hair on his chest.

"I've been meaning to tell you that I've started playing guitar again."

"Hey, that's good."

Maria wasn't sure why she hadn't mentioned this to Doug before now. She'd gotten into the habit of talking about the mundane parts of her day, but somehow avoid speaking about this exciting part.

"It *is* good. I can still play, which was a relief. I even went for a lesson at McGarrigle's the other day."

"That was a nice idea."

"You think?"

Doug kissed the top of her head again. "Definitely. It's good for you to have a hobby."

Was that what this was? Music hadn't ever seemed like a hobby to Maria, and she wasn't looking at it that way now. If she'd decided to take up scrapbooking, that would be a hobby. Blogging about being an empty nester – that would have been a hobby.

Not this, though. To Maria, the word "hobby" connoted casualness. One engaged in a hobby as a way to pass the time. She'd never felt that way about music.

She was about to mention this to Doug, but she decided to let it go instead.

❊❊∧∧❊❊

Tyler had been feeling uneasy since yesterday morning. It felt like he was coming down with something, though he was fairly sure his physical health wasn't an issue. The pleasures of Friday night had given way to the uncertainty of Saturday morning. Patrice hadn't responded to his proposal in any way, and when he hinted at it, she'd been evasive. Pushing it seemed like the wrong thing to do, but their drive home to Oldham had felt awkward. Compounding this, Patrice had cancelled their date last night, saying that the nonstop rush at the store had left her exhausted and needing a quiet evening and an early bedtime.

Feeling antsy, Tyler had awakened early this morning, gotten in his car, and pointed it east, winding up an hour and a half later in Narragansett, RI, wandering along by the water, and grabbing lunch before turning toward home. He avoided the highway on the way back, so the return drive took much longer, especially since he stopped twice to take photos. By the time he got back to town, the fall sun was lowering.

Tyler didn't know what to make of Patrice's reticence. He couldn't possibly have read what was happening between them the wrong way. And this wasn't the first time the subject of marriage had come up, though admittedly it hadn't come up often and both of them had been noncommittal. Was she just so shocked by the proposal that she didn't know how to respond? Did she think maybe they should spend more than a few days back together before making wedding plans? He couldn't fault her if that were the case, but he still wished she would say *something*.

As he pulled up to his home, Tyler resolved to get his mind on something else. He'd make himself some pasta, have a couple of beers, maybe stream a movie or two. He needed to do something to shake this mood. The weirdness with Patrice would go away in due time; they'd reignited, and that wasn't going to die down again. As long as that was true, the rest was just detail.

He heard the thud as he opened the front door. The sound was coming from his bedroom. Had someone broken in, knowing he had valuable computer equipment in his studio?

He had no idea how to deal with this. Did he pull out his phone and call the police? Did he run out the door, back out of the driveway, and let whatever was happening happen? He had insurance; there was no reason to go vigilante here.

He heard whispers. Two voices, one male, one female, both sounding young. He was either being robbed by kids or something much stranger was going on.

He stepped cautiously down the hallway toward his bedroom. When he got there, he found Ryan and a girl he'd never seen before, though there was plenty of her to see now. They were struggling into their clothes, and the girl had one leg in her jeans and nothing on top.

Ryan, obviously a faster dresser, was buttoning his shirt when Tyler stepped in the doorway. Their eyes locked, and Ryan scowled.

"You think maybe you could give us some privacy?" he said sharply.

Tyler glared back at him. "You're in *my* bedroom."

"So that gives you the right to see my girlfriend naked?"

Ryan's attitude was so outrageously disarming that Tyler found himself momentarily speechless. By the time he thought of a response, Ryan's girlfriend – and he didn't even know Ryan had a girlfriend – was no longer naked in any way, and they were striding past him.

"Just don't," Ryan said, pointing a finger at Tyler as he exited.

Five seconds later, Tyler heard the front door slam.

Feeling utterly disoriented, Tyler sat on his disheveled bed.

Well, at least now he had something else to think about.

❀ ❀ ∧ ∧ ❀ ❀

Maxwell had desperately wanted to make love to Annie when they got home from the reunion, but Joey had other plans for them. Whether he was feeling a little under the weather or he was off his game because they'd left him with a babysitter – something they rarely did – Joey was out of his bed and into their room before they'd even brushed their teeth. Maxwell tried to settle his son down and then take the boy back to his room, but Joey protested and Annie suggested that they let him sleep in the room with them. They'd done this sort of thing before, laying Joey's old crib mattress on the floor next to their bed, but they'd never done it when Maxwell was feeling this much desire for his wife. Romance was definitely out of the question with their notoriously light-sleeping child a few feet away. Annie and Joey dozed off quickly while Maxwell stared at the ceiling and wished the evening had had a sweeter ending.

Annie had seemed distracted most of the morning. He tried to debrief her about the reunion since it seemed they'd spent so much of their time talking to others in different parts of the room, but Annie didn't seem particularly interested. She even got up from the breakfast table to clear the dishes when they both still had half of their coffee left and then focused on chores she usually did when he wasn't around.

Joey was being his usual pinball self, so Maxwell just shrugged it off and played with his son.

At around one o'clock, he finally got his wife and child out of the house. The air was crisp but the sun was strong, and it wasn't the kind of day for spending indoors. They decided to have lunch at Proof, a recently opened bakery. Several people at the Chamber had told Maxwell that the breads there were outstanding and the sandwiches were inventive. Not willing to push the envelope too far, he ordered a turkey on a baguette with melted cheese and orange marmalade and got Joey peanut butter and jelly on potato wheat, even though the kid really wanted an Oreo cupcake. Annie said she only wanted a croissant. She hadn't eaten much for breakfast, either.

For the first time, Maxwell considered the possibility that his wife was hung over. He hadn't seen her drink terribly much, but they'd spent a good portion of the party apart. Maybe she had been drinking more heavily when she was catching up with old girlfriends, though she never seemed drunk to him at any point during the night.

While they waited for their food, Maxwell talked with the owner, asking her about her first month's business, offering support, and inviting her to come to the next Chamber meeting. Once they sat down to eat, first Roye Albrighton of Progressive Lighting and then Isabella Summers of Valley Appliances stopped at their table before

Maxwell could take a single bite. The conversation with Isabella went on for a bit, as she was exercised over street repairs going on in front of her store. She seemed to calm when Maxwell said he would see what he could do with Town Hall about authorizing another work crew to speed the repairs along.

When Isabella left, Maxwell smiled at his wife and then finally tried the sandwich, which was as delicious as advertised.

"Yum," he said, pointing the sandwich in Annie's direction. "Want some?"

"No, thanks. It probably tastes better now that you've built up an appetite working the room. You're the man everybody wants to talk to today."

Maxwell rolled his eyes. He hadn't actually noticed, because these exchanges seemed to happen wherever he went around town. That, presumably, was one of the reasons Mike and Will were trying to get him to run for office.

"Yeah, well, about that, there's a chance even more people are going to want to talk to me. A bunch of people are trying to get me to challenge Mayor Bruce next fall."

Annie's eyes opened wider than Maxwell had seen them all day. "You're not seriously considering that, are you?"

"I know, I thought it was ridiculous, too, when I first heard it. I have to admit it's growing on me, though."

Annie looked away from him and out the bakery's window. When she didn't say anything for a full minute, Maxwell said, "I thought you'd think this was pretty cool. If I won, you'd be Oldham's First Lady."

Annie snickered at that and then looked at Joey, who'd stuffed a good quarter of his sandwich in his mouth. She shook her head slowly and then made eye contact with Maxwell.

"That's a big job."

"Well, it's not like I'm running for mayor of New York or even Hartford. It's hardly the first step toward the presidency."

"But you'd be working long hours."

"I work long hours now."

"No kidding. *Longer* hours."

Maxwell had expected Annie to enjoy this. He imagined her delighting in the public appearances and the great clothes she would get to buy to make them.

"I hadn't really thought about it from a workload perspective."

"Yeah, well, maybe you should."

Maxwell wished he hadn't brought up this subject today. His instincts were usually better than this.

"Annie, are you okay? You seem a little off."

Annie took a sip of coffee and looked over at Joey again. "I'm fine."

"You sure? Did you have a little more wine than you planned last night?"

Annie tilted her head to the side and gazed at him. "Really, I'm fine."

"You just don't seem fine. Did something happen at the reunion last night?"

Annie dropped her eyes to the table. "This mayor thing just caught me by surprise."

That might have been true, but Maxwell knew it was only a partial explanation. Annie's body language made it clear, though, that if there were more to discuss, she didn't have any interest in discussing it.

Eleven

Monday, October 18
Thirteen days before the party

Corrina had spent most of the morning following links. Yes, she'd charged Maxwell with doing the PR for the party, but she'd had enough conversations with him about it at this point to realize that, at the very least, he needed backup. While he might be working the usual angles, Corrina knew there were all kinds of online publicity opportunities – everything from leaf-peeping sites to travel sites in other parts of the country – that might mention the party or even do a feature piece if they just knew about it. She'd already gotten two bites by following this strategy.

She'd just clicked on a mom blog from western Rhode Island when a popup ad took over a significant portion of her monitor. Didn't her computer block these things automatically? Did anyone think this kind of advertising was effective anymore?

She was about to roll her mouse over to click off the ad when she took a look at it. The ad was from a telephone florist, and it featured the exact corsage Maxwell had given her when he took her to her first formal when she was eleven. The corsage looked horribly old fashioned, but maybe it was coming back into style. Not that she'd been keeping up with corsage fashions, though she supposed she'd know a little more about them if Ryan decided to go to his junior prom in the spring.

Corrina grinned when she thought about that formal. It had been such a big deal to buy a gown, get her hair done, and put on heels. Her parents made a huge deal about it, and Maxwell, who rarely said anything to her at that point without teasing her, told her she looked fantastic without a hint of irony in his voice.

Corrina's friends thought Maxwell looked great as well. Most of them were also with older brothers, but no one mooned over other people's "dates" the way they were mooning over Maxwell. Corrina remembered catching a glimpse of him in his tuxedo as he was getting them drinks and noticing for the first time that her brother was a good-looking guy. She decided not to mention it to him.

Maxwell flirted outrageously with her friends that night. Corrina knew he was only playing with them, since the age difference was meaningful back then, but he left several girls giggly and smitten. She never knew for certain if he was doing this for her benefit or just because he turned out to be naturally charming, but it definitely raised Corrina's status among her friends to have a brother who cleaned up so nicely.

Things were different between Corrina and Maxwell after that formal. It was almost as though the event marked the point when Maxwell stopped treating her like a kid. A few months later, they even had a fairly candid conversation about sex; it took a couple of years before her sisters would do the same.

Corrina hadn't thought about her first formal in years, though she knew it would forever be one of her cherished family memories. She wondered if Maxwell ever thought about it. She considered calling him to tell her about the corsage on her screen, but their last few conversations had been so tense, and she wasn't sure he'd welcome the call. On a lark, she decided to click on the ad to see what people were wearing with corsages these days.

Before she could, though, the ad disappeared from her screen.

❀ ❀ ∧ ∧ ❀ ❀

Other than the chefs at restaurants, exactly two men had ever cooked for Deborah. One was her father, who would occasionally warm the family's souls with one of his hearty stews. The other was Maxwell, who would perhaps once a week prepare his "world famous" grilled cheese and bacon sandwiches while they were all still living at home. None of the men Deborah had dated had ever made a meal for her. Several told her they found her culinary skills intimidating, but Deborah really would have found it charming if even one of them had attempted to fry her an egg.

This was one of several things that made it so delightful to be sitting in Sage's kitchen while he prepared lunch for her. There were other pleasures for sure, including having an unobstructed view of his sexy forearms released from his rolled-up sleeves, but the part about watching him compose a dish was close to the top.

Before she arrived, Sage had started olive-oil-poaching baby artichokes that he'd shaved with a mandoline. Now he was stirring simmering chicken stock into barley for a variation on risotto. Deborah was impressed with Sage's *mise en place*. Everything he needed for the dish was chopped and waiting for him. This served Sage well when, eighteen minutes after he started, he needed to stir in finely chopped red bell pepper, Kalamata olives, and tarragon, giving everything forty-five seconds or so to come up to temperature. He then plated the risotto, layered the artichokes on top, and drizzled a balsamic reduction over the dish.

He brought the plates to the table and refilled the glass of Montepulciano d'Abruzzo Deborah had been sipping.

Deborah admired the meal in front of her. Maxwell had never presented his legendary grilled cheese with a balsamic drizzle.

"You know, if you hadn't made this for me today, I probably would have had peanut butter straight from the jar with a spoon," she said, still ogling the food.

Sage sat across from her. "You're shattering my illusions."

"Oh, it would have been very good peanut butter."

"Then we're okay."

Deborah forked a tender sliver of artichoke and then tasted it with the risotto. This dish would have been sumptuous even if a man with sexy arms hadn't prepared it specifically for her. It was nutty and earthy with an appealing blend of textures.

She closed her eyes and let the taste embrace her. "This is sensational."

"I'll bet you say that to all the boys."

Deborah grinned. "True, but I'm not embellishing this time."

Sage seemed disproportionately pleased to hear this. "So I didn't diminish myself in your eyes by taking this considerable risk?"

Maybe later Deborah would tell Sage how much the "considerable risk" meant to her. For now, she just said, "My eyes have no interest in diminishing you."

"Then that makes me happy."

Twenty minutes later, Sage got up from the table, took their plates, and set about making coffee. As much as Deborah enjoyed having him wait on her, there had been enough of that for the day. She walked up behind him as he stood at the coffee grinder and wrapped her arms around his waist.

"That was delicious on several different levels," she said softly into his ear.

He turned around, bringing their faces inches from one another. He kissed her eyebrow and then her nose. "You realize, of course, that this was all an elaborate plot, don't you?"

"You don't need an elaborate plot."

He pulled her closer. "I don't?"

She nuzzled his neck and then nibbled his ear. "And we definitely don't need coffee."

"It's extremely good coffee."

She began to unbutton his shirt. "Let's have it later."

※ ※ ∧ ∧ ※ ※

Maria had her guitar out fingerpicking softly while she waited for her second lesson with Colin. Unlike last week, she was the only person in the waiting area, so she had no concerns about limbering up her fingers.

She started out playing random chord changes, but soon transitioned into the Indigo Girls' "Least Complicated," slowing it down as she had when she used to play it regularly.

"What makes me think I could start clean slated? The hardest to learn was the least complicated."

Maria looked up from her guitar at the sound of Martha's voice singing the chorus.

"I love that song," Martha said when Maria stopped playing two chords later. "That was a great idea slowing it down."

"Thanks."

Martha sat in the chair next to her. "Colin's a better teacher than I realized. Your playing is much better today than it was the other day."

Maria wrinkled her brow. "I play better when I *think* no one is listening."

"Yeah, you should get over that. Do you know about the new artists night that I've been running at Mumford's?"

Maria shook her head quickly.

"We do it every Thursday night. It's something between a showcase and an open mic show. We get a nice crowd. You should join us."

"Yeah, it sounds great. I'll drag Doug out one of the next few Thursdays."

Martha leaned toward Maria. "I meant you should join us on stage."

The suggestion caught Maria off guard. "On stage? I haven't performed for anyone I don't know in about twenty years."

"Then you're way past due. This week's show is already booked up other than the walk-ins, and you don't want to do that. How about the Thursday after next?"

Maria wasn't sure what to think of this. She loved that playing and singing had become a meaningful part of her life again, but she hadn't considered taking it to any "stage" beyond her living room. She'd never been overly fond of playing in front of audiences, and she doubted the past couple of decades would have changed that.

"Maybe I should just sit in the crowd once or twice."

Martha threw a hand at her. "Don't be ridiculous. If you sit in the crowd, you're either going to wish you were on stage, or you're going to go running in the other direction. Just step up and do it."

Maria wasn't sure why Martha was encouraging her to do this after only hearing a couple of songs. "You're having trouble booking acts, aren't you?" she said with a smile.

Martha laughed. "Hardly. Every wannabe in eastern Connecticut wants to do these shows. I'll probably have to bump someone. I want you there, though."

"Because I slowed down 'Least Complicated?'"

"Among other reasons. Come on, Maria, knee-jerk nervousness aside, you know you want to do this."

"I should probably book another couple of sessions with Colin if I'm gonna perform next week."

"We can make that happen."

Maria pointed to her accusingly. "Ah, so this is just a ploy to get me to pay for extra lessons."

"You saw right through me. Are you in?"

Maria looked upward. "Yeah, I guess I am."

❖❖∧∧❖❖

Corrina had barely seen Ryan the past few days. He'd agreed to go to brunch with Gardner and her yesterday, but he rushed off quickly afterward. Beyond that, he'd been preoccupied with "friends," though Corrina wondered if it were really just one particular friend he'd been giving his time.

She'd gotten home late after a crazy afternoon at the visitors bureau. Mondays were normally quiet, even in the early fall, but three different tourist groups had long sessions with her on the phone, including two in close succession. That, combined with the walk-in traffic and the fact she hadn't anticipated any of this made the workday particularly wearisome. She got home and immediately started chopping vegetables for a quick curry, surprised to find her stepson picking up a knife to help a few minutes later.

She looked over at him as he sliced mushrooms. "Are you staying in tonight?"

"Yeah, of course," he said without looking up. "I never go out on a Monday."

"You don't usually go out on Tuesdays through Thursdays, either, but you went out after dinner every one of those days last week."

Ryan shrugged and grabbed another mushroom from the container.

Corrina looked down at the onion she was chopping. "I saw you on the street the other day."

"Oh yeah?"

"She's cute."

Corrina heard Ryan stop cutting, so she looked up.

"I don't know what you're talking about," he said.

Corrina grinned. "I have a feeling you do."

He went back to slicing, but he was doing it with more fervor now. "Really, I don't."

"I don't know why you don't want to talk about it, Rye. You're a good-looking sixteen-year-old guy. Why wouldn't you have a girlfriend?"

"Can we not discuss this, please?"

Corrina went back to work on the onion. "Fine with me. I just know that if I'd just started dating someone – and let me repeat, she's very cute – I'd want to talk about it all the time."

Ryan put down his knife. "Are you just gonna keep grilling me about this?"

Corrina turned to face him. "I'm not grilling you. Forget I mentioned it."

"You told Dad what you saw and he convinced you to pump me for details, right?"

"I haven't said anything to your father, actually."

Ryan picked up the knife and then threw it back down on the cutting board. "Yeah, I believe that. You love playing spy for him. Cut your own damn mushrooms."

He left the kitchen without looking at her. Corrina stood frozen for at least a minute, trying to figure out what had just happened.

Then she shook her head and continued to get dinner ready.

Twelve

Tuesday, October 19
Twelve days before the party

Deborah had been feeling very good the entire drive. Lunch and then "dessert" with Sage had been supremely satisfying on so many levels. Deborah's instincts told her that Sage would be a caring and passionate lover. What she didn't expect, though, was how *embraced* she felt afterward and how that sense of embrace would stay with her even when they were apart. She carried it with her into the kitchen that evening, which inspired a nudge from her sous chef Gina. It also inspired her to change the Moroccan-themed sauce she'd been planning for the evening's arctic char to a dill velouté. The latter sauce reminded her of being wrapped in a warm blanket.

The cozy feeling stayed with her in the car for the long trip into the Berkshires. It had surprised Deborah when Danny Kortchmar of the Sunny Skies Inn contacted her about a position as executive chef. Sunny Skies had a national reputation as a vacation spot for the rich and famous. Rooms started at five hundred dollars a night, and some culinary heavyweights had worn a toque there, including Gabe Nelson, whose *Sunny Skies Mornings* breakfast cookbook had won a James Beard Award.

The name of the inn suggested something homey and cozy, but the structure itself shouted affluence. An enormous Colonial building, it housed twenty guest rooms, each of which Deborah knew to contain thousand-thread-count bedding, original oils on the walls and sculptures on the handcrafted dressers, and granite bathrooms with Jacuzzis and body sprayers.

Danny was waiting for her in the inn's lobby when she arrived. He was in his early fifties with a full beard and casual dress that contrasted with the luxe surroundings. Deborah had heard that Danny liked to deemphasize his own wealth; he'd made a fortune selling an Internet company in the nineties before moving up to the Berkshires to start his "little B&B."

"Was the drive okay?" he said as he grasped her hand with both of his.

"Wonderful, actually. I could hardly believe that it was more than two hours."

"I'm glad. It's a nice drive, isn't it? Our trees aren't as beautiful this time of year as yours are down in Oldham, but they're still pretty."

Deborah agreed, though she truly hadn't noticed. She'd been so caught up in her thoughts that she'd barely seen the road.

Danny gave her a quick tour of the public rooms at the inn and then took her to the kitchen. Though this kitchen probably only served twice as many customers as the Sugar Maple, it was easily four times a large, and as expected, it was state of the art in every way: infrared grill, immersion circulator, even an anti-griddle. Deborah wasn't sure she'd ever feel the need to use the latter – she was still somewhat ambivalent about the whole molecular gastronomy thing – but regardless she found it impressive that Danny was willing to provide all the toys his executive chef desired.

The kitchen staff was preparing for lunch service, which was predictably low-key. There wouldn't be a huge market for forty-dollar entrees on a Tuesday afternoon in the fall, though she guessed the place would be considerably more animated in July.

Afterward, Deborah and Danny sat over espresso and biscotti discussing the position. Though Deborah already knew it, Danny explained that a number of chefs had used the dining room at Sunny Skies as a launch point for very high profile gigs. Jasper White had tabbed the current executive chef for his latest Boston restaurant.

"I know we look very good on resumés," Danny said. "I'm only asking for two years."

Deborah tried to imagine herself in this setting. She could do much worse than to spend the next couple of years – maybe longer – catering to the rich and famous and experimenting with every culinary invention that came on the market. The kitchen at Sunny Skies had a long reputation for innovation, so she doubted she would ever feel constrained. There was little question that this job would be good for her career and good for her sense of adventure.

Danny walked her back to her car a little more than an hour later. "I don't mess around, Deborah," he said as he took her hand. "I hope you'll come to appreciate that about me. You're my first choice. The job is yours if you want it."

"I'm flattered, Danny, and this place is everything it was advertised to be. Can I take a couple of days?"

"Absolutely."

They parted after that, Danny waving to Deborah as she exited the long driveway. By the time she made a left onto the street, she knew she was going to turn down this opportunity.

❀❀∧∧❀❀

Tyler had spent all of Sunday night and all day Monday trying to think of the right way to approach the situation with Ryan. Did he go hard-line on the kid, calling him out for sneaking into his house uninvited? Did he try to talk to Ryan about the emotional implications of becoming sexually active? Did he just blow the whole thing off, assuming Ryan was never going to bring it up himself and that he'd probably think twice before using Tyler's house as a love nest again?

The last option had been gaining traction when he went to bed last night, but Tyler found that when he got up this morning, he couldn't abide by it. He decided he would talk to his nephew when the kid got home from school.

He hadn't expected to find Corrina at the house. He'd been practicing a conversation in his head, but he hadn't prepared for her presence.

"What's up?" she said when she came to the door.

"Aren't you supposed to be at work?"

"What difference does it make to you?"

Tyler was still having trouble adjusting to his sister's biting attitude toward him. His experience with most family conflict was that, even if left unaddressed, it waned after a period. In this case, though, Corrina seemed to be holding an unyieldingly persistent grudge.

"It doesn't," he said. "I was just surprised to see you."

"I don't work at the bureau on Tuesdays. If you weren't expecting to see me, what are you doing here?"

"I was here to see Ryan."

Corrina's expression darkened. "Why is that?"

"I have something to talk to him about."

Corrina leaned against the doorway. "Talk to me about it instead."

Tyler took a step back from the door, wishing he could walk backward and make time reverse with him. "I'd rather keep this between the two of us."

"Really? Have you found something new to give him crap about?"

"It isn't like that – though actually it wasn't like that the last time, if we're being honest. I just need to have a talk with him."

"He isn't around. He's...I'm not sure where he is right now. He texted that he was spending the afternoon with friends."

Tyler nodded his head slowly. "All right. I'll catch up with him some other time."

He started to walk down the stoop when Corrina's voice grew sharper.

"I'd really prefer it if you went through me for anything you had to say to Ryan."

Tyler stopped walking and turned back in his sister's direction. "He's sixteen, Corrina. He's going to have private matters, even within the family."

"Not with you."

"Why the hell not?"

Corrina scoffed. "You don't get to have private matters with Ryan. Not with the way you treat him."

Corrina was talking like Tyler had been verbally abusing her stepson for years rather than raising his voice – admittedly loudly – one time in their entire relationship.

"Forget about it, okay Corrina."

He started to walk away again, and again she stopped him with her words.

"I want to know what you were coming to talk to him about."

"I really don't think you do."

"I said I *want to know*, Tyler."

Tyler looked down at the walkway for at least ten seconds. Then he walked back up the stoop.

"I was coming to talk to him about not using my bedroom as a playpen."

Corrina didn't look nearly as surprised by this as he had expected her to look.

"What are you talking about?"

"I came home Sunday night to find him in my bedroom half undressed and the girl he was with wearing even less."

Corrina's face started to color. "I don't believe you."

"I don't care whether you believe me or not. If you remember, I wasn't coming here to discuss this with you."

"You're making this up just to rile me."

Tyler looked away from his sister for a moment and then reengaged with her. "Corrina, I don't have to make things up to rile you. These days, it seems that all I have to do is breathe."

Corrina took two steps forward, though she kept one hand on the doorjamb. "I can't believe you would make up a lie like this. I don't know what you have against Ryan, but it ends now."

Tyler knew that any further conversation was pointless. Should he try to offer further evidence? Should he ask Corrina what possible benefit he could glean from fabricating this? Ultimately, it made more sense to cut his losses.

"You're right, Corrina," he said as he turned his back on her. "It ends now."

❀❀∧∧❀❀

Annie had a feeling she was supposed to feel guilty about plopping her toddler son in front of the television. It was such an easy way to dial him back, though. He could be his usual tireless self, bouncing off of everything in sight, and the vision of the Nickelodeon logo would drop him onto the sofa like she'd shot him with a tranquilizer dart. Annie would never let Joey sit in front of the set for more than an hour, but by the early afternoon, she was ready for the respite. Joey was a great kid and all, but being with him was never a stroll in the park – even when they were strolling in the park.

Annie had just popped a mug of water in the microwave and gotten the Chamomile out of the pantry when the doorbell rang. Her first thought was that it was the UPS guy with the Zappos order she placed the other day. She was looking forward to seeing her new shoulder bag since it looked so lush on the website.

When she opened the door, though, the man on the other side was not decked out in a brown uniform. He was wearing a royal blue sweater over khakis, and she'd never met a delivery person who made quite this much of an impression as he stood on her stoop.

She opened the screen door and Marty stepped into the foyer.

"What are you doing here?" Annie said hoping she expressed surprise and delight in equal measure.

"Things weren't getting anywhere in Boston. I decided to come back to Oldham a little early."

Annie hoped this didn't mean that he was going to be heading *out* of Oldham early as well. "This is a nice surprise."

Marty tilted his head and grinned at her. "I was hoping you'd think so. Wanna go out for a cup of coffee or something?"

Annie turned toward the living room. "Not really an option right now." Before she could explain further, the television exploded with a song about healthy snacking.

"Oh, you have a kid?" Marty said. The inflection in his voice suggested that this had thrown him, but Annie wondered about which part – the fact that she had a child or the fact that she hadn't mentioned it the other night.

"He's two," Annie said, as though that explained anything.

"Wow, that's cool. I hear they can be a lot of fun."

"Yeah, that's the rumor. Hey, I was about to make myself some tea. Do you want some?"

Marty nodded, his bangs flipping forward. "That would be great."

They went into the kitchen and Annie put another cup of water in the microwave. Marty seated himself at the head of the kitchen table and chose rooibos from her collection of teas.

"So I'd gotten the word that you'd married Maxwell Gold, but no one at the reunion mentioned you had a kid. Do you keep your child locked in the house away from the rest of the community?"

Annie rolled her eyes. "Hardly. I think every shopkeeper in town knows him."

"So it's a 'him,' then. Does he come with a name?"

"It varies by time of day, but he always seems to answer to Joey."

Marty seemed to be considering this as the microwave signaled that their water was hot. Annie dropped the tea bags into their mugs and joined Marty at the table.

Marty bounced his tea bag in his mug a few times. "I never pictured you as a mother."

"That's funny; I always thought I'd make a great mother."

"Oh, I'm sure you are."

Annie thought about what to say for a few seconds before responding. "I said I always *thought* I'd make a great mother."

"Do you think something different now?"

Annie smiled softly. "That varies by time of day, too."

Marty brought the mug to his lips. "I can imagine."

She watched him drink for a moment, wondering exactly what he could imagine about parenthood. "Have you ever thought about having children yourself?"

He put down the tea and ran his fingers through his hair. "There were two days when I thought an ex-girlfriend was pregnant. I thought about it a lot then."

"And what did you think?"

"I thought that I seriously hoped she wasn't pregnant."

Annie grinned. "Being a dad is not appealing?"

"Like rabies is not appealing." Marty looked skyward for a moment and then caught Annie's eyes. Marty had a way of locking into eye contact that seemed like a physical act. Annie seemed to recall quite a few "physical acts" between them coming after just such eye contact. "Is Maxwell doing okay?"

Annie nodded, dropping her eyes at the same time. "He's doing great. He's quite the man about town – he's the head of the Chamber of Commerce."

"Sounds like a good, responsible gig." Marty swept his eyes around the room. "This is a nice place."

"It works."

She could tell by Marty's expression that he'd picked up on her inflection.

"What gives?" he said.

Annie had no idea where to begin this conversation. "Let's just say I didn't have a big idea about five years ago, that I don't have an office in Vegas, and that I'm not 'scouting locations.'"

Marty shrugged. "The grass is always greener, Annie."

"Really? Does the grass on this side of the fence seem greener to you?"

Marty took another long sip of his tea and then stood. "I've gotta run. Are we still on for Thursday?"

"I'm on if you're on."

"I'm on. Is – what was his name? – Joey coming with us?"

"Hell no. I've got a babysitter and a backup."

Marty reached into his pocket for his car keys. "That's good. I'm kind of weird around kids." He pecked Annie softly on the cheek. "See you in a couple of days."

Annie got the impression that Marty didn't want her to follow him to the door, so she allowed him to let himself out. When she heard the door close, she brought his mug to the sink, noticing that he still had half a cup of tea in it. Replaying their conversation in her mind, she wondered if she'd driven him away with the manner in which she was talking about her life.

They still had their plans for Thursday, though. Annie would make sure to keep things a lot lighter then.

Thirteen

Wednesday, October 20
Eleven days before the party

Maxwell was going to be late for the meeting. He'd been running behind the entire day. Things always got a little more frantic in the fall. It was make-or-break time for so many of the local businesses, even with the surprisingly strong summer.

He took his sports coat off the hanger behind his office door and then glanced at his overcoat. Did he really need it? The air was crisp this morning, but it looked like it had turned into a beautiful day. He'd take his chances.

"I'm heading off," he said to Belinda, his assistant, as he passed her desk. Just then the phone rang. He knew he should just keep walking – he hated being late – but he'd never been able to ignore a ringing phone.

"There's someone named Lucretia on the line for you," Belinda said.

"Lucretia, really?"

"That's what she says."

He hadn't heard the name in years. "Lucretia" was what Maria called herself when she phoned him at college. She thought it sounded exotic and that his dorm mates would think he had a mysterious girlfriend. Maria spent a great deal of time telling him that he needed to be more three-dimensional back then.

"Lucretia" called often during his sophomore year. She was a senior at Quinnipiac and had started dating Doug seriously, and it seemed she had endless questions for her brother about the male psyche. From Maxwell's perspective, Doug was insanely and transparently in love with Maria, and that what was going on in his mind hardly needed to be analyzed, but maybe Maria just liked talking about him or maybe this was her way of staying in touch. Maxwell kind of liked it. Maria had never come to him for advice when they were home together.

After college, the use of the name "Lucretia" indicated that one of them required a heart-to-heart. If Maria called and introduced herself with a bad Eastern European accent, he knew they were going to be on the phone for a while. If something was troubling him, all he needed to do was ask if "Lucretia" was home to let his sister know that he had something on his mind.

It had been a while, though. Several years at least. What was going on with Maria?

Maxwell glanced at his watch. He was going to be ridiculously late now, but he had to take this call.

"Thanks, Belinda. I'll get it."

He went back to his office, closed the door, and sat down at his desk. When he picked up the phone, though, there was no one on the other end. He hung up and dialed Maria's number.

"Did you just call?" he said when she answered several rings later.

"Call who?"

More than a little baffled, Maxwell simply said, "Never mind."

❁❁∧∧❁❁

Buying sheet music online had been a revelation for Maria. The last time she'd been able to concentrate on her playing, relatively few songs were available as individual music sheets and most songs came in compilations by artist or genre. This was fine when the artist was James Taylor or Joni Mitchell, but Maria had spent too much money and taken up too much shelf space on books that contained only one or two songs she wanted to play. Now, there was an enormous selection of charts she could buy singly, and even better, she could download her choices straight to her iPad. She'd bought a couple of Jason Mraz songs this morning, along with a few Amos Lee songs, and an old Eric Andersen, song, "Is It Really Love At All," that she'd always wanted to learn.

She'd just begun to play the latter when the phone rang. Checking the caller ID, she was surprised to see her daughter's name. Olivia never called at this time of day, and Maria's first instinct was to worry.

"Olivia?"

The voice on the other end was bright, immediately easing Maria's concerns. "Hey, Mom."

"Hey, Liv. Is everything okay?"

"Yeah, great. What're you doing?"

"Just playing some music."

"Do you think you could peel yourself away for a little while?"

"Of course. Do you need me to do something for you?"

"I was kinda hoping you'd come pick me up at the train station."

Maria pulled the phone back and looked at it, as though she could see Olivia's face through the receiver. "You're here?"

"The Amtrak just got in at Old Saybrook."

"I'm getting in the car now."

Maria was giddy with the idea of a surprise visit from her daughter. It wasn't until she was halfway to the station that she began to think that something could still be wrong. Olivia had a full course load on Wednesdays and she wasn't the kind of kid who blew off classes casually. Maria was nervous now, and the tension stayed with her for the rest of the drive.

Olivia seemed completely relaxed when Maria met her at the station, though, and her hug was warm, but not in the least needy.

"You look fabulous," Maria said when she pulled back from their embrace.

"You always say that, Mom."

"It's always true."

Olivia hefted her backpack over her shoulder and went around to her side of the car. As they headed out of the parking lot, she said, "I'm starving. They had *nothing* good on the train."

"Do you want to eat around here? If you can hold on a little longer, there's a great new Thai place in town."

"Actually, what I really want is your mac and cheese."

"Really?" This was a surprise. Olivia never passed up an opportunity to go out to eat. Admittedly, though, Maria made awesome mac and cheese. "We can definitely do that. It's going to take a little while, though."

"That's okay. Are we stocked up on Wheat Thins?"

"We always are."

"Then I'll have a few of those to tide me over."

Olivia caught her up a bit on the ride home. As it turned out, Olivia's American lit and composition professors were both away at an event at Yale, and her European history professor was showing a documentary Olivia had seen in high school. Left with the makings of a wide-open day, Olivia had decided to make a quick trip home. She could catch the first train back in the morning and still make her Thursday classes.

An hour later, they were sitting down to Maria's lush macaroni and cheese, which Maria had laced with double-smoked slab bacon and yellow pear tomatoes. Olivia closed her eyes as she took her first bite, smiling contentedly.

"The mac and cheese at the dining hall is all wrong," she said after she ate another forkful. "This, however, is as perfect as it always is, Mom."

She's homesick, Maria thought. *She's not going to admit it, but that's what's going on here.* The irony of this was not lost on Maria. A week earlier, missing her daughter, she'd decided to pay her a surprise visit and came away feeling horribly awkward, yet Olivia felt perfectly fine about surprising her when she was in need of a touch of home. Obviously, this was going to have to play out on Olivia's terms. Maria was okay with that.

Maria brought out a package of Mallomars after lunch and the two stayed at the kitchen table talking about classes, Olivia's roommates, the guy Brad, who no longer seemed to fascinate, and the news Olivia had gotten from her high school friends at other universities.

"You know how I've been playing the guitar again lately?" Maria said during a lull.

"Yeah, I want you to play me a few songs after I've had maybe *two* more Mallomars."

"I ran into Martha McGarrigle the other day. She's been putting on shows at Mumford's and she told me she'd like me to play at the one the Thursday after next."

Olivia clapped her hands together. "Really?"

"I don't think I'm going to do it, though."

Olivia scowled. "What do you mean?"

Maria looked away from her daughter. "I'm not great with crowds."

"Oh, don't be ridiculous – you're doing it."

Maria laughed. "You're making this decision for me."

"Well, someone has to. Come on, Mom, how cool would it be for you to get up at Mumford's and blow people away with your music?"

"I'm not sure people get blown away by my music."

Olivia stood up. "Nope, sorry, not the time for modesty. You're definitely doing this. You're also giving me permission to cut classes next Friday so I can be here for the show."

Olivia was already planning to be down for the party, so coming a day earlier would be no big deal. "You really think I should do this?"

"Of course I think you should do it. More importantly, *you* think you should do this."

"I'm not certain about that."

"Not buying it, Mom. I can hear it in your voice. What does Dad think about it?"

"I haven't mentioned it yet."

"Well, mention it. Because you're definitely doing this and he's gonna have to come home from work early that night to take us out to dinner first." Olivia started walking toward the living room. "Come on, show me what you're thinking of playing."

Maria followed her daughter out of the kitchen, feeling exponentially happier about this impromptu visit.

❀❀∧∧❀❀

Deborah was putting her knives away and trying not to think about using them on her family. Corrina had called another Wednesday dinner. This meant Deborah had to cook on her day off, which really wasn't much of a hardship, except that it meant she couldn't cook for Sage (though he was coming by later). It also meant she had to endure more of her sister's histrionics about the party, and that was becoming increasingly difficult to do. At least Olivia was there, which was a nice surprise.

"Is the coast clear?"

Deborah looked up to see Sage grinning at her from the doorway. Her shoulders relaxed instantly. "Yes, they're finally gone."

Sage moved toward Deborah and enveloped her. She sighed and melted into him. "Do you have your new marching orders?"

She tilted her head up to kiss him. "General Corrina has explained the errors of my ways and charged me with my mission."

Sage nuzzled her neck. "I can't tell you how sorry I am to have missed this."

As Sage kissed her jaw, Deborah wanted nothing else but to have this man caressing her. Memories of Monday afternoon made her knees a little wobbly. Unfortunately, he chose that moment to pull back and reach for her hand.

"Come tell me about it," he said as he guided her toward a chair in the kitchen.

"Talk is overrated," she said as she sat. "Can we go back to what you were doing with my neck?"

Sage's eyes made it clear that his memories of Monday were as pleasant as hers. "We will definitely go back to that. Talk to me first. You looked pretty tight when I walked in."

Deborah felt herself slumping. "Oh, it's just the same garbage with some new garbage added. Corrina being autocratic, Maxwell being a politician, Tyler being befuddled – the usual. On top of that, Corrina and Tyler were sniping at each other even more than they have been. It was lots of fun. I made a pork loin with apples and currants and a brown butter pan gravy; I don't think anyone noticed, though they ate all of it."

"It sounds like the party is getting the best of them."

"I don't think that's it. I mean, it's some of it, but something tells me it would be this uncomfortable if it were June." She looked away from Sage for a moment and considered that notion. "I can't imagine what a dinner *next* June will be like. I wonder if we'll even have one."

"Your family has been close for a long time, right? Things will normalize."

Deborah nodded her head slowly. "That's just the thing. I think this might be the new normal.

What if all the tension is a symptom? What if now that my father and mother are gone – and soon the inn will be as well – we don't have any reason to stay connected?"

Sage took her hand and rubbed it softly. "I guess that's a real possibility."

"You should have seen it tonight. Corrina and Tyler looked like they genuinely disliked each other. I mean, we've always taken shots and gotten under each other's skin, but this wasn't that. This was real pissed-off stuff."

"And neither of them will tell you what's going on?"

"It's not open for discussion. If I ask one, all they do is complain about the other, but the complaints don't match the anger."

Deborah drifted back to the last time she'd broached this with Tyler. What she'd found most disturbing about the conversation was his complacency. It was as though he was already well on his way to accepting that his sister would some day be an acquaintance.

Sage squeezed her hand and then brought it to his lips. "I'm afraid I'm not going to be much help analyzing family dynamics. I haven't seen my father since a couple of weeks after my mother's funeral, and I haven't spoken to my brother in three years."

Deborah studied his eyes. "I think that might be me and my siblings soon."

Sage moved closer. "Maybe not. You're different. I never liked my brother. He eats frozen bagels."

That got a smile out of Deborah. "Frozen bagels? That's genetic, you know."

Sage's eyes few open in mock surprise. "It is?"

"It is. You're fighting your destiny. All those truffles and elderflower honey aren't going to save you, though. It's only a matter of time before you start chowing down on canned spinach. Thanks for letting me know now. I'm glad I didn't get too committed."

Sage laughed and then moved even closer. "*Too* committed?"

"Well, yeah. I was a little into you."

"Really?"

Impulsively, Deborah took his face in both of her hands. "What part of purring contentedly next to you did you misunderstand on Monday?" she said softly.

He pulled her toward him and then drew her onto his lap. "Absolutely no part."

He kissed her passionately, and the last vestige of tension over the family dinner vaporized. "Okay, maybe I'm more than a little into you."

Sage kissed her again and then started once more on her neck. "I'm not sure I have the wherewithal to make it back to my place or yours."

Deborah chuckled, surprised by how seductive it sounded. She rose from his lap and extended her hand.

"Did I mention that one of the guest rooms is empty tonight?"

Fourteen

Thursday, October 21
Ten days before the party

Maxwell called his assistant to tell her that he was going to be an hour-and-a-half or so late and then stopped at Piece of Cake for two of their signature sticky buns. He knew Tyler would never accept any kind of cash payment from him, but Maxwell could compensate him with a different kind of dough.

He hadn't called his brother ahead of time, so there was always the possibility that Tyler wouldn't be around. Maxwell hadn't planned on doing this today, but the morning had started in such an off-kilter way that he figured a change in routine might be useful. Annie, who had been unpredictable for weeks, was flat-out confounding as he prepared to go to the office. He'd made a simple request that she call the cable guy to come check why the ESPN2 signal was breaking up, and she responded by doing three minutes on how much she had going on today and how her purpose in life could not be to make sure he always had six channels of twenty-four hour sports. Taken aback, Maxwell said he'd make the call himself, at which point Annie much more calmly told him that she'd call the cable people before she got started on her day. Exchanges of this sort had become more frequent between them lately, but they still left Maxwell feeling as though he'd dropped into an alternate reality.

Maxwell pulled into Tyler's driveway, glad to see his brother's car sitting there. Grabbing the bag of sticky buns, he went up to the door and rang the bell. It took more than a minute for Tyler to answer.

"Hey," Tyler said, as he opened the door. "What are you doing here?"

Maxwell held up the bag. "I have a bribe for you."

Tyler opened the screen door and looked at Maxwell suspiciously. "Why do you have a bribe for me?"

Maxwell entered the house. "Because it's always good to have a bribe for someone when you need them to do you a favor."

"This favor wouldn't have anything to do with babysitting Joey, would it? I swear I thought I was going to pass out from exhaustion the last time."

"No babysitting. This is a photography favor. I need new headshots."

Maxwell wasn't planning to tell Tyler that the headshots were for a PR kit that would be used to get donors on board for his gestating mayoral run. Maxwell hadn't fully committed to making the run yet, but Mike had convinced him to put the kit together. Telling Tyler would make the entire thing seem as though it were genuinely in motion, and Maxwell wasn't ready for that, especially since Annie had been less than thrilled when he broached the topic with her.

"Headshots aren't exactly my thing," Tyler said.

"To tell you the truth, I'm not entire clear on what your thing is."

"Really? I've given you three framed pictures. I've seen them hanging in your house."

Maxwell flashed on the photographs Tyler had presented him with over the years. "You only do leaves?"

"Not only leaves. Sometimes other plants."

"No people?"

"No people, just natural images."

Maxwell grinned. "I've been told I'm a complete natural."

Tyler rolled his eyes. "Yes, people who make awful puns are such naturals." He grabbed for the bag. "What did you bring me from Piece of Cake?"

"Sticky buns."

"Nice."

"Does that mean you'll do the headshots?"

Tyler opened the bag and took a sniff. "These need coffee," he said, turning toward the kitchen. "I'll do the headshots if you want. I'm just not

making any promises. You might come out looking like a shrub."

"Hey, that would be an improvement over
the shot of me that's on the Chamber website."

"Yeah, I've been meaning to talk to you about
that. Did you use a disposable camera to take
that one?"

"I know it's awful. I need something better
now."

Maxwell had followed Tyler into the kitch-
en and watched as his brother ground coffee and
boiled water for the French press.

"How artsy can we be?" Tyler said when the
grinder stopped.

"Completely not artsy."

"Okay. How casual can we be?"

"Completely not casual."

"This is sounding like more and more fun by
the second. Are you sure you don't want the disposable camera guy to do this?"

"I brought sticky buns."

Tyler took an exaggerated deep breath. "You
did. You did bring sticky buns. Okay, I'll do the
shots. No tripod, though."

"I have no idea what that means."

"It means that I'm going to keep the camera
moving. I don't know much about taking pictures of people, but we're not gonna do this stiff."

"I'm in your hands."

Tyler poured the boiling water into the
French press and set a timer. "Can we lose the
tie?"

"We really can't."

"Ugh. This is why I don't shoot things that wear clothes."

An hour later, Maxwell was in his car on the way to his office. Despite his protestations, the shots Tyler took looked good, at least through the little screen on his camera. Tyler promised he'd work on the images and e-mail something later. Maybe this would convince him to consider doing more headshots in the future. There had to be more money in that than there was in photographs of plants.

By the time he got to work, Maxwell felt as though his equilibrium had been restored. He'd call Annie later to tell her that he appreciated everything she did to keep the house running. Maybe she and Joey would even meet him for a quick lunch.

❀❀∧∧❀❀

It took Annie fifteen minutes to relax into the day. The babysitter was late, which meant that the woman had arrived only minutes before Marty did at eleven thirty. This caused a bit of confusion in getting Joey settled, but Annie managed to do all of that in the den while Marty waited in the foyer. Still, she felt thrown off for a while, as she usually did when she needed her son to conform and he wanted only to do things his way.

By the time they'd gotten onto the exit out of Oldham onto I-95, though, Annie was thinking less about Joey and the babysitter and more about the darkly enchanting music Marty had on the stereo and the easy cool that her one-time lover exuded from the driver's seat. It didn't hurt that it was a magnificent Indian Summer day, easily the warmest in two weeks.

Marty had decided they were going to a beach up the coast about a half-hour, where they would picnic on a blanket on the sand. He told her he'd gotten their food from a gourmet shop in town, but Annie would have been happy with a bag of chips and a Coke. Just being out like this was enough for her.

"You still haven't told me where you got your fortune from," Annie said as she ran her hand across the buttery leather of Marty's BMW roadster. "I'm starting to think it's drugs or guns."

Marty smiled slyly. "I can promise you it's not drugs, guns, or anything else illegal."

"Then why doesn't Google have anything about you? It's like you're off the grid."

"You Googled me?"

Annie felt momentarily embarrassed. "You have me intrigued."

Without taking his eyes off the road, Marty reached over and patted Annie's leg. "Everything is set up behind holding companies. To tell you the truth, it's all pretty boring."

"But you're still not going to tell me about it."

Marty gave her leg a little squeeze before downshifting to change lanes. "Whatever you're imagining is way better than the reality."

Annie laughed and shook her head. The old Marty was never mysterious. One of the reasons they'd split was that he felt the need to say everything on his mind, including some things about her that she would have preferred not to hear. While she found his teasing a little frustrating, Annie thought this was another indication that this Marty was a considerable upgrade over the old one.

Annie was feeling completely relaxed by the time they got to the beach. The water from the Long Island Sound lapped softly onto the shore as Marty spread out their blanket and pulled food from a bag. They'd settled at a spot secluded by brush that kept them protected from the mild breeze. Other than a couple of seagulls, they had this part of the beach completely to themselves.

Marty touched her on the shoulder and handed her some red wine in a crystal glass.

"Pretty fancy for a picnic," she said.

He gestured her toward the blanket. "Wine doesn't taste right in anything else."

Annie sat down and took a look at the spread – pâté, three cheeses, some cured meats, and a jar of truffle honey. "We used to drink the cheapest wine we could find out of plastic cups."

Marty tore off a hunk of bread and handed it to her. "Times have changed."

They ate quietly for a few minutes, the wine warming Annie even more than the unseasonable sun.

"So we've discussed my mysteries, but we haven't discussed any of yours," Marty said as he drizzled some honey over a piece of cheese.

Annie looked out toward the Sound. "I have no mysteries."

"Impossible."

Annie turned toward Marty and held his eyes for several long seconds. "If I have any, they're buried under laundry and toys."

Marty smiled at her crookedly. "See? That sounds mysterious to me."

"Not mysterious. Just achingly normal."

"And you don't want that?"

"Sometimes I do. Sometimes it's even fun, like when Joey figures something out for the first time or settles enough to just cuddle with me."

"Isn't that what you signed up for?"

Annie took another sip of wine, watching the legs trail back to the bottom of the glass. "I guess I didn't realize I was signing up for this to the exclusion of everything else."

"Every gig has its downsides."

Annie tipped her head toward him. "Even running a drug cartel like you?"

Marty smiled at her again, his eyes glittering in the autumn sun. "You have no idea how tedious being an outlaw can be."

Annie put down her wineglass and leaned toward Marty. "We were never tedious, Marty."

"That was definitely true."

She turned to face him directly. "I can't even remember what tore us apart."

"Time and circumstance."

"Is that what it was?"

"That's all I remember."

Annie rose up on her knees, and before she could think about it, she moved toward Marty and kissed him, softly at first and then with increasing passion. There were several things about Marty that couldn't be improved upon, and his kisses were among the greatest. The instant their lips touched, Annie remembered how hungrily she craved his kisses, how she desired them before, during, and long after their lovemaking.

Marty's hand found the small of her back and then slid under her waistband, and she abandoned all caution. Within minutes, they were lying naked in the sand and Annie was feeling a fire she'd long believed was extinguished.

Afterward, they lay entwined while Marty tenderly massaged Annie's scalp. Only the encroaching chill and the approaching evening raised them out of their secluded cove.

They didn't speak much on the way back. Maxwell had a dinner tonight, which was good, because Annie knew she wasn't going to be ready to face him for hours. She couldn't think about the implications now, though she knew she would have to face them soon enough. All she knew was that she needed what happened this afternoon, and that she was going to need it again soon. Annie had found something inside of herself that she thought was gone; she couldn't allow herself to lose it again, regardless of the consequences.

The sun was starting to go down by the time they pulled in front of the house. The dusky light made it harder to see Marty's face, but Annie's vivid memory filled in the details.

"This was great," he said, reaching a hand out to her.

She took his hand and brought it to her lips. "Thank you."

"I wish I didn't need to be on the road again tomorrow."

"You'll be back soon, right?"

"I don't think so."

Marty's words braced her. "You don't?"

"We've gotten an amazing offer from Tampa. We're going to move the offices there."

"When did you find out?"

"We closed the deal about an hour before I picked you up."

The icy grip around her heart was the coldest Annie had ever felt in her life. She suddenly felt a desperate need to get out of the car, to shower off the smell of the beach, the smell of Marty.

"I'll keep this day with me forever, Annie."

Annie couldn't respond. She couldn't even look at the man who less than an hour before was running his fingers through her hair and reminding her of everything she'd been missing.

Instead, she opened the car door and made her way into the house quickly, not looking back once.

※ ※ ∧ ∧ ※ ※

Tyler had spent most of the afternoon applying filters to the same image, trying to make it come alive. That he was having trouble with this surprised him. It was one of the shots he'd taken on the Rhode Island coast on Sunday, and everything about it had seemed right at the time.

He saved a seventh version of the file to his desktop and decided to stop noodling with it for now. Maybe simply coming back to it tomorrow or a few days after that would show him what he was missing.

As he stood up from his workspace, the doorbell rang. He glanced out his studio window to see Patrice's car in his driveway. This was the first time she'd come to visit. All the time they'd spent together since they'd reconciled had been at her place or somewhere else.

"Hey," he said, opening the door and kissing her quickly on the lips. "Didn't we decide we were meeting at the restaurant at eight?"

Patrice walked in and glanced around the living room. "We did, but I thought I'd come by if that's okay with you."

"Yeah, of course."

"I like the way the place looks. You always had a great head for composition."

"Kind of a professional prerequisite. Here, let's go sit down. Do you want something to drink?"

"No, I'm good."

Tyler gestured her over to the couch. Patrice waited until he sat down and then sat across from him in a chair. She looked uncomfortable.

"You okay?" he said.

She pursed her lips together and then locked eyes with him. "I don't want to marry you."

The directness startled him. "You don't?"

Patrice lowered her head and then looked off to the side. "I don't, Tyler." She made eye contact again. "I love you. I feel things for you that I've never felt for anyone else. But I don't feel that I want to be your wife."

Tyler leaned forward and held up his hands. "Look, I just blurted it out. It was crazy of me to do that. It was way too soon after we'd gotten back together."

Patrice sat back in the chair as though she were retreating from him. "That's not it. If it were, I wouldn't be telling you like this, saying things this bluntly. Tyler, I'm not ever going to want to marry you."

Tyler was finding it hard to wrap his mind around this. He couldn't think of anything to say.

"What's been happening between us is a rebound," Patrice said.

"A rebound?"

She nodded. "I started dating someone a couple of weeks after you and I split. It was very intense – very intense – for a short period, and then it ended badly. That happened only two days before you came into the store. I saw you, I remembered what a good guy you are, and all of this unexpected affection came pouring out of me. And it felt great, you know? Caring for you was never an issue. I really enjoyed the two of us being together again. When you asked me to marry you, though, it forced me to think about how I saw our future – and I just don't see us as a forever thing."

Tyler continued to be dumbstruck. He thought he knew Patrice so well. How could he have possibly been unaware of how she was feeling?

"Do you hate me?" she said.

Tyler realized that he was looking far past Patrice and out the window behind her. He shifted his focus back to her.

"I don't hate you. I can't hate you."

She smiled ever so slightly. "I wouldn't blame you if you wanted to try."

"Yeah," he said weakly. "Maybe later."

"I'm sorry, Tyler. I never should have done this to you. I should have been more able to keep my wits about me, especially because it was affecting you."

All he could do was look at her. She was still as gorgeous as ever to him. This would have been so much easier if he could see her as ugly.

Patrice stood, walked over to him, and kissed him on the top of the head.

"I'm gonna go. Let's talk in a few days, okay?"

When he didn't respond immediately, Patrice kissed him on the head again. Then she turned and walked toward the door. Tyler continued to look out the window behind her chair until he heard her car back out of the driveway.

❈❈∧∧❈❈

It wasn't as though it was the first time Corrina had had a door slammed on her. Still, for some reason Ryan's doing so as he stormed out of the house after dinner continued to bother her nearly two hours later. He'd been uncommunicative at dinner, which was hardly unusual, but Corrina couldn't help think that he was being so quiet because he was hiding something. She hadn't wanted to believe her brother when he said he'd caught Ryan *in the act*, but the reality was that Tyler really didn't have any reason to invent that, and she had recently seen Ryan with his arm around a girl and had that awkward conversation with him about it. Tonight, she thought the questions she'd asked her stepson while they were eating were innocuous enough, even though she was asking them to pick up some clues. He answered them increasingly sharply, though, and finally threw down his fork, pushed back aggressively from the table, and stomped out the door.

As the echo of the slam reverberated through the house, Gardner turned to her and said, "I assume that wasn't what you were going for."

Corrina looked down at her half-finished meal. The snapper had seemed so appetizing when she bought it this afternoon. Now she'd lost interest. "You're gonna have to handle this."

"I didn't realize there was anything to handle."

Corrina hadn't mentioned Tyler's allegations to her husband, not wanting to add to the family-wide tensions that already existed between her household and her brother.

"I think bolting on us in the middle of a meal and slamming the door on the way out qualifies as something to handle."

Gardner started eating again. "At Ryan's age, I think a certain amount of acting out comes with the territory."

It dawned on Corrina that Gardner would have had an entirely different reaction if Ryan's anger had been directed at him. Saying anything of the sort was simply going to leave another member of the household pissed at her, though, so she held her tongue. Ten minutes later, dinner was over, and Gardner was back in his office working on a case. At least he bothered to mutter something about having some free time this weekend. And he didn't slam the door.

As it turned out, Corrina had plenty to take care of herself tonight. She had to follow up on the VIP invitations for the party, and she'd promised the Visitors Bureau that she'd do some maintenance of the bureau's website in preparation for the switch in focus from fall foliage to the holiday season. This kind of work often distracted her when something wasn't going right at home, but it wasn't doing so right now. She kept flashing back to Ryan's expression just before he got up from the table. It didn't say *you're getting me very angry*; it said *I don't need to take this crap from you*. It wasn't necessary to remind Corrina that she didn't have any leverage with her stepson. What would she do, though, if Ryan actually started treating her as though she were completely irrelevant to his life?

She heard Gardner's office door open and the sound of his footsteps heading toward the kitchen. She thought about meeting him there to reopen the conversation, making it less about Ryan's abrupt departure and more about her concern over his recent pattern of behavior. She thought twice about this, though, because Gardner could be so distracted and irritable when she tried to get him to think about anything other than a case while he was working. A minute later, she heard him return to his office and close the door.

Corrina tried to focus on the Visitors Bureau site, attempting to decide how to feature the various Thanksgiving events occurring in the area. However, for whatever reason, sitting alone in her office left behind by the two men in her home, she couldn't get her thoughts to extend beyond the end of October.

A few minutes later, she shut down the computer. Considering the direction in which this day had gone, heading to bed was probably the best option.

Fifteen

Friday, October 22
Nine days before the party

Tyler stood up from his desk, rubbed his eyes, and went into the kitchen to grab a glass of water. He guessed that he'd been staring at the image on his screen for a half-hour straight while he tweaked values, adjusted colors, and performed all the other subtle manipulations he brought to each of his photographs before he started printing. The challenge was always to enhance the natural without crossing over into artificial.

Sitting on the couch, he shut his eyes. When he was in a heavy work session, he found that doing this for a few minutes every couple of hours kept his vision sharp. Then he rose, rolled his neck a couple of times, and headed back to the monitor.

The image he was working on was of a carpet of fall leaves against a rise in the park. From the angle he'd chosen, it appeared that the leaves went on for miles. The only thing to break up the expanse was a tiny sliver of street in the upper left corner. Looking at that spot now, Tyler noticed a bicycle that he'd somehow missed before. It didn't surprise him that he hadn't seen the bike in the shot because his eyes naturally fell on the array of color that filled most of the screen.

Looking more closely, Tyler saw that the bike had a child seat strapped onto the back. It looked a lot like the bike Deborah used to take him for rides on when he was a little kid. Tyler didn't remember much from his preschool days, but he had very clear memories of the wind on his legs when they sped down the hill around the corner from the house. He'd squeal as they made their descent and immediately start begging Deborah to do it again when they got to the bottom.

Tyler remembered doing this with his sister from spring through fall when he was four. Deborah was an incredibly good sport about it. The spring after he turned five, though, it nearly ended with a bang.

It was the first warm day of March and Tyler immediately started campaigning Deborah for a ride. He must have gone through a growth spurt over the winter, because Deborah remarked about how much heavier he felt on the back of the bike, and she definitely seemed to be having a harder time getting up the hill. Going down, though, would turn out to be more problematic. As they picked up speed, Deborah must have noticed something in the road, because she shifted the front wheel quickly. The now-heavier Tyler threw her off balance, and suddenly the bike went crashing, Deborah flew out of her seat, and the strapped-in Tyler skidded along the road. Tyler remembered being shaken up, but he didn't feel frightened or hurt until he saw Deborah get up with a bloodied knee, look at him, and start screaming. That's when he noticed there was blood running down his face and into his eyes, and his arm was bleeding too. Deborah unstrapped him, hugged him to her chest, and ran with him all the way back to the house. There was quite a bit of blood, but all of Tyler's injuries were superficial. Mom patched them both up and they didn't even need to go to the doctor.

That didn't stop Deborah from being horrified by the experience. She spent the entire evening alternating between crying, checking on Tyler's wounds, and apologizing.

The next afternoon, Tyler asked Deborah if they could go down the hill again. Deborah immediately got tears in her eyes.

"I don't think we should, babe," Deborah said in an unusually high voice. "I almost really hurt you yesterday."

Tyler remembered his head dropping at that point. As he studied the floor he said, "So we can't go down the hill anymore?"

Deborah knelt next to him. "I just don't want to hurt you."

Tyler looked into her teary eyes. "You don't hurt me. You take care of me."

Deborah hugged him close at that point, pinning his tender arm. Now *that* hurt, but Tyler definitely didn't want to say anything about it.

Mom wouldn't let them ride that day, but they were back on the hill two days later, and they went down it dozens of times that year. The next year, Tyler was old enough to race Deborah down the hill on his own bike, something they kept doing until Deborah went off to culinary school. It was their thing.

Tyler realized he'd lost focus on the image on his monitor. He examined it again now. Doing so, he realized that the vehicle on the upper left corner of the picture wasn't a bike at all. It was a motorcycle.

Maybe it was time to get away from the computer for a while.

❀❀∧∧❀❀

Spurred by Olivia's encouragement, Maria had spent every minute that Doug wasn't around working on her four-song set for the show at Mumford's. She knew she wanted to do a James Taylor song, but picking one required playing dozens from his songbooks to choose something that felt and sounded the best. She figured she would do the version of "Least Complicated" that Martha liked enough to ask her to be in the show originally. She also wanted to do something not usually associated with acoustic performers, and had been auditioning everything from Earth, Wind & Fire to Nine Inch Nails to Coldplay.

For the fourth song, Maria decided she wanted to do something original. It wasn't that she thought she was in the same league as these other songwriters, but if she was going to perform for people for the first time in years, she wanted to do at least one thing that was distinctly hers.

What song, though? As she flipped through her songbooks, everything seemed either too personal – lullabies for Olivia, mostly – or too derivative. She didn't want to do an original song only to come off as an imitator. She tried tweaking a chorus here or a chord change there, but none of the improvements seemed substantial enough.

I'm going to have to write something new, she thought. This made all kinds of sense to her. She'd evolved so much as a person over the years. Surely her lyrics would be more sophisticated now, as would be her sense of how to build a song.

Maybe she would write something for the Halloween party as well. She'd done this sort of thing for special family occasions in the past, major anniversaries, birthdays, and other events. She could play it toward the end of the night, giving the evening an emotional sendoff and the future an appropriate start.

She picked up her guitar, spent a moment tuning, and then tried out various combinations of chords and fingerpicking styles. Though she considered her lyrics to be the most important part of her songs, she always started with a melody. She also knew from experience that the first hour or so of noodling would net absolutely nothing of value.

With less than a week before the show and only nine days until the party, she didn't have any time to waste.

❉❉∧∧❉❉

Maybe this is how you're supposed to feel, Deborah thought as she walked from her car down Hickory. *Maybe queasiness is part of the process.* She realized as she started driving toward Sage's shop immediately after getting off the phone that she had no reference point for this.

Sage was setting up a display along the left wall when Deborah entered the store. He stopped when he heard the door open and started walking toward her when he realized who it was. He must have noticed how skittish she was feeling, because his expression changed from one of welcome to one of concern just before he hugged her.

"What's going on?" he said, still holding her close to him.

"I told River Edge I'd take the job."

He pulled back, still holding her shoulders. "Hey, that's great."

"That's what they said."

"It is. Right?"

Deborah took a step away and sighed. "It is, I know. It's a great restaurant, a great kitchen, and they're going to let me do whatever I want. And the pay is good, which means I won't have to dig into my savings while I'm looking around. So why do I feel like I just got into my safety school?"

Sage chuckled softly. "Because that's exactly what happened."

"But they're *all* safety schools. That's the thing that's making me crazy."

Sage reached out for her hand and moved her toward the display he'd been setting up.

"These arrived today," he said, handing her a bottle of scotch bonnet ketchup. Deborah looked at the label, a lovely line drawing of vines and vegetables. Then she examined some of the other items on the shelf: a curry mustard, a persimmon relish, a passion fruit chutney, an apricot salsa. "They're made by a woman in the Finger Lakes. A few years ago, she was running a food truck selling artisanal sandwiches. The artisanal part came largely from the homemade condiments she put on them. Rather than expanding her catering business, she decided to start selling the condiments instead."

Deborah found this fascinating. "She gave up the food truck?"

"She had to. This is ramping up very fast. When I spoke to her at the fair, she told me that she's already in twenty-three states."

Deborah reached for the chutney and read the statement of purpose on the back of the jar. *Adding new tastes to time-honored favorites.... Complete dedication to the fullness of flavor.* Deborah had the feeling she would like this person. Maybe she would go with Sage to the next food fair he attended. If she could get the time off from the River Edge.

Sage took the jar from her hand. "Isn't this what you should be doing with your sauces?"

He completely surprised her with the suggestion. "Bottle sauces?"

He put the jar back on the shelf. "Your sauces are uniquely yours and people travel from all over to taste them. We could get the food blogosphere talking about this in ten seconds."

Deborah put a hand up to her nose, still trying to reconcile something so completely different from what she'd been considering for her next career move.

"There's nothing 'safety school' about it," Sage said.

She glanced over at him, and a smile blossomed on her face. "There isn't, is there?"

"Nothing in the least. You could fail spectacularly."

"I could," she said, her smile broadening. She gazed skyward and then looked toward the door. "They're going to be so furious with me when I tell them I'm not taking the job."

"They'll get over it."

❀ ❀ ∧ ∧ ❀ ❀

Tyler had surprised himself with his reaction to losing Patrice, especially since there was little question that it was final this time. There was no way back for them after what she'd said to him. Still, less than a minute after her car had backed down the driveway, he was back at his computer, working on images. First, he cracked the code on the Rhode Island shots and then he started refining photos he'd left unfinished for a year or more. He didn't even stop to go to the bathroom until two thirty in the morning, when he finally left his studio for the night.

Whatever had spurred that burst of productivity was absent today, though. He didn't get out of bed until after eleven, and making coffee easily took him ten minutes. At this pace, he wouldn't be showered until Saturday.

Sitting with his mug at the dining room table, he could see the couch where Patrice had kissed him goodbye. He'd known that his marriage proposal had not gone well, even if he'd been a little reluctant to acknowledge it consciously. He'd even prepared himself for Patrice suggesting to him that they set the conversation aside for the immediate future. He might have even been fine with that, as long as it didn't become an issue between them.

If he hadn't asked Patrice to marry him, would they have kept going the way they had been going since their reunion? Did he inspire her departure – and her candor – by raising the bar? Or had he merely hastened the conversation by a week or so? Maybe Patrice had already had it in her head that she was going to end things without committing to a timeline.

Tyler realized that this kind of conjecture didn't matter, even though he couldn't prevent himself from continuing with it. Right now, nothing seemed like a better option than sitting at the table, staring at the couch, and wondering about alternative ways in which Patrice might have dropped the bomb on him.

Tyler's cell phone started playing his ringtone, the opening notes from Fun.'s "We are Young." For a split second, he thought about letting the call go to voicemail, but curiosity prevailed, even in his torpid state.

The call was from an area code he didn't recognize, and the number was one he didn't know. Having already expended the energy to rise from the table to see who was trying to get in touch with him, he decided to answer it.

"Hello?"

"Hi, I'm looking for Tyler Gold."

"That would be me."

"It's a pleasure to meet you, Tyler. My name is Joe Elliott, and I run the Aperture Photo Gallery in Columbia, South Carolina. First of all, let me tell you how much I love your work."

Tyler shook his head briskly at the incongruity of this call. "Did you say you're from South Carolina? How did you even see my work?"

"From your site, of course. Beautifully designed, by the way."

"Yeah, I figured you saw my stuff on the site, but how'd you find the site in the first place? Don't tell me that search engine optimization thing I did actually worked."

The man on the other end of the call chuckled. "I don't know anything about that. A gallery owner in Silver Spring, Maryland told me about you."

Tyler had no idea how the guy in Silver Spring knew about his work either, and he assumed that asking Joe Elliott was pointless. "Well, thanks."

"I'd like to talk to you about my carrying some of your photos in my gallery."

"Really? You think there's a market for pictures of New England leaves in South Carolina?"

"I think there might be a good one. There are only so many photos of palmettos you can sell."

Tyler hadn't once considered this kind of merchandising possibility. He'd always assumed that the only market for his current work would be relatively local and that he'd have to change his style if he wanted a broader reach. It hadn't occurred to him that people might gravitate toward his images precisely because they *weren't* local.

The idea popped into Tyler's head so quickly that he barely had time to consider it before he started speaking.

"I can't believe how great your timing is," he said. "I happen to be flying down to...Charleston next week."

"Wow, that *is* great timing. Charleston's not around the corner, but it's only about a two-hour drive away. If you feel like taking a ride, let's get together."

Meeting Joe Elliott in Columbia, South Carolina sounded exponentially better than anything he was going to be doing in Oldham next week.

"Sounds great. I'm just printing some new shots. I think you might like them."

Sixteen

Saturday, October 23
Eight days before the party

Corrina put the grocery bag on the kitchen counter and started getting the produce into the refrigerator. With the door still open, she checked the pantry to confirm that she had enough rice for tonight's dinner, even though she could wind up eating alone, given how things were going in her household. Still, it would have been a complete hassle if she had to go out again.

She turned back to the canvas bag and noticed the logo imprinted on the front. "Delson's Corner Market." Delson's? The store had gone out of business when Corrina was a teenager. It really was a great place back then. Sawdust on the floor – why did old stores do that? – and a faint mustiness that said, "We've been here for decades" and, "You can feel comfortable here" at the same time. The store was small, maybe a few thousand square feet, but it was packed with fresh fruits and vegetables, a deli counter decorated with hanging dried sausages, a bakery section that always tempted her, and the coolest candy selection around that had stuff you couldn't find anywhere else like Gold Nugget bubble gum and Pixy Sticks. Mr. and Mrs. Delson ran the place for forty years until the big Stop & Shop opened outside of town and drove them to retirement. They were in Florida now if Corrina recalled correctly.

None of which explained how the Delson's logo got on the grocery bag she could swear she purchased at the farmer's market a few months ago. Was the Delson's logo some kind of nostalgia thing she'd somehow missed when she bought the bag? Certainly, there were enough people who loved the old store that there'd be an available audience for such an imprint.

Corrina remembered how her father used to go to Delson's early every Saturday morning. If she was up in time, he'd take her with him, and he'd invariably let her buy one of those cool candies. Tyler was the only other one who ever got up early enough to go with them, and it became something of a ritual, the siblings talking about which treat they planned to buy during the entire trip there. One Saturday, both of them had overslept and Dad went off without them. He always said he wouldn't wake them because if they were sleeping, that meant they needed to sleep. Still, the entire weekend felt wrong to Corrina because she'd missed the trip to Delson's. She knew Tyler felt the same way.

The next Friday night, Corrina and Tyler came up with a plan: they would take turns "standing guard" to make sure that Dad didn't leave them behind again. That first weekend, it was Corrina's job to listen and wake Tyler in time to get both of them downstairs. Of course, she barely slept the entire night. The next Friday night, it was Tyler's turn. They didn't miss a single trip with their father again until the store closed.

Corrina couldn't remember the last time she had a Jujube, one of the candies she regularly bought at Delson's. Maybe Patrice knew where she could find one.

Corrina put a can of white beans away and then set aside the grocery bag – a bag that prominently displayed the logo of the Oldham Farmer's Market. She laughed when she looked at the bag a second time.

She wondered what made her think of Delson's.

❊❊∧∧❊❊

The opportunity was too good to pass up. Maxwell and Joey were on their way back from their stroll through town when they came upon an enormous pile of leaves at a curb three blocks from their house.

Joey had been surprisingly mellow since they left the deli where they'd had breakfast. Maybe he'd worn himself out pinballing from the sandwich counter to the chips display to the refrigerator to various diner-filled tables, and under a newspaper stand he never should have fit beneath. Maxwell knew there was a risk that taking his son out of his stroller right now would toggle his on switch. Still, there was the pile.

It was time.

"Joe, here comes today's rite of passage," Maxwell said as he unclipped the boy's safety belt. He pulled Joey up into his arms and then placed him next to the pile.

"Do you know what you do with one of these?" he said, pointing to the enormous collection of leaves.

Joey looked up at him and shook his head vigorously.

"You do this."

Maxwell hoisted the boy and placed him into the pile, splashing him with leaves as though they were in the community pool. Joey laughed and started pushing leaves in Maxwell's direction, jumping up and down as he did.

Maxwell pulled his son out of the pile and set him at the edge of the curb. Joey was still jumping.

"Jump," Maxwell said, pretending to jump into the pile.

Joey jumped higher.

"No, *jump*."

Maxwell repeated the gesture, but Joey just kept bobbing.

"Like this," Maxwell said before jumping into the leaf pile himself. The leaves were mid-thigh-high on him. Joey thought this was hilarious and jumped in to join him. The leaves came up to his chin.

They tossed leaves at each other for a minute or so until Maxwell looked up from the pile of leaves at the curb to the house beyond. From a window, a woman looked out with a perplexed expression.

She thinks I'm out of my mind. Maybe I should cross this house off my list when I go canvassing for votes.

Feeling a bit sheepish – but only a bit, because Joey was having such a good time – Maxwell extricated himself and his son from the pile, straightening it out after he did so. He brushed off the two of them and tried to get Joey back in his stroller, but the boy wasn't the least bit interested in doing so. Maxwell pushed the stroller while his son bounced ahead yelling, "Jump! Jump! Jump!"

Annie still wasn't around when they got back to the house. She'd gone to bed right after dinner last night, and she was gone by the time Maxwell and Joey woke up in the morning. Something was obviously going on with her, but she had rebuffed all attempts Maxwell made to discuss it. She'd had moments like this in the past, and she'd been equally closed during those times. Maxwell had learned that the only option he had was to continue to let Annie know he was available to talk and to otherwise let her deal with the funk on her terms. Eventually, the cloud would pass.

Joey finally stopped jumping by the time they got to the living room. That did not mean, though, that he was calming down. Within thirty seconds, he'd pulled a truck, two balls, and a wind-up clown from his toy chest.

"It's nap time, Joe," Maxwell said when Joey started digging into the chest again.

Joey stopped, turned, said, "Catch," and threw a yellow toy football to him. The kid's accuracy was improving; Maxwell only needed to stretch the length of the couch to get the ball. The boy thought it was hilarious to see his father sprawling to grab it in flight.

Maxwell gathered Joey up in his arms and headed toward his son's room. It took three lullabies to soothe him, but Maxwell finally got the pinball down for his nap.

Maxwell had been on the couch reading for about fifteen minutes when Annie entered. He got up to kiss her, and their lips barely touched before she moved into the kitchen. She hadn't suggested she wanted Maxwell to follow, but he did so anyway.

"Joey's sleeping," he said as he watched her fill a large glass with water and drink it down quickly. "You were gone early."

She put the glass on a countertop and looked in his general direction. "I wanted to get out for a while."

"Yeah, I figured."

It was clear Annie wasn't interested in offering details about where she'd gone. Again, experience told him that asking would be counterproductive.

"Listen," he said, "I decided I'm going for it."

Annie looked at him as though they'd just met. "Going for what?"

"The mayor thing. I've decided that I want to run."

Annie's eyes clouded instantly. "Isn't that fantastic."

"I was hoping you'd be a little more excited than that."

Annie laughed darkly. "Really? You really thought there was any chance that I was going to be excited about this? Why the hell would you possibly think that?"

"I know you have some concerns, but –"

"– I don't have *concerns*, Maxwell. I have something much bigger than *concerns*. You want me to be the happy little supportive wife? It's not happening – not for this. I want to go back to work. I want to spend less time strapped to Joey. I want to be *something*, and by that, I don't mean that I want to be the freaking First Lady of Oldham. I want to be doing something with my future that's a little more meaningful than going to a bunch of public functions with my husband pretending that our family has the perfect little life."

The outburst set Maxwell back on his heels. He knew Annie was going to have some issues with his running for public office, but nothing she'd said before prepared him for this tirade.

"This obviously doesn't have anything to do with my running for mayor," he said after the silence between them extended for an uncomfortably long time.

"You can think what you want."

Maxwell took a step toward his wife. "Talk to me, Annie."

Annie headed out of the kitchen. "I don't want to talk. And while it seems that what I want doesn't matter much these days, if I want to not talk about this, there's nothing you can do about it." She grabbed her purse. "I'm going out again."

"Where are you going?"

"I haven't decided yet. Have a good afternoon with your son."

❊❊∧∧❊❊

Since she had gotten to the kitchen an hour and a half ago, Deborah had been working on variations of Béarnaise to go with the roasted pork she was serving at the inn tonight. If you took out the tarragon, could you technically call it a Béarnaise? She decided to flout convention by switching out green peppercorns in one batch, sorrel in another, and even lavender in a third. The latter didn't work at all, but the other two were delicious. For the next batch, she was going to try both tarragon and green peppercorns, walking the line between traditional and daring.

She'd been thinking about sauces nonstop for the past day, running endless combinations in her mind. This was a variation on the nonstop thinking she'd been doing about what to serve for the last meal at the inn. Or the nonstop thinking she had been doing about where she was going to work starting in November. Deborah wasn't sure you could be thinking *nonstop* about multiple things, but it certainly felt as though she'd been doing that.

If this tarragon-green-peppercorn Béarnaise works, will I be able to figure out a shelf-stable version of it that still has the right flavor profile?

She had just started chopping tarragon for the new trial when Tyler came into the kitchen. He'd called this morning saying he wanted to stop by for lunch, which he used to do all the time, but hadn't been doing for the past few months. She smiled up at him while she continued to chop.

"Yum, tarragon," he said, "one of my favorites."

"Too bad. You're not getting any of this."

"You can be very cold. Did you know that, sis?"

Tyler said this lightly, which surprised Deborah, since she wasn't sure there'd be anything lighthearted about their conversation today. Deborah assumed her brother was hurting badly over Patrice's leaving him and that lunch would involve quite a bit of hand holding.

She finished chopping and set the herb aside, moving to another cutting board to begin prep for their lunch. A few minutes later, she was sautéing garlic in olive oil before adding crumbled homemade chorizo. A short time after that, diced red and yellow peppers went into the pan along with a minced Vidalia onion and some fresh peas. After that came a healthy dose of Sherry. While that reduced, Deborah grabbed some linguine from the refrigerator and threw it in a pot of water. When the pasta was ready, she tossed it in the pan with a knob of butter and turned it out into two bowls, topping each with some thyme leaves.

Tyler had been standing next to her during the entire process, saying virtually nothing. He'd always been somewhat star struck while she cooked, starting from when they were much younger, which she had always considered endearing.

"Do you want some wine?" she said as she put the plates on the table in the kitchen.

"Nah, I'm good."

Tyler got some sparkling water for both of them and then settled down to eat.

He twirled a forkful of linguine. "So I'm going to South Carolina on Monday."

"Why South Carolina?"

"Some guy called."

"Good thing the call wasn't from Bogota."

Tyler finished chewing. "A gallery guy."

"Great. Why do you need to see him?"

"To show him some of my new stuff."

"Isn't that what the Internet is for?"

Tyler twirled up some more pasta, but held it in front of him rather than eating. "I don't know; something just told me I should go to see him. I just got a little vibe about this one."

"Then you should go with it. Following your instincts has always worked well for you."

Tyler tipped his head sideways.

"I wasn't being sarcastic," Deborah said. "I mean, following your instincts with Patrice didn't go so great, but following your *professional* instincts usually pays off for you."

Tyler seemed satisfied with that clarification and ate hungrily.

He sighed. "I always love it when you make this dish."

Deborah smiled, remembering the first time she came up with this combination for her brother on one of her weekends home from the CIA.

At that moment, inspiration electrified her. "That's it! I'm know what I'm going to do for my final dinner here. I'm going to make a meal where each course is a favorite from each member of the family. I'll have to tinker with a few ingredients to balance things out and bring things up to fine dining level, but it'll be great."

She started playing out the progression of courses in her mind. She hadn't initially considered her sisters' husbands, but she probably should. Gardner had a thing for cauliflower; maybe she could build a side around that.

Doug loved her cold watercress soup; she could do shooters of it as an intermezzo. Joey didn't have any favorites yet, but Olivia loved her caramel-stuffed bomboloni. She could do that for dessert.

Pleased with how well this was coming together, Deborah didn't immediately register that Tyler was staring at her.

"That's a cool idea," he said once she looked at him, "but isn't it a little strange that you're going to make this dinner on a night when none of us are there?"

Deborah allowed the question to steep for a few seconds. "No," she said slowly. "Actually, it seems completely appropriate."

❀❀∧∧❀❀

After Corrina reminded him about their eight o'clock dinner reservation at seven fifteen, Gardner had come out of his office looking a bit peeved, showered quickly, and jumped in the car with her, barely saying a word. He seemed more than agitated about needing to leave his cases for a night out with his wife. He seemed disquieted, as though his internal system was roiling. Corrina wondered if there was something especially troubling in the case that was about to go to trial. If so, he would never tell her, so the best she could do was hope that a Scotch or two might bring him back toward equilibrium.

They didn't speak much while they looked through the menu and ordered, but once that was done, and once Gardner had downed three quarters of his first drink, he took an exaggeratedly deep breath, held a hand out to her from across the table, and smiled.

"So?" he said, letting the word out as a long exhale. "How are things?"

Corrina snickered. That was as close as Gardner would ever come to an apology for sequestering himself. She caught him up a bit on the party planning, telling him about a confounding conversation she'd had with the cleaning service that afternoon, and then mentioned a coffee date she'd had afterward with her friend Terre. This was nothing more than the usual end-of-day debriefing, but it felt good to be able to speak to Gardner without feeling as though his eyes were constantly glancing over to his office.

It was also nice to have a dinner conversation that didn't include either scowls or dismissiveness from Ryan. Since the door-slamming incident, he'd been even less communicative. Tonight, he'd simply left a note on the kitchen counter while Corrina was showering that read, "I'm going."

"By any chance," Corrina said as their appetizers arrived, "has Ryan said anything to you about having a girlfriend?"

Gardner's mystified expression suggested that he thought the idea of a son discussing this with his father was entirely inconceivable. "No, of course not. Ryan has a girlfriend?"

"Not that he would acknowledge to me, but I saw him walking with his arm around someone a little while ago."

"Hmm. Well, he's certainly old enough to have a girlfriend. Maybe she'll warm him up a bit."

Corrina took a forkful of her tomato salad and thought about whether she should take this conversation any further.

"She might be warming him up more than a bit," she said.

"What's that supposed to mean?"

She put down her fork and gestured with her hands. "Tyler came to see me the other day. I immediately got my defenses up because he's been such a jerk lately, but he told me something that seems more and more plausible the more I think about it."

"What's that?"

"That Ryan and a girl snuck into Tyler's house while he was away and that he came home to find the two of them semi-naked."

Gardner's eyes widened. "Is this girl under eighteen?"

"I have no idea. I saw her in profile once. For that matter, I don't even know if the girl I saw and the girl Tyler saw are the same person."

Gardner looked down at his plate, pushed a bit of food around, and then dabbed at his mouth with his napkin. "I don't like this. Does he understand the risks?"

"Which risks are you talking about? The pregnancy risk? The getting-your-heart-broken risk?"

"I was thinking specifically about the statutory rape charge risk."

Corrina's nerves prickled. "That sounds like something a lawyer would mention to him. Too bad we don't know one."

Gardner sent her a gaze intended to wither. "Don't give me any of that crap, Cor. Why don't you know more about what he's doing? Teenaged boys can screw up their lives in a millisecond."

Corrina had the presence of mind to acknowledge their environment – and the fact that the tables on either side were very close – before she responded. "Why don't *I* know more about this? You do remember that I'm his stepmother, don't you? I assume you also remember that every time I've tried to make a decision regarding Ryan – even really little ones – you've contradicted me."

"You're being unnecessarily dramatic."

"I really don't think I am. You won't even let me have my say over little things like whether he can go to a concert in the city. Why don't I know more about what Ryan is doing? Because you've sent him the very clear message that I have no parental role whatsoever."

Gardner wiped at his mouth again, though he hadn't taken a bite since the last time. "Cor, ratchet down the angst a little."

Corrina wanted to throw something, but she didn't want the rest of the restaurant to know she was that angry. "Okay, Gardner, I'll ratchet it down. Let's just leave it at this, okay? Your son – *your* son – might be screwing around. There are all kinds of reasons to be at least a little concerned about this, including your legal reasons. If this worries you at all, you – and only you – need to deal with it."

With that, Corrina returned to her meal, wanting nothing more than to be done with the food and back home.

Less than an hour earlier, as they were driving to the restaurant, she'd imagined that she and Gardner would go straight up to the bedroom after they got home.

Now she just hoped he'd go back to his office.

Seventeen

Sunday, October 24
Seven days before the party

The resonant echo of something striking her guitar's hollow body woke Maria. Her first thought was to turn toward Doug to see if he'd heard the sound as well, but his head was buried deep in his pillow; he probably hadn't moved for hours. She looked in the other direction, toward the rocking chair in the corner of the bedroom.

To find her mother rocking softly with the guitar in her lap.

Maria startled for a moment, but she found this vision surprisingly comforting. Hadn't she been hoping for a "visit" since her mother died?

"Mom?" she said softly to avoid waking her husband.

Her mother picked a few notes on the instrument. "Hello, dear."

She fingerpicked several chord changes.

"Mom, you never played guitar."

"I sound pretty good, though, don't I?"

She did sound good. Her touch was delicate, but even though she was playing quietly, there was a sense of dynamics.

"Have you been taking lessons in heaven?"

Mom offered a tiny grin, but no other response. Instead, she started humming a melody that complimented the chords she was playing. The melody was familiar, but Maria couldn't remember where she'd heard it before.

"That's pretty," she said, speaking a little louder. Obviously Doug was sleeping very hard or this entire thing was a vivid dream. In either case, she didn't need to worry about waking him.

"I'm glad you think so. You should like it. After all, you wrote it."

Mom hummed another couple of lines and Maria tried to pick it out from her many compositions.

"I did?"

"For Corrina's fourth birthday."

As soon as Mom said that, the song sprang to Maria's mind. She'd only been writing songs for a short while and she wanted to do something special for her little sister. Corrina reacted as though Maria had presented her with a truck full of candy. She made her sing the song four times in a row, even though birthday cake was waiting, and then asked her to sing it repeatedly over the coming weeks.

This was the first time Maria had given a gift of a song, something she would do often afterward. She'd lost contact with this memory, but now that her mother had given it back to her, she remembered how good it felt to be Corrina's big sister, to be able to give her something no one else could give her.

Did Corrina remember this? If so, did she think of it as fondly as Maria was thinking of it now? When was the last time either of them mentioned it to the other?

Maria closed her eyes and sang along with her mother now, accessing the lyrics from some dusty file in her brain. By the time she got to the chorus, though, she realized she could no longer hear the guitar or her mother's humming.

She looked at the rocking chair. Her mother was no longer there. Nor was the guitar. Maria remembered that she'd put it in its case Friday afternoon.

※ ※ ∧ ∧ ※ ※

Deborah didn't get out of bed before six in the morning very often. She especially didn't often get out of bed at that time when a beautiful and very cozy man was in there with her. For whatever reason, though, something jogged her awake at five-thirty with thoughts of Espagnole sauces. This kind of thing happened to her. Others might bolt up in the middle of the night thinking about an unpaid bill or a difficult relationship. For Deborah, it was cooking challenges. Usually, she could set such things aside after a few minutes and get back to sleep. Not now, though. Not with this particular challenge.

Deborah always kept frozen Espagnole in her freezer. This wasn't the kind of thing she mentioned to casual acquaintances, but it did come in handy because Espagnole took so long to make. It was especially useful now because she needed to find a way to put her own stamp on the sauce if she were going to put her name on it and market it to the food world.

Since she didn't do all that much cooking at home, Deborah had a limited range of fresh ingredients at her disposal. She thought about taking a run to the inn – it would be much easier to test recipes there, anyway – but it was very early and there was the matter of not wanting to run out on the beautiful man in her bed. She had some dried porcini and sun-dried tomatoes in the pantry. She could do something with those. She had several good balsamic vinegars; that could take her in an interesting direction. Might as well roll up her sleeves and see where things went from here.

While she slowly thawed the frozen Espagnole in a saucepan, Deborah tried to imagine a future where making sauces was a full-time profession. Could she sell enough to make a living? Certainly she was well enough connected in the food community to have a decent profile on the food fair circuit and to get in front of the necessary distributors. She'd also built up enough of a relationship with food sites and blogs over the years that she could get attention for the product line when she was ready to launch it. After that, it was up to the consumers, and that was a tremendous unknown to her. Devising menus that drove people to her restaurant was one thing; she understood that world. Packaging things for people to use in their own homes was something else entirely.

As Deborah soaked the mushrooms and tomatoes in hot water and minced some onion, she thought about something else she hadn't considered until this moment. She wouldn't be able to experiment nightly with these sauces. Once she launched a product line, she'd have to keep making *those products*. She'd never build up an audience if the sauces she shipped the first week in December were completely different from the sauces she shipped the third week in February.

This thought caught her up short. So much so that she turned off the burner on which she'd been thawing the Espagnole and sat down. For the next several minutes, her thoughts paralyzed her. This had seemed like such a liberating idea, a way of staying true to herself without having to work in someone else's restaurant. Now, she wasn't at all sure.

"Your bed is considerably less comfortable when you're not in it with me," Sage said, walking into the kitchen. He was wearing the jeans and polo she happily remembered removing from him last night. "Wasn't the plan to sleep in this morning?"

"I know, I'm sorry. I started making sauces."

Sage sat next to her and reached for her hand. "That's nearly an acceptable reason to be up this early on a Sunday morning."

"But then I stopped."

"Really? It smells great."

She turned to face him directly. "I don't think I can do this, Sage."

"Every entrepreneur worries about whether they're going to be successful."

"No, that's not it. I mean, that's an entirely different set of worries. What hit me a few minutes ago is what it would mean if I *were* successful. I had this vision of myself making gallons and gallons of brown sauce with porcini and sun-dried tomatoes every week. That isn't me. How many sauces can I realistically think about selling? Four? Five? Maybe a new one every nine months or so. How am I going to do the same thing over and over and over?"

Sage sat back. It was clear he hadn't thought of this, either. For more than a minute, the kitchen was silent. Then he brightened. "What if you did something no one else is doing? At least no one I know of. What if you had your line of four or five staple sauces, but then had a subscription program where stores could get a limited edition sauce from you every other week. You could even sell the subscription direct to consumers online. The sauces would show up every Tuesday or something and people would be lining up to get them for that night's dinner."

Deborah found it impossible not to chuckle at Sage's enthusiasm. "Line up. Really?"

"Absolutely. Except for the people who are buying direct. They'll just be sitting by their mailboxes."

Deborah laughed out loud now. Still, the idea was intriguing. Of course, if no one else were doing it, it could mean that it was unworkable. It was worth a try, though.

"Okay, well since you're coming up with brilliant solutions this morning, come up with this one: how am I going to start a food business in this lousy kitchen?"

Deborah looked around the room. Her appliances were rudimentary at best. This had never mattered to her because she did so little cooking at home and she always had access to a great professional kitchen.

"You're not going to do it here."

"Yeah, I know, I can rent out a restaurant kitchen for a few hours every day, but I'm always going to feel like I'm in the way."

"You're not going to do that, either."

"You know that when people call me a wizard in the kitchen that they're not actually saying I'm Dumbledore or something, right?"

"You're going to use mine."

The implications were obvious. And even though they'd only been together for a short while, the implications didn't feel wrong to Deborah in any way.

Sage leaned toward her. "Come on, you know you've been lusting after my kitchen from the minute you saw it."

"You do have a great kitchen," Deborah said, kissing him. "But that is definitely not what I'm lusting after right now."

❀ ❀ ∧ ∧ ❀ ❀

Tyler was walking to the park to take some more shots when he saw Ryan coming toward him from the other direction. The kid was walking with his eyes toward the pavement and didn't seem to notice Tyler, even as they got within twenty feet of one another.

"I'm sure the ants appreciate that you're trying not to step on them," Tyler said.

Ryan looked up, immediately registering discomfort when he realized who was talking to him. "Oh, hey."

"Did Corrina mention that I came by looking for you the other day?"

"I don't think so."

"You don't *think* so?"

Ryan looked down at the ground again, and then off to the distance. "I try not to listen too much to what Corrina says."

"Fair enough. That strategy never worked for me. How's it going for you?"

Ryan shrugged in response.

The park was maybe a hundred yards in the distance. Tyler gestured in that direction. "Come on, let's go sit for a few minutes."

"I really have to be somewhere."

"Pretend that you don't."

Making his reluctance apparent, Ryan followed Tyler to a bench and sat on the end opposite.

"We need to talk about last Sunday," Tyler said, turning to face his nephew.

Ryan's expression tightened. "Not if you don't want to."

"Yeah, we do. First of all, how did you get in?"

"The window in your office wasn't locked."

"How did you know that?"

"I tried a few other windows first."

Tyler made a note to himself to latch all the windows shut when he got home. "What made you think this was a good idea?"

Ryan studiously avoided eye contact. "I thought you'd be cool with it."

The response seemed ludicrous to Tyler on so many levels. "You did? I didn't think you thought I was *cool* with anything anymore. And what part did you think I'd be cool with? The breaking into my house part? The screwing around with a girl in my bedroom part? The running out without a word when I came in part?"

"Look, I was wrong. About all of it. I'm sorry – is that what you want me to say?"

The response was standard-issue teenaged bluster. However, Tyler saw something behind it that he hadn't seen from his nephew in months: genuine emotion. There was just a hint of it, but it was noticeable.

"Ryan, what the hell is going on?"

"Nothing."

"I'm guessing it's not nothing."

Ryan glared at him as though he was going to snap, but then he pulled back. A long silence ensued, but Tyler refused to stop looking at him.

"Everything is weird, okay?" Ryan said. When Tyler didn't respond, he continued. "The only conversations I have with my father are about 'staying focused' and 'staying on track' and crap like that. Meanwhile, I think I was nine the last time he asked me how my day was. Corrina's trying to give me this 'I'm your friend' garbage, but then she sells me out to my dad. Nobody in this whole family gets me. I just have a feeling my mother would have gotten me if she were still around."

Tyler inched a bit closer. "She probably would have. But, you know, I thought I got you, too. How come you stopped checking in with me?"

"Because you started to sound like *them*."

"Because I disagreed with you?"

"Because you started going into a 'teenagers suck' rant."

Tyler tried to remember enough of the conversation to call up a quote from it and then realized that this wasn't the point. "You thought that was a 'teenagers suck' rant? It was definitely a '*some* teenagers suck' rant, but I'm pretty sure I wasn't talking about everyone."

"Certainly sounded like it."

"I think you might have missed the point of that exchange, Rye. I was trying to have an adult-level debate with you about something that mattered to both of us."

Ryan locked eyes with him for a second and then looked off again. "Maybe I don't know what those are like."

"Then we should talk more often."

"Yeah. Maybe we should."

Neither of them said anything for a short while. Tyler watched a little girl and boy playing soccer together, the girl stopping play regularly to tell the boy what he was doing wrong.

"So, who's the girl you were with?" Tyler finally said.

"Her name is Amy."

"You into her?"

"Yeah, I think I am."

Tyler turned away from the soccer siblings and looked back at his nephew. "She's kind of a babe."

Ryan's eyes widened and he guffawed. It was easily the most unguarded gesture Tyler had seen from him in months. "You were checking out my girlfriend."

"She was in panties in my bedroom and I have a heartbeat."

"Solid point. Yeah, she's a babe. She's also funny and smart."

"Seems like you might not want to screw this up."

"I'll keep that in mind. So now that you and I are friends again, you wanna give me a key to your house so I can use it when you're not around?"

Tyler smirked and stood up from the bench. "I think you mentioned something about needing to be somewhere."

❀ ❀ ∧ ∧ ❀ ❀

Maria checked the radio on her way back from McGarrigle's to confirm that the Patriots had won their game this afternoon. That meant that Doug would be in a great mood when she got home. It always baffled her how her normally even-tempered and rational husband could have his moods completely influenced by a sporting event every fall Sunday. Fortunately, the Pats had been very good for a long time, which meant that bubbly Sundays far outnumbered the glum ones.

Doug wouldn't be the only household member in high spirits. Maria had been at McGarrigle's running through her set for Thursday night's show for both Martha and Colin, including the original song she'd written. She even threw in the new song she'd written for the party as well. Their response was appreciative, encouraging, and genuine, as indicated by Martha's dabbing at her eyes during the last tune.

Their feedback was invigorating. Yes, Colin was completely right that her fingerpicking wasn't as fluid as it needed to be on one of the new songs, and Martha nailed her tendency to over-sing during emotional passages, but those were easy fixes. The point was that she didn't trip over herself. She was beginning to regard Thursday's show with something other than trepidation.

Doug was watching the post-game show when she entered the living room with her guitar.

"45-17," he said when he saw her. "Brady was merciless today."

"I heard. Four touchdown passes?"

"Would have been six if he didn't stick to the ground game for the entire fourth quarter."

Maria put the guitar in the living room closet and walked over to kiss her husband. He gave her a post-victory squeeze.

"How was your music lesson?"

"Fantastic. Really fantastic. It wasn't a lesson, though. It was more of a run-through."

The show went to commercial and Doug switched to another game. "Run-through for what?"

"Thursday night at Mumford's."

"Oh, that showcase thing? You feeling good about that?"

"Better after today. I'm a little nervous since I haven't been on stage in such a long time, but this run-through really has me feeling confident."

"It's nice. It'll be a fun little event."

The television caught Doug's attention and Maria looked over at it. Seattle versus Phoenix, not something he would have any special interest in.

Maria sat back on the couch. "Martha Mc-Garrigle was very encouraging. She told me there's a whole series of venues between here and Rhode Island that feature live acoustic artists. I had no idea – tells you how out of it I've been. She said if things go as well on Thursday as she thinks they're going to go, that she can help me book some more dates."

Doug had seemed to be listening with one ear, but now he turned away from the TV. "You're not considering doing that, are you?"

"I know. It's a little weird to think about, isn't it? And I'm completely getting ahead of myself. But I've been really enjoying playing again."

Doug seemed mystified by her words. "You mean you actually want to *pursue* this?"

The chilliness in his tone set Maria's nerves prickling. "Maybe. As I said, I've been loving it."

Doug stared at the TV for a moment and then looked in her general direction. "I thought you were just screwing around."

"I might have been at the beginning, but I'd forgotten how much making music means to me."

"But these performances would all be at night, right? So just when I'm getting home from work, you'd be taking off. That's not exactly how I pictured things."

"You pictured me just sitting home waiting for you every day?"

"That's not exactly fair, Maria. I've been encouraging you to find something that mattered to you. It would have been nice, though, if the hours coincided with mine."

So much for being in great moods. "We don't need to discuss this now," she said, getting up from the couch and heading toward the kitchen. It was premature to make an issue of her getting deeper into her music, but it was something she hadn't expected to contend with.

❀ ❀ ∧ ∧ ❀ ❀

Tuesday, October 26
Five days before the party

The flight from Providence to Charlotte yesterday afternoon had been uneventful, Tyler's favorite kind of flight, and the drive to Columbia had been scenic. There were so many trees and flowers here that he couldn't see in Connecticut. The very fact that he could see flowers at all was something of a treat in late October. Based on what he'd read about the area online, the temperatures stayed in the seventies or above all but three months of the year and rarely dipped

below freezing, even at night. That led to a different type of growth and a different kind of
color. There weren't rusts and umbers here. The
shades were much more vital.

Tyler had spent some time walking around
the University of South Carolina campus in the
late afternoon and then grabbed some barbe-
cue from a food truck for dinner. Afterward, he
walked around the downtown area, peering into
the window of Aperture Photo Gallery, though it
had closed at six. It definitely looked like a legit
place.

Tyler's hotel was less than a ten-minute walk
from the gallery, so the next morning he left his
car in the parking lot, grabbed his portfolio, and
trekked over, stopping for coffee along the way.
Tyler liked the activity of this downtown area.
It was hardly a major metropolis, but it was so
much more of one than a town like Oldham.

Joe Elliot was a tall, thick man with longish hair, maybe in his early fifties. His voice was
more resonant in person than it had seemed on
the phone, which was a little surprising to Tyler
since he found the opposite to be true in most
cases.

"Great to meet you," Joe said. "Good trip?"

"Very good. The flight and the drive were a
breeze."

"Yeah, it's a pretty straight shot from Charleston. What brought you down here, anyway?"

Tyler had forgotten he'd told Joe that he was
already going to be in South Carolina. He was so

glad the man mentioned it before he blundered. "Just a little away time."

"Well, I consider it serendipity. Hey, can I get you a cup of coffee."

"Thanks, I just had one."

"Have another. I roast my own beans."

"That sounds like a very good reason to have more coffee."

Joe went to the back office and Tyler looked around the gallery a bit. There was an interesting blend of styles here, very different from the galleries near Oldham. There were plenty of formal images, but also a number of edgier ones. That told Tyler something about the market here. Because Aperture was in a college town, it could make room for more cerebral work. Tyler had no trouble imagining his shots hanging in this environment.

Joe came back with the coffee and the two of them sat at a table near the back of the gallery. The only other person present was a young woman, presumably a college student, who worked there. Tyler would have been surprised to find customers here on a Tuesday morning.

He opened his portfolio and pulled out a few pieces that he'd printed and matted. Joe reached out for them as though Tyler were offering up a tray of delicacies from an exotic land. He flipped through the work slowly, smiling and nodding at each new piece.

"I'm addicted to the leaves," Joe said when he got to the end of the collection. "That piece with the single upturned leaf you just put up on your site is stunning."

Tyler had added that shot to his slideshow after his phone conversation with Joe, which meant the man had been back to the site since then.

"Thanks."

Joe handed the photos back to him. "I'm thinking we'll start with a dozen pieces. I have the perfect spot for you."

Tyler hadn't expected Joe to have made a decision about carrying his work before Tyler got there. "You really think people want this kind of thing down here?"

"No question in my mind."

Tyler couldn't help but laugh. "I don't suppose you have five or six more galleries nearby."

Joe raised a finger. "That's something I want to talk to you about, actually. I'm something of a networking freak. I'm in constant touch with photo galleries all over the country – gotta stick together, you know? How would you feel about my brokering your work outside of your home region? I've been doing that with –" Joe pointed over Tyler's left shoulder, causing Tyler to turn in that direction "– that guy, and he's now in twenty-four galleries. I even got him into a place in Calgary."

Tyler had never had any kind of representation. People who worked on his scale rarely did. The idea was exciting.

"Yeah, I'd be open to discussing that."

"That's great. I think we'll be able to do some really good stuff with your work. Let's get you rolling here, though. I'd like to have some kind of launch event. Maybe right before Thanksgiving. Do you think you could come down again for that?"

Tyler gave the briefest consideration to whether there might be anything on his calendar for the last week of November. "Yeah, I can definitely come down again for that."

He spent another hour in the gallery. Joe introduced him to Lily Campbell who was in fact a student at South Carolina, but also the daughter of one of the gallery owners in Joe's network. Together, the three of them walked through the shop discussing the various photographers. Joe talked about each as though he'd had close personal relationships with them for decades.

By the time Tyler got ready to leave, the gallery was getting busy. Joe promised to send a contract within the week and then went to attend to a potential customer.

Walking back to the hotel to check out, Tyler considered the possibility that this meeting might have marked the beginning of the next phase of his career. It was possible, of course, that Joe's confidence in his ability to sell and market Tyler's work was unfounded, but there was the very real chance that Tyler would remember this morning as the point when his footprint genuinely started to grow.

Twenty minutes later, he was back in his car. As he was about to turn the key in the ignition, though, he realized he wasn't ready to leave. Maybe he'd walk around a bit more before going; the vibe here felt so good. As long as he was on the road by three o'clock, he'd get to the airport in time.

On the other hand, he didn't absolutely need to fly back tonight. Before he left yesterday, he handled the last details on the party decorations. Everything was under control on that end. He didn't have any pressing business in Oldham. And he certainly didn't have anyone waiting for him.

Maybe he'd hang around South Carolina for another couple of days.

Eighteen

Thursday, October 28
Three days before the party

Martha signaled Maria to come backstage ten minutes before she was scheduled to go on. She got a quick peck from Doug and then a huge hug from Olivia.

"Crush this, Mom," her daughter said.

Maria smiled nervously, "I'm just hoping not to *be* crushed."

"Backstage" at Mumford's was little more than an office down the hall. The guy who'd been on just before the current performer was sitting in one of the three chairs in the room, smoking a cigarette. Maria told him she liked his set, even though she found it a little passionless. He nodded as though he anticipated her compliment and fully deserved it. The guy couldn't have been out of college more than a year or so. Maria could imagine him thinking he'd be receiving much bigger accolades in much bigger venues by next spring, having no idea that for most aspiring musicians this was as big as it ever got.

Maria took out her guitar to check the tuning as Martha entered the room.

"Are you ready to go on?" the woman said, touching Maria on the shoulder.

"I guess we'll find out in a few minutes."

"About five. Damien is finishing his last song and then I'll go out to introduce you."

Maria simply shook her head in acknowledgment.

"You're gonna be great," Martha said. "You know that, right?"

Maria smiled, but she had been growing increasingly nervous since she entered this room, and Martha's encouragement was only elevating that.

"Thanks."

Martha patted her shoulder. "Gotta get back out there."

A couple of minutes later, Maria heard enthusiastic applause, the singer thanking the audience, and then Martha thanking the singer. As Maria listened for her introduction, the singer passed her to come into the office and their eyes met appreciatively for a second. He was probably only a few years younger than Maria and she could tell by the way he carried himself that the response he'd gotten meant something to him. If he was still here when she finished, maybe they'd compare notes.

At that point, Maria heard her name and the polite applause of the audience. She walked up the four steps to the stage and exchanged a smile with Martha before she sat at the stool, adjusted the mic, and checked the tuning on her guitar one more time.

She looked out from the stage. The room was perhaps two-thirds full, maybe seventy-five or eighty people. That was a decent crowd for something like this, a testament to Martha's ability to get attention for these showcases. Maria recalled doing similar things twenty years ago in front of gatherings of no more than a dozen.

Just before she started playing, she looked over at the table where her family was sitting. In addition to Doug and Olivia, Corrina and Maxwell had come as well. Deborah was cooking at the inn, of course, and Tyler was still out of town. Maria assumed that Gardner wouldn't be there, since he always seemed to be working, but she was surprised that Annie hadn't come. Maxwell said something about a babysitter, but he seemed to be having trouble explaining the matter. Maria wondered if he'd be asking to see Lucretia some time soon, though Lucretia hadn't made an appearance in a very long time.

Maria checked her tuning a third time, superfluous because the guitar had been in tune when she first checked, and then started her slowed-down version of "Least Complicated." As she sang the first verse, she realized that it had been decades since she'd last sung into a PA system. She'd used microphones to record, but not to amplify her voice. For some reason, she found this disorienting, as though what was coming from the speakers was not originating from her, and this distracted her to the point that she botched the last line of the first verse.

This led to a cascade of errors. Thinking too much about the lyrics caused her to slip up on her fingerpicking. Concentrating on her mechanics caused her to blow a chord change. By the time she got to the third verse, she half expected the strings to start popping from the bridge one at a time.

Olivia whooped at the end of the song, but applause in the rest of the room was sparse. Maria considered it to be generous.

Just then, her eyes connected with Doug's. He pantomimed taking a deep breath and letting it out slowly. It was precisely what she'd done for him when, during one of his infrequent public presentations, he'd stumbled badly at the beginning. Maria understood that the gesture was much more than an attempt to pay her back, and she appreciated it more than she realized she would.

Feeling bolstered, Maria regarded the rest of the audience. "Here's some James Taylor," she said before launching into "Song for You Far Away." She handled the fingerpicking at the beginning of the song without incident, and this served as her own metaphoric deep breath. By the time she came to the last words of the first verse – "people keep talking 'bout a different line but it never seems to fit" – she felt she was channeling the song rather than playing it. This was the seamlessness she remembered from her favorite times on stage. Her guitar, her voice, and her spirit were all merged. She didn't need to think about directing things, or even worse, remembering or noticing things. She could just go along for the ride.

The applause was much stronger after this one. She stole a quick glance at her daughter, who offered her an exaggerated thumbs-up, and her husband, who smiled appreciatively. Then she went directly into her greatly rearranged version of Queen's "Keep Yourself Alive." The pace of the song was considerably faster than the previous two and the crowd seemed to connect with this, even though she could tell that most of them had never heard the song before and likely wouldn't have recognized it even if they had. By the second verse, her family was clapping along, and this caused several others to join them. Maria found herself moved to the edge of her stool, and she would have stood for the last verse if she could only think of a way to raise the mic while still playing.

The cheering after this one seemed genuinely enthusiastic. Maybe she'd found her calling in acoustic reinterpretations of hard rock hits. Probably not. Still, the fact that several people she didn't know were smiling after this song warmed her.

"Thanks," she said as the applause died down. "You're very polite, and I'm adding all of you to my Christmas card list. I'm going to risk your disapproval now and do an original song. It's something I just wrote, and it's called, "What If I Told You."

Maria played the twelve-bar opening with her head down to the guitar, as she tried to inhabit the song. Playing her own material had always been different for her than covering others. While she could attempt to place herself in the songwriter's head when she did other people's songs, there was no distance between her own material and herself, and it was important that anyone listening feel this.

This was especially vital with this song, as it was more than a little confessional.

> *What if I told you I've started*
> *dreaming new dreams again?*

There was a certain sense of standing naked and vulnerable in performing this song, but it was liberating as well. Then there was a third thing she hadn't anticipated: it was nostalgic. Singing these new words that gave voice to what she was feeling at this stage in her life reminded her of why she'd started writing songs in the first place, of why this particular form gave her a level of expression that she'd never found in anything other than the unspoken communication between mother and infant child.

For a moment, right before the third verse, the emotion of this realization threatened to overwhelm her. She tucked her chin into her chest, improvised a sixteen-bar break, and gathered herself enough to finish strong.

> *You say to me that you don't know*
> *where I'm going.*

> *Well, what if I told you?*

As the crowd began to cheer, Maria leaned her forehead on the mic for an instant before looking out and thanking everyone. Then she blew quick kisses to her family and walked off the stage.

❀❀∧∧❀❀

The house was dark when Maxwell returned from the show, even though it was only a little after ten. He'd been half-hoping that he and Annie could talk for a while. He'd tried to convince her to get a babysitter so they could go out to see Maria together, but she'd refused. How could she complain about being tethered to Joey all day and then have no interest in untethering herself to go out with him for the night?

He got ready for bed and slid under the sheets, leaning over to kiss his wife, whose back was toward him, on the cheek. She didn't move. Whenever he got home after she was already asleep, no matter how late, he would kiss her and she'd turn over and move into his arms. That's how he knew she wasn't asleep now.

"Annie," he said softly.

She didn't answer.

❀❀∧∧❀❀

"Hey," Corrina said as she stepped into Gardner's office. He was studying a brief and kneading both of his temples.

"How was it," he said without looking up.

"Fantastic, actually. I don't remember Maria being this good."

He continued to rub his head. "It's nice that she didn't tank."

"Yeah. Are you okay?"

Gardner tipped his head back and breathed deeply. "As long as you define 'okay' as 'certain I'm going to lose this case.' I also have a monster headache."

Corrina moved closer and started massaging the base of Gardner's neck. He groaned appreciatively. "Do you really think you're going to lose?"

"Would it be possible for you to keep doing that for about an hour? No, I don't really think I'm going to lose, but I think I might not have any hair left by the end of this trial."

"Sorry. Can you take off fifteen minutes to have a cup of tea with me."

"I really can't. I'm panning for gold here. I might not make it to bed at all tonight."

She kneaded his neck for another minute and then gave his shoulders a squeeze. "I'll leave you alone. I'm gonna spend a little time taking care of some things for the party – Tyler screwed up in a big way on the decorations – and then I'm calling it a night."

"Lucky you."

Corrina scoffed as she left Gardner's office.

❀❀∧∧❀❀

Tyler didn't turn his cell phone back on until he was in his car and heading toward his house from the airport. He saw that there was a voice message and he instructed his hands-free device to play it for him.

"Tyler, it's Corrina. I got a call from Celebrations because they couldn't get you. The thing with the flying bats is a total disaster. I'm taking care of it, but –"

Tyler clicked off the phone. It was exactly the kind of "welcome home" he should have expected.

❀❀∧∧❀❀

Saturday, October 30
The day before the party

Deborah had been in the kitchen since ten this morning, and her legs had only now started complaining, eleven hours later. The fourth course had just gone out, and she took a moment to wipe her brow and check in with her staff before beginning final preparations for the first meat course.

The dining room was filled with many of the inn's most dedicated patrons from the years that Deborah had been running the kitchen. She'd reserved one table for four diners from Manhattan who ran a hugely influential food site, her only concession to marketing for her next endeavor, and a table for two for the writers from the *Post* covering this. There was no space for the casual or the curious. There was also no space for her family. Deborah had made it abundantly clear that this night wasn't for them, even though they'd inspired the menu.

Sage had come by after he closed the shop, about an hour before the single seating began at seven-thirty. He was willing to offer more than moral support, but understood when Deborah explained that all the cooking had to be from her and her team tonight. Still, she reveled in wandering past his table in the kitchen for a quick kiss whenever possible. In the past, having a boyfriend hanging around while she was working would have been distracting and annoying. She felt neither distracted nor annoyed now.

Deborah started working on the lemongrass gastrique for the roasted chicken. When she'd first learned the ideal way to roast a chicken at the CIA, her mother had insisted on eating it unadorned. "It doesn't need anything else, sweetie," she would say. "This is perfect." Deborah eventually convinced her that the chicken wouldn't be *hers* unless there was a sauce on it, and she'd topped the meat with several over the years. This was always Mom's favorite, though, and it had shown up on the inn's menu numerous times.

The same was true of the cream of parsnip soup with rapini oil and raisin bread croutons that started the meal. Even though Corrina requested it often in the fall for Wednesday night family meals, Deborah would still bring it out for other diners on occasion. That was also the case with the roasted garlic soufflé she offered after the soup, a personal favorite that she present-ed with an aged Gouda béchamel that servers spooned into the center. Tyler's pasta had never gone out to the inn's dining room – at least not for patrons – and it required a bit of dressing up tonight. Maxwell's diver scallops with hazelnut butter, on the other hand, was already formal and elegant enough, even though Deborah had never served it to anyone other than family previously.

Once the chicken had gone out, it was time to work on the Aleppo pepper bordelaise to go with the beef tenderloin. This one was a favorite of her father's, and he requested it nearly every hol-iday, even in the face of Deborah's suggestions that they try something different. Once this was done, it was just a matter of stuffing the bom-boloni. Gina was already frying the doughnuts and Evan was finishing the caramel.

Twenty minutes later, as the last of the ten-derloin plates were leaving the kitchen, Nancy Wilson, the head of the wait staff, came in.

"They want you outside," she said.

Deborah had just started filling a pastry bag with caramel. "Who wants me outside?"

"Practically everyone. Lots of people have asked during the night, and I kept telling them that I assumed you'd come out at some point, but now I'm starting to wonder if you're just planning to hide in here."

Deborah often took a walk around the dining room at some stage in the evening. That she hadn't tonight had much to do with the scale of the menu, but it was also at least partially deliberate.

"I'm getting dessert ready," she said.

Gina took the pastry bag from her hands. "I'll stuff the donuts. Go bathe in adulation."

Deborah offered her soon-to-be former sous a *gee, thanks* smirk. Then she turned to Sage. "Are you coming?"

He sat upright, but he didn't rise from his chair. "They aren't asking for me. You should do this solo."

Cringing inside, she headed for the door. As soon as she entered the dining room, it erupted in applause with several diners standing.

"You do realize you're paying for your meals tonight, right?" she said to laughter when things quieted. "I hope you've enjoyed your dinner. After the beef, there's dessert, after which we have a little something for you to take home and then we'll have used all the food we have left in the kitchen. If you're still hungry – and if you are, you might want to talk to a doctor – the diner down the street is open all night, and they make very good omelets."

Deborah paused and looked at her hands. She hadn't planned to give a speech tonight and she'd prepared nothing. She was hoping someone would simply start applauding so she could wave her thanks and get back to her work, but that wasn't happening.

"You know, cooking in this kitchen is the only job I've ever had. Unless you count the time when my mother paid me to spend an hour playing Candy Land with my little brother. Now *that* was work. My parents put their souls into this place and I felt that it was only appropriate that I do the same. Since the day we decided to sell the inn, I've been thinking about how I would soon not be cooking here anymore, and I've been dragging my heels as much as I can.

"I guess I can't avoid it any longer. As each dish has gone out tonight, I've been thinking, *last soup, last appetizer, last fish course*. You really should eat your last meat course before it gets cold, by the way. I'm sorry I didn't come out earlier tonight to see how everyone was doing, especially considering that all of you have had a special relationship to the inn. I had a feeling that if I did I'd never make it through the entire meal.

"So thank you for your patronage, thank you for your kindness, thank you for not sending anything back tonight – that would have been tough. There will never be another place like this for me, and I appreciate your being a part of it more than I could possibly express."

With a slight bow, Deborah turned to go back to the kitchen as the applause started again. When she got back, Gina was waiting for her with a hug, and each of the staff followed her. Finally, she walked over to Sage and collapsed in his arms.

It was a good thing someone else was handling dessert, because Deborah wasn't sure she'd survive it.

Nineteen

Sunday, October 31
The day of the party

Inspired by his multiple conversations with Joe Elliot while he was in South Carolina, Tyler had been out with his camera since nine this morning. He'd decided not to phone Corrina about the "disaster" with the party. By tomorrow, none of that would matter. Instead, he was treating this day as another, more meaningful occasion, and he needed to take as many shots as he could.

There were lots of children in the park, several of whom were in costume. There were two kids in Patriots jerseys throwing a football. Was that a Halloween thing for these two, or did they always dress that way to have a catch?

Tyler got to the huge oak in the northeast corner of the park and camped under it. As he settled, a leaf dropped down, flipping in the light breeze toward him. Tyler lay on his back and caught the leaf making several turns until it landed on his stomach.

He looked through his lens up the branches of the oak, and then did the same without the camera. The branches were now completely bare. Brushing the last leaf from his shirt, Tyler snapped dozens of frames of the tree in its winter guise.

❀❀∧∧❀❀

Joey was on his third shirt. The first had fallen victim to a yogurt tube explosion. The second had proven no match for the toy truck the kid thought it would be fun to stuff underneath it. Joey didn't as much outgrow his clothes as vanquish them. Having re-dressed his child yet again – maybe he should have just left him in the tattered shirt until they were about to go – Maxwell sat his son in front of the television, hoping Joey would mellow out for a bit. Maxwell needed to get ready for the party.

When he got to the bathroom, he saw that Annie had blown her hair dry and was now applying eyeliner at a glacial pace.

"He's neat again," Maxwell said. "I'm hoping Bob the Builder can sedate him long enough for us to get out of the house."

Annie now seemed to be just staring at the mirror, though she did manage to say, "Good luck with that."

Maxwell changed quickly. At one point, Corrina had the idea that all of them should show up at the party in costume this year as they did when they were kids. Maxwell squashed this immediately. The last thing he needed was an opponent flashing pictures of Maxwell dressed as an eighties rock star or some such thing while he was trying to convince voters that he had the gravitas to be mayor. When he went back into the bathroom to brush his teeth, his wife was still gazing at her reflection.

It was more than obvious that Annie had no interest in coming to this event. He hadn't pushed her about Maria's show, but this was different. If everyone didn't show up tonight, Maxwell wasn't sure when they'd all be together again.

Maxwell stood next to Annie at the mirror.

"You're still the fairest of them all."

Annie broke eye contact with herself to smirk at him. "Yeah, like you actually believe that."

The darkness in her tone shook him. He took her by the shoulders and turned her in his direction. "I do believe that, Annie. There's never been a time when I didn't believe that."

Annie shook her head slowly.

"Annie, talk to me."

She locked eyes with him for a moment and then looked away. "We don't need to talk."

He realized he was still holding her shoulders, and he gave them a light squeeze before stepping back. "We *do* need to talk. Look, I know I've been spending a lot of time thinking about my future lately, but in case I haven't made it as clear as I thought I'd always made it, I want you to be happy and I want you to have all of the things you want. We'll figure out whatever we need to figure out."

"You're just saying that because you want me to be a bouncy, smiling accessory for your campaign."

Maxwell looked down at the floor for a second, unsure of how he could have ever let his wife believe this. "I'm saying that because I'm deeply in love with you and I have been for as long as I can remember. I have lots of agendas, Annie, but you're not one of them. My desires for your happiness are as pure as anything I've ever felt."

Annie turned back toward the mirror and tried to get back to her eyeliner. She couldn't do it through her tears, though.

"Annie, tell me what's going on."

She turned back to him and threw herself into his arms, nearly knocking Maxwell backward. Momentarily stunned, he recovered and pulled her close.

"I can't," she said, "But –"

"– Daddy, Bob made my pants dirty."

Still hugging Annie, Maxwell looked down at Joey, who'd somehow managed to draw all over his khakis.

"Pinball, I need a minute with your mom."

Annie patted his chest and wiped at her eyes. "Go. Get him cleaned up again. I'll be ready in a few minutes."

❋❋∧∧∧❋❋

The canapés put Corrina over the top. The party had been going for about an hour and a half now. As happened every year, the first people to show up were the families with young children. The kids went straight for the huge bowls of candy and seemed to love the animatronic ghouls, cackling witches, and "scary" sound effects. They even showed an interest in Tyler's flying bats, though Corrina herself had to prevent them from being a major insurance liability.

About an hour into the party, families with older children and people with no children at all started showing up. A surprising number, including several of Oldham's most notable citizens, showed up in costume, which made Corrina regret even more that she'd allowed Maxwell to talk her out of having all the hosts in costume. The press showed up around the same time, with video cameras chronicling the event. Corrina was slightly miffed that when they needed a member of the family for an interview they went for Maxwell instead of her, but it was probably better that way, as her hands were full keeping everything running.

At this point, there were easily more than a hundred people in attendance, walking through the haunted house, listening to the ghost-storyteller hired for the event, dancing to the DJ on the makeshift dance floor, or mostly standing around and chatting while nibbling canapés.

Or at least they would be nibbling canapés if there were anywhere near enough to go around. Corrina found it frustrating at the highest level that her sister – who knew how important this event was, and who had had all the notice she could possibly need – hadn't prepared enough food for the crowd she knew was coming. Coming into the night, Corrina had convinced herself that Deborah was the least of her concerns. That had obviously been an enormous mistake.

She headed off to the kitchen.

Deborah was buzzing around from workstation to workstation when Corrina got there. She certainly looked busy, even if she wasn't producing anything.

"What the hell is going on with the food?" Corrina said, pulling her sister away from one of her staff.

"What are you talking about?"

"There isn't enough of it for how many people are out there. Please tell me you didn't underestimate this entire thing."

"I didn't underestimate anything. We've just had a little bottleneck getting it out. One waiter called in sick, another cut himself and had to be bandaged up, and a third had a crisis with his new employer that we had to talk him through. We've called in a replacement for the sick one, we've patched up the wounded one, and we've pulled the one in crisis back from the ledge. A lot more stuff will start going out now."

Corrina wasn't mollified. "You should have prepared for contingencies on a night like this."

"I never would have prepared for losing three members of the wait staff."

"Well, the lack of food is destroying the party."

"For who? Are people walking out? Are they collapsing from starvation?"

"I'm not saying they are."

"What are you saying, then?"

Corrina watched the motion around the kitchen, an awkward ballet of spinning chefs and weaving waiters. It was a wonder that people and dishes weren't splayed across the floor every few minutes.

She took a deep breath and turned back to her sister, whose confrontational glare had not diminished.

"First the music was too low, then it was too loud, and now the DJ is just being obstinate. The smoke machine was pumping so hard that a toddler nearly disappeared. The storyteller has told the same story five times already. The candy is disappearing way too fast. And the video guy has caught all of this so we can be mocked later tonight on the local news."

Deborah threw her head skyward and then took Corrina by the arm to lead her back out into the party. "Look at this," she said, pointing. "Does anyone here seem to be having a bad time?"

Corrina scanned the area. Kids were laughing, adults were talking animatedly, and there now seemed to be a dozen waiters delivering food in every direction. "No."

"Then just calm down. You can't manage this anymore, Corrina. It's happening – and by all indications, it's happening the way we hoped it would happen. Just lighten up."

With that, Deborah pivoted and went back into the kitchen. Corrina stayed where she was for another couple of minutes, simply watching the revelers. They did seem to be, well, *reveling*. Maybe it was time to take her foot off the pedal.

As she started to walk back into the main function room, Gardner came up to her.

"I'm gonna go home," he said.

Corrina couldn't believe what she was hearing. Her husband had shown up an hour late and now he was bolting. "What? You want to leave already?"

"I think I've got something. My head is pounding, and the noise in here isn't helping. I'm gonna go to bed."

Corrina knew that wasn't it. He was going back to the house to work on his case. He'd probably been calculating exactly how long he'd need to be here to make a decent showing. He'd calculated wrong.

"This is a big night for me, Gardner."

"So you've mentioned a few thousand times. I'm sorry. I feel miserable. I've been feeling like

I was coming down with something for a while, and it really hit me tonight."

"Then go. I'll see you when I get home."

Gardner kissed her cheek and then left without another word. As she watched him cross the room, Corrina caught sight of Ryan, who noticed Gardner's exit and then turned to her and rolled his eyes. Clearly, he was thinking the same thing she was thinking, though she was surprised that he was willing to acknowledge it. There would be a conversation about this as soon as she could grab her husband's attention again.

"The gravlax is spectacular," Etta Colter said as she walked past.

Corrina smiled at her. "Thanks. I'm so glad you're enjoying it."

❀ ❀ ∧ ∧ ❀ ❀

Deborah rarely made cakes. Her pastry skills were not up to her other culinary skills, and she tended to keep her desserts on a less ambitious scale than the savory dishes she served. Still, tonight was an occasion for a cake – and not just any cake, but a very large one. Once she'd figured out what last night's menu was going to be, constructing this cake had become her most nagging obsession.

The dark chocolate cake with orange buttercream was done now, though. She'd just finished garnishing it with frosted cranberries, and it was ready to roll out to the guests.

Deborah glanced around her at the still-bustling kitchen. There was still plenty to do: washing, cleaning, sanitizing, putting everything in place for the chef who would take over this spot when the new owners reopened the inn. This was the last dish that was ever going to leave this kitchen with Deborah in charge, though. How ironic that the last thing she would serve at the inn would be so far from her strengths. It would easily be the least refined item she'd presented all evening. Maybe she should have started with the cake and then moved on from there.

Deborah began to unbutton her jacket. Corrina told her that she wanted her with the rest of the family for the last hour of the party. Deborah wanted to disagree just because Corrina suggested it, but her sister was right. Once she'd finished with the food service, she needed to switch from chef to co-host.

As she shrugged off her jacket, Sage came up to her. He'd been flitting in and out of the kitchen all night, obviously unsure of whether he was here as Deborah's emotional aid, a part of the Oldham community, or a member of the inner circle. All of those roles were so new to him, though he maintained each with a level of grace that was one of the hundreds of things Deborah found so endearing.

"Do you want me to take this?" he said, reaching for her jacket.

She smiled at him. "Thanks."

"The cake looks fantastic."

"It tastes like Plaster of Paris."

"I doubt that."

She kissed his lips softly. "That's because you're a good man."

She kissed him again, then looked down at the cake, and then around the room.

"I think I need a minute alone," she said.

He touched her arm. "I'll leave you to it."

"No, I mean completely alone."

She called out to her staff. It took a full thirty seconds for the clattering and washing to stop. She asked them to give her the kitchen for a moment, and they respectfully cleared out, Sage included.

When the room was empty, Deborah closed her eyes and let the room fill her soul. She remembered the first time her mother let her come in here to do more than beg a chocolate chip cookie. It was a few weeks after her fourteenth birthday and she wanted to try to make a stir-fry. She'd cooked things in the family kitchen before, but she'd read in a magazine that real stir-frys required a level of heat that most people didn't have in their homes. She guessed that if most kids told their parents they wanted to play with fire in the parents' place of business they would be shunted aside, but that didn't happen to Deborah. The stir-fry was a mess that day, but the power in the kitchen thrummed through her. She knew it was where she was meant to be.

Deborah opened her eyes and slowly walked from station to station. They'd replaced nearly all the equipment over the years, but the basic layout of the room had remained the same. That made it very easy to envision her days as an apprentice under Chef Marco, or the way her hands shook as she sent out her very first amuse bouche as head chef, or the way she leaned her head against the door to the walk-in when she learned that her father was gone.

Would the new management decide that the kitchen needed a facelift, maybe an expansion into the storage space beyond the walk-in? Would Deborah ever come back here to see this kitchen in someone else's hands, even though she'd sworn to never set foot in the inn again? Right now, she couldn't think about such things. She just wanted to feel this place, this home, one more time.

Again, she closed her eyes, keeping them closed for an unknowable stretch.

Then she walked over to the cake. Sage was right; it looked okay. And it probably didn't taste too much like paste.

She rolled it out to the party.

❀ ❀ ∧∧ ❀ ❀

Maria thought Deborah's cake was gorgeous, and she couldn't have been happier for her for the ovation she received when she brought it out. It was a nice moment for her and for the entire family. Now Maxwell was speaking. He was so much better at this sort of thing than Maria was.

To her, a crowd was only addressable if there was a guitar between her and it.

Maria hadn't mentioned to anyone that she'd written a song for the event, though she'd snuck her guitar behind the front desk earlier in the evening. Maria assumed that Corrina would want to say something after Maxwell, after which she could get her instrument. She was very pleased with the way the song had turned out. It was less nuanced than "What If I Told You?" but she thought the chorus might be stronger. She could even imagine others singing along by the time she got to the third refrain, as she'd kept the message very simple and clear there.

The entire evening had run the spectrum of emotions for Maria. So many people had come up to her to share their favorite stories about the inn, and Maria found these warming, even if sometimes bittersweet. She also loved watching Olivia "work the room," impressed with how her daughter had added an extra layer of polish to her social skills since going off to college. At the same time, though, it was impossible to forget the occasion behind the occasion here. Yes, this was the annual Halloween party at the Sugar Maple Inn. That was impossible to mistake between the costumed attendees and Tyler's very prominent decorations. But it was also a wake. Everyone here was in some ways paying their last respects to the Gold family's presence at this place that had been theirs for so long.

Corrina was speaking now, explaining to all in attendance how much effort went into putting on this celebration, thanking others in a way that made it clear that she'd masterminded everything. As Corrina continued, Maria noticed something she hadn't seen earlier. Corrina was holding court in the middle of the room, partygoers extending out from her in concentric circles. Maxwell had addressed the crowd from a spot near the buffet on the far wall. Deborah was still near the cake in the back of the room closest to the kitchen entrance. Tyler, camera around his neck, had one leg up on a chair near the wall opposite Maxwell. And Maria was situated closest to the exit out to the front desk.

Had she said much of anything to her siblings tonight? She'd kissed Maxwell hello when he came in with Annie and Joey, and she'd spent a minute with Tyler talking about his trip to South Carolina. Deborah was in the kitchen until now, and Corrina was, well, everywhere, but never in one place for long.

The chorus of the song she'd written for the party came to mind. It was all about the legacy of families and unbreakable bonds. She'd written it in major chords with a key change coming out of the bridge to give the entire thing the feel of a soaring anthem, and just a few minutes ago, she'd imagined the entire room singing it. The chorus had come to her so easily and had practically written itself. She thought she understood why now. She had written a song about the mythology of her family, maybe even about the family they once were.

It was not reflective of the family they were now, though.

As the room broke into applause, Maria's attention drew back to the gathering. Corrina was smiling and attempting humility. Then Corrina looked around the room and caught sight of Maria. Pointing in her direction, Corrina said, "Maria, do you want to say something?"

Heads swiveled in her direction. Maria considered the song one more time and then said, "No, I'm good, thanks."

❉❉∧∧❉❉

Tyler had been toting a camera around most of the night, snapping candids of the party, even though he'd never gotten good at that. He especially loved shooting the kids interacting with the flying bats. He had no idea what Corrina's issue had been with them, but he thought they were a great touch.

Now, as the last few partiers got ready to leave, Tyler went to his car to retrieve his tripod. He knew he couldn't let this event pass without a portrait.

He'd enjoyed himself at the party tonight, even though he'd spent much of it staying out of Corrina's way. He'd gotten the chance to tell a few gallery owners about what was going on with Joe Elliott, and they seemed genuinely happy for him. He also got the opportunity to have some hangout time with Ryan (though the girlfriend was nowhere to be found), which was a good thing. It would sustain them. It was so good not to be tussling with the kid anymore, though he had a feeling that Ryan would be engaging in a bit of tussle with Corrina and Gardner soon.

He half-expected Patrice to make an appearance tonight, if for no other reason than that she should have been here as an Oldham entrepreneur. It would have been nice to have some additional closure, but maybe it was right this way. Tyler wasn't an everything-works-out-for-the-best kind of guy, but that might just be the case here.

When he got back to the main function room, Corrina was calling out to Ryan from across the room, Maxwell was chatting up Mike Mills while Annie sat in a chair watching Joey run in circles, Deborah and Sage were in a corner making love with their eyes (*get a room, will ya? – there's a dozen of them upstairs*), and Maria, Doug, and Olivia were preparing to head out.

"Wait up, guys," he said, foisting the tripod. "I want to take a couple of shots."

Doug sighed deeply, but they all halted and Olivia shouted, "Hey, everyone, Uncle Tyler wants to take a picture."

Slowly, the family coalesced from various spots in the room. Mike Mills said goodnight and exited. Sage tried to stay on the sidelines, but Deborah pulled him into the group. Tyler liked

Sage and he especially liked Deborah with Sage; he hoped it worked out for the two of them.

"Where's Gardner?" Maxwell said.

Corrina's reply was terse. "Buried under a deposition in all likelihood."

Tyler arranged everyone and then looked through the viewfinder. In spite of how tired everyone must be, they seemed to pull themselves together for this one last thing. *They all look so beautiful right in this moment*, Tyler thought. *Like leaves in the fall.*

Though they'd been taking timer pictures since before Tyler was a photographer – Dad used to love to bring out the old Nikon – he explained how things were going to work. Then he hit the timer button and ran to his place.

The timer counted down and the flash went off. Rather than a quick explosion of light, though, it rose slowly from the bulb, cascading outward. At the same time, Mom's voice resonated in Tyler's ears as though she were calling everyone into the dining room.

You may think you don't need each other anymore, but this love will prove important again. More than you could possibly know.

With that, the flash reached its apex. Tyler stood stock still, momentarily bewildered. Then he ran behind the camera to check the shot. In it, others reflected the confused expression on his own face. What had that been about? There had been other weird stuff like this in the past month. Maybe they were all going crazy together. They tended to do things very well as a unit; they'd be world-class lunatics.

He thought about taking another shot, but then realized that he couldn't possibly get a better one.

"We're all set," he said.

❀ ❀∧∧ ❀ ❀

Tyler took one last walk around the inn as the cleanup crew set about prepping the place for the new owners. They'd be at it all night. It was a wreck in here.

He stopped nearly every ten feet to recall something that happened in a particular spot. There had been lots of goodbyes lately. He was looking forward to some hellos.

Finally, he went out to his car. He'd just placed his camera and tripod in his trunk when Corrina walked over to him. His first thought was that she was going to let him have it for whatever he'd done wrong with the decorations, but he could tell from her relaxed gait and posture that she wasn't on the attack.

"The party was great, Cor," he said as she got closer. "People are going to remember this one."

She stopped a few feet from him. "I think so. The decorations were fantastic, by the way."

"Thanks. Hey, sorry about the screw up with the bats. What was the problem?"

"A stupid detail about our insurance. Nothing major, really. It was just my thing to freak out about at that moment. I guess I'll need a new outlet for my anxiety now, huh?"

She smiled and he smiled back at her. It had been so long since they'd had a conversation that wasn't contentious, that Tyler wasn't sure how to proceed.

After the silence stretched a bit, he said, "You heard that thing from Mom, didn't you?"

Corrina's eyes widened. "You heard it too?"

"Based on the picture I got, I think everyone heard it."

Corrina laughed. "Now we're having joint hallucinations."

"Well, we always were a close family."

His sister smiled warmly. It was an image he'd nearly forgotten. "She's right, you know. There are always going to be times."

"I know. I think we all do. We'll get that part right."

Corrina nodded, and they stood together quietly for a moment.

"I guess this is a good time to tell you I'm going away. I've decided to move to Columbia, South Carolina. Things are happening for me down there and I want to be in the middle of it, at least for a while."

Corrina's expression toggled through four emotions in a blink. "Wow. Other than college,

I think the furthest any of us have ever gone to live is Manhattan."

"It's not that far. I'll be back for Christmas. Maybe I can crash at your place."

She stepped toward him and hugged him. "You're welcome any time."

Tyler held Corrina tightly and then took a step toward his car. He looked up at the inn one more time.

"This was a good sendoff," he said, opening the door. He had a long drive ahead of him.

Twenty

Monday, November 1

Deborah's internal clock woke her somewhere around six thirty. She was still in Sage's arms and immediately snuggled closer. She hoped she never took for granted how good this felt.

There was work to do, though. Upon leaving the inn last night, she officially became an entrepreneur. If she was going to succeed in the food product business, actually coming up with a food product was a fairly important part of the process.

She started to slide her left arm out from under Sage. As she did, he stirred and she stopped for a moment to let him settle down. It took a bit of effort in her attempts not to wake him, but she eventually rolled over to her other side and pulled the sheets back.

"Where are you going?" Sage said.

She turned to him; his eyes were still closed.

"Sorry, I was trying not to disturb you. I need to get started. I'm going to give that hot rod kitchen of yours a whirl."

"Tomorrow."

Deborah knew that one of the traps of self-employment was thinking you could always put things off because you didn't have a boss standing over you. She wasn't going to let that happen to her.

"I can't, Sage. I don't want to get off on the wrong foot."

He opened his eyes now and propped his head up on his arm. "You can get off on the right foot tomorrow. My store is closed today, remember? I was hoping we could take a ride up the river."

With everything that was going on in her head, she'd forgotten that the store was closed on Mondays. "I don't want to fall into a –"

"– Deborah, do you really think you're suddenly going to become a slacker? You've had an intense month. A drive up the river will be restorative. I promise to show you a very good time."

He was right, of course. There was no way Deborah was going to take this enterprise anything less than seriously. However, a one-day break before launching into her new career wasn't going to hurt her.

She slid back under the sheets. "Did you say a *very* good time?"

❊❊∧∧❊❊

Maxwell awoke to his son doing a belly flop on his chest. No matter how many times it happened, he never got used to that. Joey started playing with Maxwell's face, contorting it and laughing.

He slipped out of bed and grabbed the boy up in his arms. If Maxwell got Joey some milk, the kid would calm down a bit. Then they could take a shower together and give Annie a few more minutes of sleep.

Except that Annie wasn't there.

Worry prickled at Maxwell instantly. He thought they'd made a breakthrough last night. What was going on?

Joey was now banging the side of Maxwell's head. He really needed to get the kid some milk. Maxwell carried his son into the kitchen and set him down. The note was waiting for him.

I'll be back, but I need a few days.

Maxwell took in a deep breath and let it out very slowly. He guessed he was going to have to get used to complicated.

Then he went to the refrigerator.

❊❊∧∧❊❊

There were times when Maria wished the Old Saybrook Amtrak station weren't so close.

She hated sending Olivia back to school. Fortunately, Thanksgiving was only a few weeks away and Olivia would be home for winter break not long after that.

"Are you sure you don't want to stop for breakfast?" Maria said as they got on the highway.

"If we stop for breakfast, I'm going to miss my train."

"What's your point?"

Olivia gave her a soft push on the shoulder. "So what's on the agenda today?"

"You mean after sobbing for an hour on the steering wheel when the train pulls away?"

"You know that this doesn't make me feel guilty, don't you?"

Maria grinned at her daughter. "I have a meeting with Martha at eleven. We're going to talk about her setting me up with some more gigs."

"You're really gonna go for this, huh?"

Maria gave herself a moment to feel herself back on stage at Mumford's last Thursday night. "I really love this, Liv. All of it: the writing, the practicing, the performing. I think I might even look into doing some recording. That whole process is so much easier than it used to be."

Olivia squeezed her arm. "I think this is great, Mom. It might take Dad a little while to come around on this, though he seemed pretty proud of you Thursday night."

Maria took the Old Saybrook exit. The Amtrak station really was too close. "He did, didn't he? Eventually he'll get used to having a pop star in the house."

❊ ❊ ∧ ∧ ❊ ❊

It wasn't even eight and Corrina was already on her second cup of coffee. She thought maybe she'd be able to relax a little now that the party was behind her, but her mind was still racing. She'd spent the entire night fidgeting in bed, amazed that she hadn't awakened Gardner. Surprisingly, he'd actually been asleep when she got home last night. Maybe he really hadn't been feeling well.

Ryan had blown in and out of the kitchen ten minutes ago before going to school. At some point soon, she was going to have to tackle him on his way out the door and force him to reenter the family orbit. It was obvious that Gardner wasn't going to do it, and it was unhealthy for them to continue the way they'd been for most of the past year.

Gardner was usually out of the house by now as well. He never even used an alarm clock, since he naturally woke up around five thirty. Obviously, he needed to recharge a little. Corrina thought about letting him sleep in, but she knew he'd be furious if she did. Even if he were under the weather, he'd insist on spending all day and all night on court prep. Maybe when this case was over, she'd convince him to go away with her for a week in Cancun. They certainly could use it.

Taking one more sip of coffee, she rose from the kitchen table and headed toward the bedroom to wake her husband. Even though he could still make it to his office by nine, he would complain about losing so much time.

She jostled him and he didn't move. She jostled him again. That's when she noticed his body didn't give the way it normally did.

Corrina's blood chilled and tears sprang to her eyes. She sat on the side of the bed and put her head in her hands.

❀❀∧∧❀❀

Tyler woke up in a motel near Baltimore and glanced at the clock on the nightstand. Eight twenty-four. He needed to get going. He'd driven more than five hours last night after the party and then crashed here for a little sleep. Now it was time for a quick shower and an even quicker stop at the coffee shop down the block that he'd noticed on the way in.

Then it was back on the road. He'd be in Columbia by the evening.

❀❀∧∧❀❀

A brisk breeze blew through the streets of Oldham. It was like this every year. The moment the calendar turned to November, the air grew sharper and the wind more insistent.

All along Hickory Avenue, shopkeepers prepared for a quiet few weeks as they dressed their windows for the holiday season. The tourists were gone now, but things would pick up again after Thanksgiving.

Sanitation crews were out in force today, gathering the last of the leaves that had been piled at roadsides all over town.

And a moving truck pulled up to the inn at the corner of Oak and Sugar Maple.

A note from the author

I hope you enjoyed *Leaves*. It's the first of a series of novels I'm going to be writing about the Gold family. There's plenty to explore here, as all the Gold siblings are at the start of something new. Maria needs to find out where her music will take her. Maxwell has a campaign to run and a marriage to save. Deborah has her new business and the first serious romance of her life. Corrina must confront widowhood with a boy who has made it clear that she isn't his mother. And Tyler needs to find his way in a place that is very different from home.

There's more, of course, as the lives of these siblings diverge and intertwine. Bethany's pronouncement at the end of the party will prove prophetic on numerous occasions, though.

This is by far the largest cast of characters I've ever had in a novel, and I feel as though I'm just starting to get to know all of them. Because of this, I'm sure their exploits will surprise me as I develop them. Toward that end, I'd be very interested in what you'd like to see me explore with the siblings as well as Doug, Annie, Sage, Olivia, Ryan, and even Joey. If you'd like to share your questions or ideas, please drop me a note at <u>michael@michaelbaronbooks.com</u>.

Thanks.

Warmest regards,
Michael